Reykjavík

Reykjavík

RAGNAR JÓNASSON *and*
KATRÍN JAKOBSDÓTTIR

Translated from the Icelandic
by Victoria Cribb

MICHAEL JOSEPH

MICHAEL JOSEPH

UK | USA | Canada | Ireland | Australia
India | New Zealand | South Africa

Michael Joseph is part of the Penguin Random House group of companies
whose addresses can be found at global.penguinrandomhouse.com

Penguin
Random House
UK

First published in Iceland by Veröld Publishing 2022
First published in Great Britain 2023
001

Set in 13.75/16.25pt Garamond MT Std
Typeset by Jouve (UK), Milton Keynes
Printed and bound in Great Britain by Clays Ltd, Elcograf S.p.A.

The authorized representative in the EEA is Penguin Random House Ireland,
Morrison Chambers, 32 Nassau Street, Dublin D02 YH68

This book has been translated with a financial support from:

 ICELANDIC LITERATURE CENTER

A CIP catalogue record for this book is available from the British Library

HARDBACK ISBN: 978–0–241–62599–6
TRADE PAPERBACK ISBN: 978–0–241–62600–9

www.greenpenguin.co.uk

This book is dedicated to Agatha Christie,
who inspired our love of detective stories.

Contents

Main Characters

Lára Marteinsdóttir	1941–?
Valur Róbertsson	journalist at *Vikubladid* newspaper
Sunna Róbertsdóttir	literature student, Valur's sister
Margrét Thorarensen	politics student, Valur's girlfriend
Jökull Thorarensen	lawyer, Margrét's father; former Minister of Justice
Nanna Thorarensen	lawyer, Margrét's mother
Gunnar Gunnarsson	theology student, friend of Valur and Sunna
Katrín Gudjónsdóttir	Margrét's friend at the National Registry
Kamilla Einarsdóttir	Sunna's landlady
Kristján Kristjánsson	police officer
Gudrún Reykdal	Kristján's wife
Snorri Egilsson	police officer

Dagbjartur Steinsson — editor of *Vikubladid*
Laufey Karlsdóttir — Dagbjartur's wife
Baldur Matthíasson — journalist at *Vikubladid*
Sverrir and Kiddi — employees at *Vikubladid*

Ólöf Blöndal — former resident of Videy
Óttar Óskarsson — lawyer, Ólöf's husband
Thórdís Alexandersdóttir — actress
Finnur Stephensen — wholesaler, Thórdís's husband
Páll Jóhannesson — city councillor
Gunnlaug Haraldsdóttir — Páll's wife
Elísabet Eyjólfsdóttir — Páll's secretary
Högni Eyfjörd — developer

Marteinn and Emma — Lára Marteinsdóttir's parents

PART ONE

1956

6 August

The grey hat flew out to sea.

Kristján had stepped out of the wheelhouse to admire the view over Faxaflói bay and watch the island approaching, low and green against the backdrop of mountains. When the squall hit the little fishing smack, he had reacted fast, but not fast enough, grabbing for his hat only to snatch at thin air. Though he'd have never admitted it aloud, he thought that it could have been worse: the hat, a Christmas present from his fiancée, hadn't really suited him. Now he would have an excuse to buy a new one.

It meant he would be bareheaded for his visit to the little island of Videy, just off the coast near Reykjavík, but what did that matter, when the whole thing was bound to be a waste of time anyway? Still only in his twenties, Kristján wasn't usually entrusted with anything important, but he was on duty this August bank-holiday weekend as his superior officer was away.

It felt as if the brief Icelandic summer was already over that August morning on the boat, with no shelter from the wind and the sun hidden by cloud. As there was no regular ferry service to the island, Kristján had had to improvise and do a deal with an old fisherman he knew.

'Almost there, Kristján,' the captain called from the wheelhouse, his voice hoarse.

Kristján nodded, though there was no one to see, and did up another button on his overcoat to keep out the cold. If nothing else, at least the trip made for a change of scene, he thought, trying to look on the bright side.

A woman, probably in her early thirties, was standing by the jetty to meet him. Kristján had asked his fisherman friend to come back for him in an hour and a half. By the time he got back to town, the whole morning would have been spent on this visit.

The woman held out her hand. 'I'm Ólöf Blöndal. Welcome to Viðey.' Her face was grave and she didn't smile.

'How do you do? The name's Kristján,' he said. There was something slightly off about Ólöf's manner, he thought. She looked a little shifty, yet at the same time he could have sworn she was relieved to see him.

'It's this way,' she said diffidently, and set off up the grassy slope from the jetty. He followed, noting that she had short red hair and was wearing a thick woollen jumper.

Two striking white buildings with red roofs came into view between the island's twin green hills: the old Danish colonial mansion and the little church beside it. As they drew closer, Kristján noticed how dilapidated they looked, the paint peeling from their walls and window frames.

Beyond them he noticed some tumbledown outbuildings, one of which looked like a cow shed; relics of the days when there was still a farm here. Halfway there, Ólöf stopped, turned and said: 'We're not actually going there. My husband's at home – we live nearby.'

Kristján nodded. 'Does nobody—'

She interrupted: 'We have keys to the mansion, but no one lives there. It's a bit run-down but in pretty good nick considering its age. It's two hundred years old, you know – the oldest stone building in Iceland.'

'This girl, Lára—'

Again she cut him off: 'It's best you speak to my husband.'

Kristján walked along beside her, neither of them saying a word. There was a blustery breeze blowing on the island, but it was warmer than it had been on the crossing, despite the lack of sun. After they had been walking for a couple of minutes, he asked: 'Excuse me, but you said you live here, you and your husband?'

'We moved here in the spring to a house that belongs to my family. We spent last summer here too. It's . . .' She paused. 'There's nowhere quite like it.'

Kristján didn't doubt it; the island was certainly a picturesque spot, its green meadows surrounded by the blue waters of the bay and set against the great hulk of Mount Esja, but Ólöf's words lacked conviction to his ears.

She went on awkwardly: 'It's not far to our house. It's more or less halfway between the mansion and the old school.'

As they walked, he let his mind wander. Being in the

open air agreed with him, but he would rather have been spending this late summer's day doing something quite different. In recent years he and a couple of old friends had taken up mountaineering in their spare time, inspired by the news three years earlier of Edmund Hillary and Tenzing Norgay's conquest of Everest. While Kristján had no hope of ever achieving those heights, he was making good progress. Only a few days ago news had come in that the north Icelandic peak of Hraundrangi in Öxnadalur had been climbed for the first time. Kristján was acquainted with the two Icelanders who had made the ascent along with an American. What he wouldn't have given to be there right now, rather than here in the tame environs of Videy.

Still, gentle though the terrain was, he was careful where he set his feet as he picked his way over the tussocky ground. He remembered how his mother used to laugh and say that Icelandic men always walked as if they were stepping over tussocks, even when the ground was perfectly flat. But his main concern was to leave here without twisting or spraining an ankle – or dirtying his suit, for that matter. He owned three suits: the light grey one he was wearing now was the newest; the pinstripe was looking a little threadbare these days; and the black one he saved mainly for formal occasions like funerals.

An old wooden house appeared ahead, its black paint flaking. It had obviously seen better days. At that moment an Arctic tern swooped over Kristján's head and he made a grab for his hat to ward the bird off, only to remember belatedly that the hat was now floating somewhere in Faxaflói bay.

'Don't worry,' Ólöf said. 'The breeding season's over, so it won't attack you.' Her tone was momentarily lighter, as if she had forgotten that she was in the company of a policeman on duty.

Her husband didn't come outside to greet them. Noting this, Kristján wondered why it was Ólöf who had been sent to meet him off the boat. Was this the way the couple normally did things, or could there be something else behind it?

'Come in,' Ólöf said, rather curtly, once they reached the house.

Kristján entered a hall that turned out to be part of the sitting room. It was warm inside; almost uncomfortably so for the time of year.

'Óttar?' Ólöf called. 'Óttar, he's here.'

Kristján heard a noise upstairs, then footsteps boomed through the old wooden house. Without saying another word, Ólöf walked into the sitting room and pulled out a chair from a large oak table, indicating that Kristján should take a seat.

He did so and waited. She sat down as well.

'Good morning,' said the man who had come down the stairs. 'I'm Óttar. I take it you're Kristján?'

'I am, indeed. Thank you very much for agreeing to meet me. I only managed to explain briefly over the phone, but the thing is, we're worried about Lára.'

'She decided to leave,' Óttar said flatly. 'She gave up on her position here. I don't know why. We were so pleased with her at the beginning of the summer; she seemed hard-working and conscientious. Still, young people today . . .' His face was expressionless as he produced this speech. Kristján shot a glance at Ólöf, who dropped her gaze.

'How old was she again?' Kristján asked, though he already knew the answer.

'Fifteen,' Ólöf answered quietly.

'Fifteen,' Kristján repeated. 'And she'd decided to go back to Reykjavík, you say? Back home?'

'Yes,' Óttar replied.

'When?'

'On Friday. Friday morning. Naturally, I objected. We had an agreement that she would stay the entire summer as our help, but there was no talking any sense into her.'

Kristján glanced at Ólöf again. She was sitting unmoving, staring down at her hands.

'As I mentioned on the phone, no one's seen or heard from her in Reykjavík . . .' Kristján left the words dangling as he watched their reactions. Ólöf didn't raise her eyes; Óttar's face remained impassive.

'Maybe I should have put it differently: did you see her leave on Friday?'

'We can't see the jetty from here,' Óttar replied. 'And it was hardly my job to give the girl a send-off. If people want to leave, that's their business, as far as I'm concerned.'

'What about you, Ólöf? Did you see her go?'

Ólöf shook her head. 'I didn't see anything,' she said, her words ringing a little hollow.

'How was she intending to get back to town?'

'I have absolutely no idea. She said someone would be coming for her – some friend or relative, I assume. I don't keep an eye on the boat traffic.'

'Do you have a boat of your own?' Kristján asked.

'Yes, of course,' Óttar said. 'But the girl didn't ask for a lift back to shore and, quite frankly, after the way she'd inconvenienced us, I wasn't inclined to offer her one. Besides, as I said, she told me she'd made her own arrangements.'

'Are you sure she left?'

'What kind of question is that?' Óttar asked, bridling. 'Of course we're sure. She said goodbye and we haven't seen her since.'

Kristján looked at Ólöf, waiting for her to answer. She was silent at first, then said: 'Yes, she's definitely gone. She took her belongings with her.'

'Her parents used to hear from her regularly,' Kristján said, 'so when she didn't ring at the weekend, they started to get worried. Haven't they been in touch with you?'

'Yes, they have,' Óttar replied. 'And I told them the same as I'm telling you. I simply can't understand why you've put yourself to the trouble of coming all the way out here. We could have answered your questions over the phone. You can see for yourself that the girl has gone.'

'I'd need to take a walk around the island to be sure on that point. Videy's quite large, isn't it?'

'Three kilometres from end to end,' Óttar said.

'The biggest island in the bay,' Ólöf added.

'And I expect there are plenty of hiding places?'

'Well,' Ólöf said, 'there's our house, and the mansion, of course. And the church. The old school too. And . . .'

'I don't think we need to list all the buildings on the island, Ólöf,' Óttar intervened. 'Let the man do as he likes if he feels obliged to make sure. Though I can't imagine why on earth he thinks Lára would have been hiding on the island for the whole weekend.'

'How was she?' Kristján asked.

'How do you mean?' Óttar countered.

'Was she in low spirits? Is there any reason to believe she might have been hiding something? Keeping a secret from you?'

Óttar opened his mouth to answer, then seemed to think better of it. After a lengthy pause, he said: 'There was nothing wrong with the girl. She was simply bored of being here with us. Well, good riddance, I say. We'll be more careful about choosing our help next summer.'

'I see. At any rate, she hasn't turned up at her parents' place. Which raises questions, that's all. Of course, it's always possible she left here on Friday and—'

Óttar interrupted: 'Possible? I'm telling you, she left, and anything that may have happened afterwards has nothing to do with us. There's been no news of a boat going down, so it stands to reason she must be somewhere.'

'No, I'm sure we'd have heard if something like that had happened,' Kristján said. 'The trouble is, there are no reports of any boats coming out here on Friday, though that doesn't rule out the possibility that someone came and picked her up. Did she live here in the house with you?'

'Where else would she have lived?' Óttar asked impatiently.

'Could I see her room?'

Óttar shrugged. 'It's upstairs. But there's nothing to see.' He showed no signs of budging, but Ólöf rose to her feet.

'I'll take you up,' she said, her tone a touch friendlier than her husband's.

Every stair creaked in the old wooden house. The guestroom was small but reasonably cosy, with a sloping ceiling, a bookcase and a dormer window with a view of the sea.

'Did she bring the books with her?' Kristján asked.

'Oh, no, those are ours. We put books in all the rooms. It creates a nice atmosphere. My husband collects them. He's a barrister, as you're probably aware. Quite well known, actually.'

Kristján was indeed familiar with the name. He nodded.

'Óttar wanted to cut down on his legal practice and devote himself to academic work for a while. We're planning to try and live here more or less in the summers. It's good to be near . . .' She trailed off, looking away.

'Did she take all her belongings with her?' Kristján asked.

'All of them, yes,' Ólöf said. 'There's nothing here.'

'Did she say anything to you?'

'I'm sorry?'

'Lára. Before she left?'

'What do you mean?'

'How did she explain her decision?'

Ólöf hesitated. 'She didn't explain,' she said eventually. 'She, er, she just left.'

'She must have said something before she left. According to your husband, she told you she was leaving.'

'Oh yes, I'm sorry. I didn't mean it like that. She just said she wanted to give up her position early. She asked our permission. Naturally, we granted it, but we weren't happy.'

'Aren't you worried about her?'

'Worried? Er, no, we've only just learned that she hasn't turned up at home. But I'm sure she's fine.'

'Let's hope so.'

'Shall we go back down?'

Kristján nodded and followed Ólöf down the narrow, creaking staircase.

When they entered the sitting room, Óttar was nowhere to be seen. Kristján looked around, then jumped when Óttar coughed behind him. He spun round, his heart beating uncomfortably fast.

'You're wanted on the telephone.'

'What?' Kristján exclaimed.

'Telephone. For you,' Óttar repeated, as though nothing could be more natural. 'In here – in my study.'

'Oh?' Puzzled, Kristján followed Óttar into the book-lined room. His eye fell on a shelf of volumes containing Supreme Court judgements. On the desk he saw a black telephone with the receiver lying beside it. There was a noticeable smell of mildew in the room. It seemed the house was as dilapidated indoors as it had looked from the outside.

'Who's trying to get hold of me?' Kristján asked.

'Someone from the police, of course,' Óttar replied.

Kristján raised the receiver to his ear. Feeling nervous, he shifted from foot to foot, noticing, as he did so, that the floorboards emitted a hollow boom. There must be a damp cellar under there. He reflected that he wouldn't want to live in an old wooden house like this.

'Kristján Kristjánsson speaking,' he said into the receiver.

'Kristján, hello. Eiríkur here.' Kristján knew instantly who it was. The man was two rungs higher than him in the police: his boss's boss.

'Hello . . .' he replied diffidently.

'Óttar got in touch. He'd like an explanation for the rather odd questions you've been asking him and his wife.'

'They were purely routine questions. I'm investigating the disappearance of a girl, a fifteen-year-old, who hasn't been seen for several days . . .'

'A girl who ran away from home, in other words?'

'Well, we can't be quite sure of that. She was in service here on Videy. Her parents are worr—' He didn't get a chance to finish the sentence.

'There's no call to cause Óttar and Ólöf any unnecessary inconvenience over this. You've gone to the trouble of visiting the island in person?'

Kristján wanted to protest, to try to explain, but reflected that it probably wouldn't do any good. 'Actually, I was about to leave. My visit here was just ending.'

'Excellent. Give Óttar my regards, would you? And Ólöf Blöndal too. You'll do that for me?'

Eiríkur hung up.

Kristján replaced the receiver carefully, trying to act as if everything was fine.

'Nothing urgent,' he told Óttar.

Ólöf was standing in the sitting room when they emerged from the study.

'Well, I think that's all for now. Unless you happen to have remembered anything else?' Kristján looked at the couple in turn.

'Nothing else,' Óttar replied.

'Then we'll just have to hope the girl turns up,' Kristján said.

Óttar answered for both of them again. 'She's bound to. I assume we won't be receiving any more visits like this.'

'Just one more thing,' Kristján said. 'The boat won't be back to fetch me for a while yet. Would you mind if I took a stroll around the place while I'm waiting?'

'Do as you please,' Óttar said. 'We don't own the island.'

'I think I'll go for a short walk, then. Thank you very much for your time.'

Kristján set out for the schoolhouse Ólöf had mentioned, at the eastern end of the island, the sole remnant of a village that had been abandoned during the Second World War. As he made his way along the grassy path, he was struck by the solitude. In the Middle Ages, Videy had been the site of a wealthy monastery; later, it had become the seat of governors, but nowadays the only inhabitants apart from Óttar and Ólöf were the seabirds screeching from the shore. The walk took him longer than expected.

When he reached it, the schoolhouse, a wooden, two-storey building, turned out to be empty of course, with no sign that Lára had ever been there. He started off back towards the place where he'd been put ashore, pausing on the way to try the door of the small eighteenth-century stone mansion, but he found it locked. He remembered Ólöf mentioning that they had a set of keys but he couldn't face bothering the couple again to ask if he could borrow them. He pondered what to do. Videy was split almost in two by a narrow isthmus, the Eid, and Kristján toyed with the idea of walking across it to explore the northern half of the island but realized he didn't have time on this trip.

Anxious not to keep the boat waiting, Kristján walked briskly back in the direction of the jetty. There was a fine view of Reykjavík across the narrow sound. The town was fast developing into a city, new neighbourhoods springing up on every side and the ambitious modern church beginning to take shape on top of the hill. In the event, he reached the jetty early. The boat hadn't arrived yet, so he would have a chance to go back and take a quick look inside the island's little church, which he guessed would be unlocked. Although he was pretty sure he wouldn't find the lost girl there, he wanted to check anyway.

Despite its tiny size and stale air, the interior was surprisingly attractive, featuring an unusually high wooden pulpit painted in blue and green, and similarly colourful pews. It occurred to Kristján that this might be a good place to get married to Gudrún, though it was bound to be a palaver having to ferry the wedding guests to and fro. He would bear it in mind as a possibility. He and Gudrún had been engaged for six months now and were beginning to discuss their future, marriage and children. They lived in the west end of Reykjavík, where Gudrún had recently started work in a grocery store. Yes, maybe one fine day they would find themselves standing before the altar in here . . .

There weren't many hiding places in the small church, and, from the musty smell, he guessed the door hadn't been opened in a while. It could do with an airing. Having checked behind the pulpit and under the pews, Kristján stepped outside again and gratefully filled his lungs with fresh air. His gaze wandered to the churchyard. Just then, his thoughts were interrupted by the faint throb of an engine. Looking out across the water, he spotted the fishing boat in the distance, making steady progress towards the island.

Kristján walked slowly down to the jetty, trying to relax and enjoy the moment, despite having received what almost amounted to a dressing-down from his superior, Eiríkur. Completely undeserved, of course. Kristján was only trying to do his job, but people like Óttar and Ólöf had influential friends. He told himself there was no point letting it get to him.

Reaching the jetty ahead of the boat, he stood and waited. The sun was breaking free of the clouds now and the blustery wind that had greeted him was dying down to a gentle breeze. He gazed out across the bay, feeling a faint regret, after all, for the hat that had been snatched away.

His thoughts returned to the missing girl. She was

probably holed up safe somewhere and her parents were making a fuss about nothing. It occurred to him that he didn't know what she looked like. He would have to ask for a photograph of her if she didn't turn up.

Yes, more likely than not she would be found safe and sound, and this would be his last trip to Videy for the foreseeable future. But as the old fishing smack came to rest against the jetty, Kristján had a powerful intuition that the case was far from closed.

1966

8 August

The woman was sitting at one of the little tables in Café Mokka, reading a newspaper. In front of her was half a waffle with cream and jam, and a cooling cup of coffee. On the wall beside her there was a print depicting a nuclear mushroom cloud and the terrified faces of children. But none of these attracted her attention, so absorbed was she in that day's copy of *Vísir* with its news of an unsolved crime.

DETECTIVE KRISTJÁN KRISTJÁNSSON: LÁRA'S DISAPPEARANCE STILL CASTS A LONG SHADOW

Ten years ago, Kristján Kristjánsson was the first police officer on the scene when Lára Marteinsdóttir went missing. The experienced detective told our reporter that Lára's disappearance still casts a long shadow over the nation. Lára was working as a maid at the home of the Supreme Court barrister Óttar Óskarsson and his wife, Ólöf Blöndal, on the island of Videy when she vanished without a trace. Only fifteen years old at the time, Lára was described as a lovely girl, well liked by everyone who knew her. Ten years later the mystery of what happened to Lára remains unsolved. As Kristján Kristjánsson explained to *Vísir*, the police pursued various lines of inquiry at the time, none of which produced any results. They never discovered who could have given Lára a lift to Reykjavík in their boat, and no physical remains have ever been found that could be linked to the missing girl. At one time there was talk of requesting help from foreign police agencies but in recent years there have been no new developments. It is as if Lára has vanished off the face of the earth.

Accompanying the report was a grainy photo of a pretty teenage girl with dark hair and eyebrows, wearing a velvet dress with a high collar. There was a photo of Kristján Kristjánsson too, with horn-rimmed glasses and a receding hairline. His expression was simultaneously kind and careworn, as if he were exhausted by the search for Lára. The woman stared at the two photos for a while before closing the paper and rising to her feet without finishing her coffee or waffle. She was filled with a creeping sense of unease, as always when she heard Lára's name, and had completely lost her appetite. She would have to distract herself by thinking about something else.

Leaving the paper on the table, she walked quickly out of the café onto Skólavördustígur, where a chilly wind was sweeping along the pavement and the scaffolding for the imposing new Hallgrímskirkja church dominated the view at the top of the hill.

Kristján Kristjánsson, meanwhile, was sitting in the old police station on Pósthússtræti, in the very centre of Reykjavík, also reading a copy of *Vísir*.

He hadn't yet moved to the brand-new police headquarters on Hverfisgata but was looking forward to working in an up-to-date building with all mod cons. Even better, it would take him almost no time at all to walk to work in future from his home on Stangarholt. And he would probably be given his own office too. For a moment his thoughts continued along this pleasant path before returning to what he'd been reading.

> What did happen to Lára? Could some unknown person have taken her in his boat from Videy to Reykjavík? Did she vanish in the sea along with all her luggage? Or did she make it to Reykjavík, only to fall victim to some unscrupulous individual there? Or could she have staged her own disappearance and still be alive today, on the other side of the globe perhaps, with a new name and family? Might some of our readers even know the fate of the girl in the picture?

Kristján sighed. The reporter's speculation got on his nerves. He felt it trivialized the seriousness of the fact that a young girl who had never hurt a soul had disappeared, and, he feared, suffered some terrible fate. But what could you say in an interview like that? Except that you had done your best.

Was it true, though? Had he done his best?

Rising abruptly to his feet, he went over to the window. It was a raw sort of day, hinting that autumn was coming early this year, an ominous wind blowing down Austurstræti and the faces of the passers-by pinched from battling against the gale as they ran their errands in the nearby shops and bank. That August had been unusually cold and stormy, and, with the sun hidden behind the clouds, the grey buildings and the street outside looked bleak.

Kristján's thoughts travelled ten years back in time, to August 1956. To the days when he had first got an inkling, then still a relatively new recruit to the police, that there were powerful forces out to influence the investigation. To the moment when the phone had rung in Óttar's study and Eiríkur, one of the most senior figures in the force, had told him that the case didn't merit any particular attention. Kristján had gone back to town, feeling chastened by the reprimand, since he believed he had only been doing his duty, as any conscientious policeman would. But what could you say to your superior officer in a situation like that? It was a question Kristján had returned to repeatedly over the past decade, though he had never discussed it with anyone else apart from his wife, who had shrugged and said that he shouldn't dwell on it; he simply needed to move on. Then there was Högni. Kristján was all too aware that he hadn't pursued the tip about him either . . . But there had been no appetite at the time for importuning prominent members of society with uncomfortable questions.

Of course the case hadn't been closed that August day on Videy, far from it.

When Lára didn't come home, she had been reported missing on the radio and in the papers. The girl's disappearance had caused a stir, as it wasn't every day that a young girl vanished in Iceland. Her large, dark eyes in the photo that was circulated in the papers had seemed to speak to the public, as if Lára were in possession of some terrible secret. There was intense pressure on the police to find the girl, and the responsibility for that lay with Kristján, but he had failed in his duty.

Kristján had worked on the investigation with a number of other officers. Together with a colleague, he had visited Lára's parents in Grjótathorp, a tangle of old wooden houses and narrow streets climbing the hillside from the centre of town. They had started to get worried as soon as they didn't receive their regular phone call from their daughter the weekend she went missing.

'She always rang us,' her mother had said. Mother and daughter were extraordinarily alike, to judge from the picture of Lára in the papers. 'She's a homebody and has always confided in us. Then she got it into her head that she wanted to work as a maid over the summer, so she applied for a position with the couple on Videy and got the job. Not that I was surprised – seeing as she's so hardworking and presentable.'

Lára's father was a little older than her mother. Both were teachers and Lára was their only child. The girl's room had been spick and span, containing a white metal bedstead covered in a colourful quilt that Lára had crocheted herself in her needlework classes at school. She had good taste in colours, Kristján had thought to himself at the time. Strange how these unimportant details remained with him a decade later. The wardrobe had been full of clothes that she hadn't taken with her to Videy, winter garments mostly, but also the velvet dress she was wearing in the black-and-white photo, which turned out to be green.

Against one wall were a simple dressing table and chair, both of which looked home-made, and in the drawer were some postcards from a cousin of Lára's who lived in Copenhagen. The bookcase had contained a Bible and several novels, including works by Halldór Laxness, the Icelander who had recently been crowned winner of the Nobel Prize in Literature.

Nothing in the room had provided any clues about Lára's fate. Kristján had found a diary behind the novels in the bookcase, but it had turned out to be for the school year of 1954–5. Inside, he'd read in Lára's careful handwriting her descriptions of the main meals she had eaten each day, as well as comments about her classmates at Austurbær School, particularly the good-looking boys.

Kristján had asked Lára's mother if the girl had been in the habit of keeping a diary and the woman had said that she had, adding that she'd encouraged her daughter to write about her life on the island. 'It was supposed to be an adventure,' the mother had continued. 'My Lára hasn't led a particularly eventful life. She's planning to take her school-leaving exams and had been working as a shop assistant at a dairy in her free time. The job on Videy was a chance for her to have an adventure and perhaps grow up a bit.' The mother's eyes had filled with tears as she said these last words. 'As far as I'm concerned, she'd have done much better not to go. Only fifteen, and now . . .' From what Kristján could remember, the woman never did finish the sentence.

He also recalled asking if there was any chance that Lára could have been planning to meet someone in Reykjavík that fateful weekend. The girl's father had replied that his daughter didn't have a boyfriend. 'Lára's always been close to us. I can't imagine her coming to Reykjavík without letting us know.'

Kristján could think of countless examples of young people who had their own reasons for not confiding in their parents about what they were up to. But, as it turned out, none of Lára's girlfriends had been able to give the police any information about possible boyfriends or other men in her life who she could conceivably have run away with.

According to Lára's parents, she had made the acquaintance of Óttar and Ólöf, the couple living on Videy, through a girl who'd been in service there the previous summer. It had occurred to Kristján that it might be worth talking to the girl in question, but it hadn't been a priority. After all, he'd reasoned, what could she know about Lára's fate?

Lára had telephoned her parents every week and sounded happy with her life. Admittedly, she would never have complained in her employers' hearing, but her parents agreed that she had sounded contented. She had taken a boat out to the island at the beginning of May with the intention of staying until the end of August. Then, according to Óttar and Ólöf, she'd unexpectedly announced that she wasn't going to see out her contract. Lára's mother had shaken her head over this: 'I can assure you, it's most unlike Lára not to finish something. She always turned up punctually to work at the dairy and would never have wanted it said of her that she was the type to quit.'

Kristján snapped out of his reverie to find himself still standing by the window in the police station. He finished the cold coffee in his cup, grimacing at the bitter taste. Lára's story continued to haunt him. He had no intention of closing the case, although it had happened a long time ago and all the clues had probably disappeared by now. The grief in her parents' eyes had been so piercing that he felt he would do anything he could to alleviate their suffering.

At the time it had been considered most likely that Lára had accepted a lift on somebody's boat and that her fate had been sealed, either on the way back to shore or later in Reykjavík. He supposed it had been the most convenient explanation: an unknown villain, a terrible crime that would never be solved.

Yet Kristján couldn't help wondering if they wouldn't have done better to focus their attention on Viðey. Of course, they had searched the island at the time, without finding any sign of the girl. And Óttar and Ólöf had stuck to their story: that Lára had decided to give up her position and return to Reykjavík. But he was aware that the police could have conducted a more thorough search and subjected Óttar and Ólöf to far more rigorous questioning.

The police had put out an appeal to anyone who could have given Lára a lift in their boat that weekend, but no one had come forward. Nor had the harbourmaster in Reykjavík been able to provide any useful information about vessels sailing between Videy and the mainland that Friday. Since the island was only a bit over four kilometres from the shore at the nearest point, it would have been possible to take a small vessel out there without attracting attention, and the boat wouldn't necessarily have put in at Reykjavík on the way back. The police's inquiries had drawn a blank. Search parties had been sent out to comb the beaches but no sign of a body or any of Lára's belongings had ever been found. The girl had simply vanished into thin air.

No wonder the case had caught the popular imagination. Nothing could be found to discredit Lára; she'd had no secrets and seemed to have been a girl anyone could identify with; a girl who had simply wanted a change of scene. A girl who had left her family home for the summer in the hope of gaining a bit of maturity and independence, and performed her duties conscientiously, right up until she had decided to quit her job early – if that claim was true.

Her departure from Videy was a genuine mystery – unless, of course, she had never left the island at all.

1976

7 August

'It'll be good for the department, Kristján; good for you and good for the police,' his boss had said. The words were still echoing in Kristján's head as he sat in his flat in a Kópavogur apartment block, offering the journalist a cup of coffee.

'I'd prefer tea, if you have any,' his visitor had replied politely.

Good for you . . .

How could it be good for him to rake up the details of Lára's disappearance all over again? Personally, he'd do anything to forget about the case. It had been like a lead weight hanging around his neck these last twenty years. Although he'd achieved a certain degree of promotion within the police, he'd always had the feeling that he could have gone further if he hadn't messed up that inquiry. And now here he was, forced to be the face of that failure all over again. 'They'll be discussing the case whether we like it or not,' his boss had added, 'so it's as well to make sure that we get a chance to tell our side of the story.' It didn't seem to have occurred to the man to speak to the press on his behalf: no, it was always Kristján who got thrown to the lions.

As it happened, interest in Lára's fate had been over-shadowed in recent months. That summer, the headlines in Iceland had been dominated by the disappearance of two men, Gudmundur and Geirfinnur, and the dramatic story of the four suspects in the case who had been arrested, then subsequently released. Kristján had come nowhere near this investigation.

The journalist, Ólafur, who was also the newspaper's editor, had a pleasant manner, and Kristján assumed the interview would at least be fair. A loyal reader of *Vísir*, he was generally satisfied with the paper's approach. The interview was to feature on the front cover of the weekend edition.

Dusk was falling outside the windows. The return of the darkness in August after weeks of the midnight sun always filled Kristján with a sense of foreboding, and had done ever since he'd embarked on the investigation into Lára's disappearance twenty years ago. He sometimes had the fanciful idea that she'd simply been swallowed up by the night.

'I'd like to start by thanking you for inviting me into your home, Kristján,' the editor said. 'That's not something I take for granted. Anyway, the plan is to remind readers about the tragic case in Sunday's paper, with your interview as the core of our coverage.'

Kristján nodded, trying to ignore his misgivings about the interview and hoping it wouldn't take more than an hour, as he wanted to watch the latest episode of *Columbo* at half past nine. All he was missing on Iceland's only TV channel at the moment was a Swedish documentary on arms production.

'Could you take us through the events of the fateful day when you first heard Lára's name?'

Kristján was silent for a while. Eventually he began: 'Of course, at the time it was just an ordinary day at work as far as I was concerned. I remember that it was chilly, like it sometimes is in August. And I also remember assuming that the girl had just run away from home – or rather from her job as a maid.'

'So there was nothing to suggest that this would be a case you'd still be talking about two decades later?'

Kristján shook his head. 'I was young and inexperienced, only twenty-four. Of course, I thought I knew everything, but then I was really dropped in at the deep end.'

'Do you often think about Lára?'

The question sounded sincere but Kristján couldn't bring himself to give an equally sincere answer. The editor had made himself comfortable in the patterned armchair, part of the three-piece suite. On the coffee table between them were teacups and a black tape recorder. The man, who was in his early thirties, had dark hair and was dressed in a tasteful grey suit. Kristján felt as if he knew him, but that was only because he'd seen him reading the news so often during the first years following the introduction of television to Iceland in 1966. Then he had been in black and white, but now suddenly he was here in Kristján's living room in full colour, although his suit was grey.

'Naturally, I often think about her,' Kristján replied after a pause, though the true answer would have been that he thought about her every day.

Because the fact was that he hadn't actually done his best. He hadn't been allowed to follow up their most promising lead as it had been considered too far-fetched. That damned closing of ranks – it extended across the entire political spectrum; no cause to rock the boat if there was any risk of people 'who mattered' being subjected to any unpleasantness. And Kristján had played along. He had wanted to hold on to his job, to keep his bosses happy. *Are you mad? Of course Högni Eyfjörd has nothing to do with it . . .* That had been the refrain.

His mind roamed back across the intervening years. A fisherman had given him a lift to Viðey for his third and, as it turned out, final visit in the course of his inquiries. Naturally, the man had heard about Lára's disappearance and asked if they were still looking for her. Kristján had said they were. He'd been wearing a new hat. In his memory, the weather had been perfect, only a light wind, the late-summer sun shining brightly.

I once took that Högni out to the island – you know who I mean?

Kristján had realized at once who the fisherman was talking about.

Högni Eyfjörd?

A developer and more; from a good family, well connected, a contemporary of the lawyer and his wife on Videy.

Yes, he was all dressed up. He'd missed his boat, he told me, and needed to be ferried over to the island at short notice.

Was this recently?

No, about a month ago. On a Friday evening, if I remember right. It probably doesn't matter but I just wanted to let you know, seeing as you're in the police.

But Kristján hadn't pursued the lead ... He'd given way to pressure.

The editor and former TV newsreader coughed and Kristján let his memories float away, returning to the sitting room and the present.

'I'm sorry?' he said, realizing he'd dropped out for a moment, become caught up in the past.

'I was just asking, Kristján, what *you* think happened to Lára?'

Strange as it might seem, Kristján hadn't actually been prepared for this question, but he answered without hesitation: 'I believe she's alive.'

'Do you really mean that?' the editor exclaimed, astonished.

No doubt that had given him the headline for his article, Kristján thought.

'Yes, I do. I have a hunch.'

'Could you explain why you believe that, Kristján?' The editor had such a friendly manner and came across as so genuinely interested that Kristján felt he had no choice but to answer.

'Well . . . there's nothing to indicate that she came to any harm. She was a young girl in service with a decent family who treated her well. Then she goes and vanishes, along with her belongings. She'd hardly have thrown herself in the sea with all her luggage. That's most unlikely. No, I think she left of her own accord, but I don't know why.'

He looked up and saw his wife, Gudrún, watching him from the kitchen with a disapproving expression. He knew what that was about. They had discussed this theory of his before and she had repeatedly warned him against expressing it in public. It would only open up old wounds and make life difficult for Lára's parents, since he seemed to be implying – indirectly – that the girl might have been fleeing something at home.

Well, he'd gone and done it now. And he didn't regret his spur-of-the-moment decision. Perhaps this would get the case moving again – give somebody a push.

'That's news to me,' the editor said. 'Was the possibility investigated at the time?'

'We had very little to go on, you know. Nothing but guesswork. The girl simply disappeared. Look, I'd like to ask a favour, if I may . . .'

'Of course, Kristján.'

'I'd like to get a message to Lára, if she is out there, all grown up and living somewhere under an assumed name.'

The editor nodded.

All of a sudden, Kristján felt as if he were taking part in a TV interview, as if the sitting room was a studio and he was in the spotlight, gazing into the camera, speaking directly to Lára.

'What I want to say is, just let us know you're all right, wherever you are . . . It would give peace of mind to a great many people.'

Not least me, Kristján thought.

He knew it was wishful thinking, but sometimes it was all right to wish for something. He knew too, deep down – didn't he? – that of course Högni Eyfjörd had had nothing to do with the disappearance of a teenage girl. The idea was totally absurd. Why would an entrepreneur, involved in the construction of half the buildings in the city, have wanted to harm an innocent kid?

Kristján felt a little better. He had managed to convince himself, yet again, that Lára was alive.

He tried changing the subject briefly: 'Can I ask, is there much difference between this sort of thing and making TV programmes?'

The editor smiled. He probably hadn't expected to find himself being interviewed. 'To be honest, I'm enjoying this more right now. It was a tremendous adventure helping to launch TV in this country, but we all need a change of scene. In ten years, maybe I'll want to do something completely different. What about you?'

'In ten years?'

'Yes, in 1986.'

'That's a long way off,' Kristján said. 'But I'll still be in the police.' He didn't even need to think twice, as it was self-evident. Once a cop, always a cop. He'd done his job well; obeyed orders. He and his wife were looking for somewhere bigger to live – a detached house, this time. His pay might not be that good but at least it provided a reliable income. They both put money aside every month, ignoring advertisements for foreign holidays, and, with luck, in a few years they'd be able to move into a house of their own. The problem was that the current galloping inflation was eating up their savings almost as fast as they could put them by. The new aluminium króna coins were so flimsy they could float on water, which said it all. In spite of this, he'd started thinking about building his own house or perhaps buying somewhere with a roof and walls in one of the new suburbs and doing it up in stages.

'I gather you're happy in the police.'

'Yes, I think I've always belonged there. My grand-father was a policeman back in the day and, although my father wasn't, you can safely say it's in the blood. I feel at home there and I hope I'm of service to society.'

'Did the original investigation into Lára's disappear-ance go smoothly? Could you tell us a bit about that?'

Kristján was brought up short for a moment. 'Yes, it went smoothly, or . . . maybe that's the wrong way to put it because we weren't successful. We didn't find Lára, though I believe that, viewing it objectively, we left no stone unturned: we talked to everyone involved and, well, we conducted a professional inquiry.' He was aware of a bad taste in his mouth as he said this but tried not to show it.

'Did you get enough support?'

'I'm sorry?'

'From upstairs? From your superiors?'

'Oh, yes, all the support I needed.' This was the correct answer, or at least all that was fit to print. 'The most important thing, when conducting an investigation, is to be given the freedom to look into every corner, and that's what we did. But naturally there are times when you need help, so you ask for it.'

'I see. Could you describe Videy for us as it was in those days? A lot has changed since then.'

'No doubt. The couple who employed Lára have moved away, for one thing . . . They were there for several summers, I believe . . .'

'Óttar and Ólöf, yes.'

'Exactly. I remember thinking what a peaceful life they led there, though of course the girl's disappearance upset everything. I expect that was one of the reasons why they moved away in the end. May I ask, have you spoken to them as well?'

'I'm afraid they weren't prepared to talk to us. Not everyone cares to rake up the past.'

Yet again, Kristján regretted having agreed to this interview, having let himself be put on the spot. 'Understandably,' he said, rather dryly. Though it wasn't the editor's fault; he was only doing his job. Not the first and certainly not the last journalist who would write about Lára.

'Did you visit them often, Kristján? On Videy?'

It occurred to him, just for a moment, to tell a lie, but that wasn't a realistic choice. A policeman couldn't lie to a journalist. That sort of thing always got found out in the end, and, if it was, the consequences would be obvious.

Kristján had no intention of losing his job on account of a lie, however ashamed he was of his rather perfunctory working methods at the time.

He wondered if he should resort to saying that he wasn't permitted to divulge the details of the investigation, but he doubted his bosses would be pleased with that answer. A long time had passed and it mustn't look as if he – or the police – had anything to hide.

'As often as necessary,' he replied, after a pause. 'I went to see them three times. The first time, alone, when we received notification that Lára was missing. Then there was an organized search of the island, as was mentioned in the news. A group of people combed the island from end to end – police officers, volunteers, the family . . . I don't suppose you'd remember that, being so young.'

The editor smiled. 'I read up on the background before coming here and saw photos of the searchers in the newspaper archives. It must have been a hell of an operation.'

'We were extremely concerned about Lára by that point, as nothing had been heard from her for several days, and the public were demanding answers. We had no alternative but to conduct a thorough search. The poor girl was nowhere to be found, though.'

An odd silence followed this statement, as if it hinted at terrible secrets and an immeasurable burden. It was true that it had been weighing on Kristján for the last two decades. Although he wasn't a particularly religious man, he did pray to a higher power almost every evening, and the prayer was always the same: that the riddle of Lára's fate would be solved. For her and her family's sake, of course, but deep down he knew that it was no less important for his own sake. He felt he could hardly bear to live with the mystery any longer, and yet he had no choice.

Now and then he sat in his office late in the evening, when everyone else had gone home, and opened up the old files. He would try to work out if he could have overlooked something, some minor detail, mentally reviewing the interviews as far as he could remember them: the people involved, their expressions even, hoping that time hadn't blurred the distinction between reality and imagination.

He continued: 'I have a vivid memory of the day we went out to search for her. It was a freezing autumn day, as if the weather gods were against us and didn't want her to be found. We split up into groups, taking experts with us, people who knew the island well, though it's not easy to get lost there as Videy's pretty small. There aren't many buildings: the church, the mansion, the old schoolhouse, the farmhouse and a few ruins. For some reason I always pictured her seeking refuge in the church – I don't know why – but of course she wasn't there. She wasn't on the island at all.'

'If it hadn't been for her missing luggage, I suppose most people would have concluded that she'd deliberately drowned herself, wouldn't they?'

'Yes. Her luggage, quite. It just didn't fit.'

'Then, later, you went out to the island once more, you said?'

Kristján nodded. That had been the time he sailed out

there with the fisherman, when the subject of Högni had
come up.

'Yes, I crossed the sound one more time to talk to
the couple. By then the trail was growing cold, if it was
ever warm. There had been no sign of her, no leads, no
one had seen or heard from her. But I felt I had to put
in one final effort and check if there was anything they
could have forgotten, even if it was only some minor
detail—'

The editor interrupted: 'Were they suspects, then?'

Kristján was wrongfooted by the question. How was
he supposed to answer that? Of course they'd been
suspects – in his opinion. Though it had been another
story with the top brass; with Eiríkur, the senior officer
who had made it abundantly clear that Óttar and Ólöf
were to be left alone. A while after the initial disappearance, Kristján had taken a look at Óttar's career. He was
a barrister with what appeared to be a spotless reputation. It was almost unthinkable that a man like that
would have harmed a young girl. In addition to his legal
work, Óttar had been prominent in the public debate
and made an impact in the business world. He was well
connected in political circles too. In fact, a man like
Óttar doubtless had a web of connections right across
society, although he had been relatively young at the
time, in his early thirties. He had taught contract law at
the University of Iceland, as well as working as a consul,
and the couple had owned a detached house in the
centre of Reykjavík in addition to the farmhouse on
Videy. Ólöf came from a good family, the origin, no

doubt, of their wealth: there were wholesalers, members of parliament and government ministers wherever you looked in the Blöndal family tree. Prominent citizens who would never hurt a soul – that was what appearances had suggested, but of course Kristján couldn't rule the couple out entirely. The girl had gone missing right under their noses. As far as he knew, they had been the only three people on the island, then suddenly there had been only two of them left. It reminded him of a whodunit he'd once read by Agatha Christie.

A scrupulous police officer would have taken this aspect of the inquiry firmly in hand, summoning the couple for a formal interview at the station and giving them a real grilling, serving Lára's interests rather than those of his superiors. But Kristján had failed the test, again and again.

'There were no actual suspects,' he said eventually, taking care over how he phrased it. 'There was never any indication that a crime had been committed, you see. We were looking for a missing girl, not investigating a murder . . .'

But if Lára had been murdered, wasn't it obvious that the couple on Videy must have been involved? Weren't they the only ones who would have had the opportunity? They could have got rid of her luggage and disposed of her body. Had it perhaps been a terrible accident, a fight that had ended in the worst way possible, which they had been forced to hush up to protect their reputation? Unbelievably, they had emerged fairly well from the news coverage. The public hadn't dared to believe that the lawyer and his wife could have had anything to do with the girl's disappearance. Kristján remembered reading an interview with Ólöf Blöndal in the *Morgunbladid* newspaper in which she had begged the public to assist with the search, lavishing praise on Lára and saying how hard-working she had been. *Such a pretty, lively girl* was the description that stood out for him from that interview. And that's how he pictured Lára, though they had never met. It was strange what a strong bond he felt with the missing girl.

'I see. There were no suspects. Was there never any question of changing the status of the inquiry, of elevating it to a murder investigation?' The editor's voice had developed an edge.

Kristján hesitated, looking around, unsure how to answer. He could just picture the headlines.

At that moment Gudrún emerged from the kitchen and said without warning: 'Kristján and I need to get going, I'm afraid. We're supposed to be meeting friends.'

'I'm sorry?'

'Oh yes, did he forget to mention it?' she asked blithely, as if nothing could be more natural than this blatant lie.

'Yes, actually, but it's not a problem. I didn't mean to take up too much of your time.'

'You haven't,' she said.

'We'll also need a photo of you – a new one, I mean,' the editor said, turning back to Kristján. 'Can I send round a photographer?'

Kristján dithered a moment, running a hand over his head. His hair was thinning fast these days – he could have done with the hat that had blown away over Faxaflói long ago. The photo of him they used whenever Lára's case was dredged up was an old one, and he had aged in the interim. He wished he could refuse the request but didn't like to seem disobliging.

'Yes, I suppose so . . .' he said, and shrugged.

1986

1 August

Thórdís Alexandersdóttir was still a glamorous woman, with luxuriant dark hair and eyes that seemed capable of expressing the entire spectrum of emotions. One of her talents was the ability to take on any number of guises. She could don a severe suit, draw her hair back in a bun and put on only the subtlest of make-up. Or wear brightly coloured dresses with plunging necklines, loose hair and the reddest lipstick money could buy. Although she had put on a few kilos these days, she still carried herself well, disguising her more ample figure by clever dressing. At this moment she was examining her appearance in the mirror at home in their detached house on Laugarásvegur. Today's outfit consisted of a red woollen shawl over a black dress and black leather boots. She applied some lipstick and smiled at her reflection.

Her mother had brought her up to believe that you should always look good, especially in a crisis. It didn't do

49

to wear your distress on your sleeve. Thórdís sometimes snorted disapprovingly when she saw the woman next door, a French teacher, going to work in jeans and a jumper, her hair looking as if she'd been dragged through a hedge backwards. This was letting the side down, Thórdís thought. She herself always made an effort to look well turned out, always wore nail varnish, whatever the occasion, even if she was only popping out to the shops.

No doubt the theatre had exaggerated this tendency. In her day, Thórdís had been one of Iceland's leading ladies, garnering critical acclaim for her performance in countless starring roles, from Shakespearean heroines to more contemporary parts.

But the roles had started to dry up as she got older. While the bloody men who had been at drama school with her were still thriving, playing opposite much younger women, she herself was rarely called on these days, except to play aged aunts or nurses wrapped in grey woollen shawls, with only a handful of lines to be spoken in a shrill, cracked voice. And when word got round that Thórdís was overfond of a tipple, the parts had become even thinner on the ground – not that the same behaviour did anything to prevent her male colleagues from being offered their choice of roles.

As far as Thórdís was concerned, her drinking was perfectly under control. And anyway, she thought, what about all those studies showing that red wine was good for you – like chocolate?

After another glance in the mirror, she nipped back into the bedroom and put on a necklace with an enormous silver cross pendant. It seemed fitting, given that she was on her way to hospital to sit by her husband's deathbed. She imagined the nurses eyeing her with unfeigned sympathy and talking about her admiringly in the cafeteria next day.

Her eyes brimming with tears at this thought, Thórdís hurried out of the house. In her red cape, with the cross on her chest, she felt almost like a Roman Catholic cardinal.

Finnur Stephensen had been in hospital for eight weeks now. He had been diagnosed with cancer of the colon and, by the time they opened him up, the disease had spread to his entire digestive system. When it became clear that nothing could be done, his health had taken a rapid turn for the worse and now he didn't have much time left.

Thórdís floated into the room, where he was lying under a white hospital duvet, his face ashen, his eyes dull. She reached out and caressed his cheek. She would miss Finnur. They had met more than forty years ago at the Reykjavík grammar school, where Thórdís had been one of only a handful of female pupils. He had been the son of a Reykjavík wholesaler and had, in due course, taken over his father's business, going on to run it with great success. He'd always had a good eye for what was likely to prove popular, whether it was sports clothing, kitchen appliances or alcoholic drinks. She and Finnur had parted ways for a while, only to get back together when he was approaching forty. She was two years younger than him.

They'd quickly become a couple at school. He'd been shy and unassuming where she was bold and assertive.

They'd balanced each other out. Eventually, though, Thórdís had tired of him. She'd been bored by the gang of friends he hung out with, feeling they had nothing to offer – all they talked about was money, politics and plotting; they'd hardly had a cultural bone in their bodies. In the emotional breathing space the break-up had given her, she'd fallen in love with one of her fellow actors.

After a brief and stormy relationship, she had gone back to Finnur. And he had accepted her with respect and understanding, making a genuine effort to show an interest in her artistic ambitions and theatrical career, and supporting her in everything she did. They had travelled together, visiting foreign art galleries, enjoying gourmet food, learning about life. Thanks to the success of the wholesale business, they hadn't had to deny themselves much. He had always regarded Thórdís with admiration and she in turn had enjoyed regaling him with anecdotes about thespian life and discussing the personalities and controversies of the day on the cultural scene.

She supposed Finnur had been the closest she would ever have to a soulmate. What would her life be like without him? Rattling around alone in the house on Laugarásvegur, knocking back red wine, with no one to talk to. In an attempt to shake off this sudden mood of despair, she concentrated on picturing his funeral and herself dressed in black, grief-stricken but glamorous, in a packed church, the Motet Choir – and perhaps a single soloist – providing the music.

She sighed. She was going to be dreadfully lonely.

*

Finnur was lying in his room on the oncology ward at the National Hospital, his eyes turned to the window, but he looked round when his wife came in. She made such a contrast to the cold sterility of the sickroom: a vision in red and black, accompanied by a waft of perfume, mingled with a faint whiff of alcohol. He knew his Thórdís, knew all her virtues and flaws, and he loved her just the way she was. She perched on a chair by his bed, took his hand in hers and held it tight.

He was tired. Conscious of the disease inside him, consuming his body from within. How he missed the pleasure of eating good food, of appreciating the bouquet of a fine wine and enjoying it with Thórdís. Instead, he was stuck lying here, doped up on morphine. Whenever the fog wore off, he became aware of the pain in his abdomen and was reminded – as if he could forget it – that the disease was pursuing its merciless course. Little by little he had lost interest in life. With the morphine flowing through his veins, he dozed, his mind wandering back in time, showing him pictures of events, some of them real, others – he wasn't so sure.

Thórdís, radiant with laughter, the centre of attention at theatrical parties where he had been happy to take a back seat. His parents on the farm where he had grown up. They had been so diligent, forever toiling away, his mother kind but serious, his father permanently on the go. When he was ten, his father had been offered a job in Reykjavík and the family had moved to the capital, living first in a basement flat on Hringbraut, then gradually moving up in the world. His father had begun by importing pots and pans, but his business had flourished and expanded until it became one of the largest wholesalers in Iceland. And Finnur had continued the work of building it up, demonstrating even more flair for the job.

He and Thórdís had already agreed on the disposal of his estate: Finnur's nephew would take over management of the wholesale business, while Thórdís retained the majority share. Finnur had his doubts about his nephew's ability. The young man lacked Finnur's drive; he was too interested in the good life. A bit like Finnur's old pal, Högni Eyfjörd. Always with a new girl on his arm, ever the jaunty bon viveur.

Finnur's mind continued roaming to and fro, clouded with morphine.

'Finnur, darling. How are you today?'

He mumbled in an effort to speak, trying to smile at his wife.

A nurse put her head round the door, regarded them sympathetically, then offered Thórdís a coffee.

'Thank you,' Thórdís said, and followed her out into the corridor, where she was handed a coffee in a mug marked with the logo of the National Hospital.

'He's going downhill quite fast now,' the nurse warned her. 'Can you stick around today?'

'Yes,' Thórdís said. The whole thing felt so unendurably cruel.

'Are there any children or other family members or friends who might want to come?'

'No,' Thórdís said wearily. 'Not today.'

'He's been talking a lot, though we can't always follow what he's saying. About all kinds of stuff, like the cost of living, inflation, and so on. But there was one thing that stuck out. He started saying he needed to go to Videy.'

Thórdís was startled. 'Videy?'

'Yes, he said he needed to go there,' the nurse repeated.

Thórdís's eyes strayed briefly to the window. Then she smiled and said: 'That must be the morphine confusing him.'

She went back into Finnur's room. The sun was shining outside, flooding the ward with that unforgiving late-summer light that illuminates everything with such stark clarity – from which nothing can be hidden. Every line on Finnur's face was accentuated as he lay there by the window, his skin so pallid it was almost grey.

Finnur rested his tired eyes on Thórdís. She had come back into the room, the smell of coffee now overlaying the scent and wine fumes. He smiled faintly. His sense of smell seemed to be the only one still functioning properly. He'd always had a sensitive nose. What made hospital so alien was the lack of normal smells. Everything was disinfected, scrubbed and washed using soap without any fragrance. Finnur loved the way Thórdís smelled.

His mind started wandering again. The scent of newly mown grass on the farm. The scent of earth when he was picking potatoes. Of Paris, the first time he visited; a complex assault on the senses, composed of red wine, perfume, garlic and the sewer stench rising from the Seine on hot days. The fragrance of pink roses. The shore smells of salt and seaweed. The smell of death mingled with that of soil and grass.

His eyelids had closed. Could he open them? He felt his breathing grow laboured. Yes, Thórdís was there, he could sense her still: the perfume, the coffee, the lotion she applied to her skin every day. She loved pampering herself.

There was something he needed to say to her, something urgent . . .

Thórdís noticed the change in her husband's breathing and realized with a jolt that he might be going. Tears sprang into her eyes, but she no longer cared what she looked like. Her husband was about to leave her.

She clasped his hand, fixing her gaze on him as if to imprint on her memory the image of that dear face that had been her companion for so many years.

Finnur opened his eyes. At first he stared hazily at the window, then he looked straight at Thórdís. As he did so, his gaze cleared and appeared for an instant so animated that he might never have been more alive than in that moment.

'Videy. You have to go to Videy.'

Thórdís met his gaze.

Finnur released a long breath. The spark in his eyes went out.

As it did so, the room seemed to darken.

Finnur Stephensen had departed this world.

1986

14 August

Valur Róbertsson was sitting in Café Mokka with that week's issue of the paper.

It was hot off the press, the heady smell of ink mingling with that of freshly brewed coffee. There weren't many customers in Mokka, just a few regulars Valur knew by sight, but he wasn't here to be sociable. Mokka was Reykjavík's attempt at a cosmopolitan coffee shop, serving customers espressos since the late 1950s, and although Valur hadn't been born then, it felt as if the place probably hadn't changed much in the interim, with its retro furniture, the art on the walls and the low-hanging copper lamps. He wanted a chance to take a leisurely look through the paper; savour this week's harvest. After that he was expecting his sister. They met at least once a week, at Mokka, to catch up on each other's lives over coffee and waffles.

There was the front page, in all its glory. He was proud

of it. Eyecatching, but tastefully so. Dagbjartur, the editor of *Vikubladid*, always stressed that it was the cover that sold the paper – it was absolutely key for sales on the street, and there was no denying that they crossed a line sometimes. But Valur was ambitious: he had no intention of getting stuck in tabloid journalism for ever. He wanted to be the best investigative reporter in Iceland, so he played by his own rules as far as possible, while doing his best to please his boss. In a year or so he reckoned he'd have made enough of a name for himself to move to a daily paper, maybe even into television. Radio held no attraction for him, as his instincts told him the future lay in television, especially now that Iceland's first private TV station was due to start broadcasting soon. Things were on the move; society was changing for the better and there was a world of opportunity out there. Although he was only twenty-five, he'd been employed in journalism since he was twenty. He'd worked his way up the ladder and been with his current paper for more than two years, almost since it was launched. The life expectancy for a weekly paper wasn't particularly long. But now their sales figures had broken records two weeks running and there was every sign that they would do the same this week. And, for the third issue in a row, Valur was responsible for the entire front page.

It was all down to Lára.

The unfortunate girl who had vanished without trace thirty years ago.

Like most people, Valur had grown up with the story. The same old photo of the girl cropped up in the press at

regular intervals, as if imprinted on the nation's soul.
Everyone knew that picture of Lára. Valur had been fas-
cinated by the riddle ever since he was a kid; he didn't
really know why. There was something indefinably mysterious about Lára's story, as if the girl were not quite of
this world. As if she'd never really been flesh and blood,
although of course she had – and perhaps she still was.
That was the secret power of her story, he sometimes
thought: the fact that no one could say for sure whether
she was alive or dead.

He and his sister, Sunna, used to speculate about the
case when they were younger. Born only two years apart,
they had always spent a lot of time together and were still
best friends in their twenties. They'd come up with all
kinds of theories about Lára's fate. No doubt many of
their contemporaries had done the same, as Lára had
been a household name in those days, but he had to admit
that he and his sister were blessed with unusually vivid
imaginations. He'd found an outlet for his creativity in
journalism, Sunna in her studies; she was doing a degree
in comparative literature at the University of Iceland.
One of these days she'd become a poet, she used to say.
He believed her. He actually thought she'd make a pretty
good poet, and was ready with encouragement whenever
she needed it.

It was more than a month since Sunna had presented
him with the idea on a silver platter – over coffee at
Mokka, naturally.

August marked the thirtieth anniversary of Lára's disappearance. Valur had started doing the spadework a

month earlier. He'd taken a seat in the office of his editor, Dagbjartur, who was in his early sixties, had survived any number of changes in the newspaper business and apparently had every intention of ending his career as editor of *Vikubladid*. He'd been unimpressed at first when Valur pitched the idea. *Everything that can be said about Lára has already been written*, Dagbjartur had argued, adding that he doubted she'd ever be found now. But Valur had persevered, pointing out that the mystery of the girl's disappearance had united the nation and an in-depth report would be guaranteed to shift papers. Valur had envisaged dedicating a whole month exclusively to a re-examination of her story, interviewing everyone he could get hold of who had known her and hopefully digging up some new clues along the way.

No doubt it was the point about increased sales that had swayed Dagbjartur when he reluctantly gave Valur the green light to write a series of features about Lára.

Three weeks and three issues later, it had to be acknowledged that Valur had been right. The paper had been flying off the shelves and interest in Lára was at its highest for years. Valur had even made it into the news himself, being invited to do interviews on TV and radio. It was as if he had become the face of the investigation that had never really been closed.

Yet, in spite of everything, no new leads had emerged. All Valur's painstaking detective work had achieved was to rehash a variety of interesting details linked to the case. While he had added new interviews to the mix, the information he got from his interviewees hadn't brought to light anything that wasn't known before. But his presentation was good, Dagbjartur had admitted, giving him a pat on the back. Deservedly, Valur thought.

He was going to write one more article. *I've saved the best till last*, he'd promised Dagbjartur, who was now distracted by the city of Reykjavík's upcoming two-hundredth anniversary celebrations.

Valur didn't really expect to be able to deliver on his big claim: he'd already used up most of his ideas and tried speaking to the main people linked to the case. The most difficult conversation had been with Lára's parents. So far, his repeated attempts to talk to Óttar and Ólöf, the couple who had lived in the house on Videy, had failed. Perhaps he would have another go before the weekend; see if he could collar Óttar in his office, for example.

There was one other possibility he still hoped might yield results. He hadn't yet managed to get hold of the policeman who'd led the original investigation. The man was still alive, as far as Valur knew, but he was proving elusive. Valur had called him at home. A woman had answered and taken a message, but no one had returned his call. Valur had rung again, without success. He hadn't yet tried door-stepping the man, but perhaps that would be worth a go . . . Because he had to do something to fill up next Thursday's paper. Right now, though, it was time for a coffee to celebrate a job well done, and then there was the weekend to look forward to. Not that Valur ever really took time off; he was always on duty in one way or another, angling for gossip from his sources at various cafés and bars, over glasses of that uniquely Icelandic cocktail – non-alcoholic beer with a shot of vodka. As the sale of alcoholic beer was illegal, this was the closest Valur could get to the real thing.

Valur didn't notice Sunna until she sat down at the table opposite him.

'Hi, have you ordered for me?' Sunna asked. She had a sunny disposition, which was reflected in her voice.

'No, I didn't know exactly what time you were coming.'

She smiled, laying down her notepad, pen and a slim, dog-eared volume.

'What are you reading?' he asked.

'Elías Mar. It's a poetry collection. About ten years old. I've just been round for coffee with him.'

'At his place?' Valur asked, duly impressed. Elías Mar was a leading modernist writer, in his sixties now.

'Yes, in the west end. It was a bit like walking into a junk shop, with books everywhere and a bit of a fug. But he's lovely. I'm writing my dissertation about him and there's nothing like meeting the subject in person.'

'Isn't that cheating?' he asked jokily. 'Meeting the subject – is that allowed?'

'Life's a competition, remember?'

'So, how was he?' Valur asked, to show an interest in his sister's life, though all he really wanted to talk about was the weekend issue of the paper and the case. After all, that was something they were both interested in.

'Elías? He was on good form. Anyway, what about you? Have you found Lára yet?' She stood up. 'I'm going to get a coffee.'

This was typical of Sunna; always in a rush. Either

answering her own questions or not bothering to wait for a reply. Valur sat there patiently, waiting for her to come back.

'Anyway, what's new? Have you found her?' she asked again as she sat down with her coffee.

'This sort of thing takes time.' He smiled. 'I'm in a bit of a fix, actually.'

'A fix?'

'I need to spin the story out for at least another week.'

She laughed. 'Spin it out? You can't make news out of nothing, Valur. Either you've got more material to work with or you haven't . . .'

'Of course, you've never had a proper job – being the eternal student,' he said, joking again. 'Take it from me – this is how things work. There are times when you have to create something out of nothing to hang on to your job.'

'You're not in any danger of losing your job. The whole country's talking about Lára, and it's all down to you. Your articles have been a big hit – the paper must be raking it in, thanks to you.'

Valur knew she was probably right. Perhaps he should grab this chance to ask for a pay rise.

'Have you trawled through the old newspapers?' she asked, ever helpful.

'Of course I have, ad nauseam. I've spent days cooped up in the National Library when I should have been outside enjoying the summer weather. I've ploughed through whole stacks of papers from August 1956 and in some cases right through September too. It looks like it was a while before people starting taking her disappearance seriously. The first report I can find is from several days after she vanished, and that's only a brief notice in *Morgunbladid* saying that the police had put out an appeal for information about a missing teenage girl. Shortly afterwards it had blown up into a big story, splashed across most of the front pages. I made a note of all the names, all the people interviewed at the time, and since then I've been trying to talk to as many of them as possible.'

He reached for the slim satchel on the floor beside him; the modest, scuffed brown-leather bag that their parents had given him the day he started his first job as a journalist.

'Here . . .' He held out his notebook. He always used the same kind, getting through several a year. The notebooks were his most treasured possessions and he rarely let them out of his sight.

'What, you're actually letting me have a look?' Sunna asked in surprise. She took it from him and opened it. 'Wonders will never cease.'

'Yes, it's all in there – all the stuff that's come in useful on this strange journey. But there are bound to be things I've overlooked, ideas . . .'

'Valur, don't tell me you're hoping to crack the case?'

He smiled. Of course the possibility had occurred to him, but not very seriously. He had let himself imagine the prestige it would bring. The fame and fortune . . . In his heart of hearts, though, he knew it was totally unrealistic.

'No, of course not, Sunna. Don't be silly. I just need to flog some papers.'

'I thought it was the paperboys who did that. They're out there selling *Vikubladid* on the street in all weathers while you sit in the warmth at your typewriter.'

He smiled.

'Can I borrow it?' she asked.

'What?'

'Your notebook.'

Valur thought about it. That hadn't been the intention, but the truth was he'd hit a brick wall and was feeling uninspired. Perhaps what he needed was a complete break from Lára for a day or two while Sunna looked through his notes. No doubt her dissertation could wait. All he needed was one or two good ideas. A fresh angle on the case; enough to fill one more article. Something to capture the public interest . . .

'Fine, take it. But make sure you give it back to me on Monday, OK?'

'Yeah, yeah.'

'I'm not kidding. Guard it with your life, Sunna.'

'Come on, it's not like it contains military secrets. By the way, have you spoken to the lead detective? I remember seeing him on TV. He's given interviews about the case in the past, hasn't he?'

'He's not answering my calls.'

'You just haven't tried hard enough.'

'Oh, shut up. It's not like I'm throwing the towel in. It's on the agenda for next week. I'm going to drop by the office this afternoon, then take tomorrow off. I'm feeling knackered after the last three weeks.'

'It's a tough life being a star reporter.'

'All right, take the notebook and show me what you can do. I'm open to ideas. I must have overlooked something. I'm not expecting to be able to drop any bombshells next week, but anything's better than nothing . . .'

Sunna smiled. 'You can rely on me. Incidentally, have you been out to Videy?'

Valur hesitated. 'No, actually. It . . .'

'Yes, you have – I read about it in one of the articles: your description of the weather, the summer birdlife and the lush green grass in the place where Lára vanished.'

'Oh, yeah, I made that up. I couldn't be bothered to go. I've visited Videy several times in the past. There's nothing useful there now.'

'You shouldn't lie to your readers, Valur,' Sunna said sternly, though her voice held a teasing note.

'It was a white lie. I'll visit the island next week, I promise. And you must promise to give me some good ideas.'

1986

14 August

The office was quiet when Valur got in. The only other person there was the editor, Dagbjartur Steinsson, a veteran newshound. *Vikubladid* had recently acquired rooms in an old house on Kárastígur with an easy-going landlord who was a friend of Dagbjartur's. Valur had a desk by the window that looked out over Faxaflói bay. The view was restful, and that afternoon the sea was a calm, beautiful blue. One day Valur hoped to realize an old dream and invest in a small yacht. His friends had been talking for several years about clubbing together to buy one. They all had sailing licences, but something always got in the way; usually the fact that one or all of them were broke.

'How are you doing, Valur, my boy?' Dagbjartur's manner was matey, as usual. Bald and fleshy – he liked his food – he always went home for lunch, strolling over to the old Thingholt district where he lived with his wife.

Valur suspected him of putting away at least two large cooked meals every day. He drank endless cups of coffee too and smoked a pipe, but had long ago given up alcohol, even going so far as to have the serenity prayer engraved on his lighter. Dagbjartur never seemed to take life too seriously. Valur had the feeling he wasn't unduly worried about money. If the paper went bankrupt, presumably one of his useful contacts would fix him up with another position.

'Great,' Valur replied. 'I was just over at Mokka, looking through the paper. We did a pretty good job.'

'You can take the credit for that. It's a miracle that we can fill the paper with good copy in the middle of the silly season.'

'Is there no news then?'

'Things are pretty slow. The Fisheries Minister has been getting involved in the whaling issue, but no one wants to read about that in August. No one wants to read about anything, really – except Lára, of course.'

'Don't forget the new radio station; that'll be going on air in a few days.'

Dagbjartur snorted. He was temperamentally opposed to innovation, Valur knew. If Dagbjartur had his way, everything would carry on the same: the thought of a free market in radio broadcasting filled him with dismay. He'd lectured his staff on the subject often enough. Valur had sometimes pointed out the inherent contradiction in being opposed to a private radio station while working on a privately owned newspaper, but this argument hadn't cut any ice.

'Then there's Reykjavík's two-hundredth anniversary, of course,' Valur said, tactfully changing the subject.

'The anniversary, yes.' At this, Dagbjartur's face brightened. 'That'll be something. Apparently they're expecting sixty thousand people to turn up. It's the big news story of the month – not that I feel like going along myself.'

'Well, I'm going anyway,' Valur said cheerfully.

'Oh, I suppose I'll have to put in an appearance,' Dagbjartur said with a long-suffering air. 'I gather the festivities are going to take over the entire city centre, so I don't suppose it'll be possible to set foot out of doors without being dragged in.' He shook his head. Although Valur was amused by Dagbjartur's grumbling, he knew that when it came to the crunch the old editor was a professional to his fingertips. 'You'll come up with something meaty about the anniversary for us,' Dagbjartur added.

Valur smiled. 'I'll try.'

'Let's have none of this *try* – you'll do it, and you'll make a success of it, my lad. We don't have any room for passengers on this paper.'

'Don't worry. And there's one more article about Lára to come, remember. I'm going to have another go at getting hold of that policeman who's not answering his phone.'

'Right. Anyway, I was thinking of knocking off early today. You'll be around a bit longer, won't you?'

In fact, Valur hadn't been intending to stay once Dagbjartur had left.

'Yes, I was planning to stick around,' he said, swallowing

his disappointment. 'Try and hammer out a few ideas, you know – get a bit of a headstart on the week.'

'Excellent, my boy. You're on duty, then.' Dagbjartur glanced at the clock. 'I think I'll work from home for the rest of the day.'

'Sure, sounds good to me,' Valur replied.

Dagbjartur took himself off and Valur remained at his desk, rather regretting having lent Sunna his notebook. He could have used the time to leaf through it in search of inspiration. Still, he tried to look on the bright side: perhaps Sunna would pick up on something he hadn't spotted.

Reaching for the telephone directory, he reminded himself of the number for Kristján, the policeman who had been in charge of the Lára case. Really, you could say that Lára's disappearance had dogged the poor man's whole career. That one case, unsolved for thirty years. When the story first hit the news, photos of Kristján had begun to appear in the papers as he gave press conferences, cutting quite a dapper figure in a suit and hat in spite of his youth – only twenty-four years old. All the photos were in black and white. In 1966 Kristján had been dragged back into the spotlight to answer questions from reporters about why the girl still hadn't been found. Valur doubted he'd managed to track down all the reports about the case in the newspaper archives. To begin with, he had confined himself to reading the coverage from the autumn of 1956, then from August 1966 and August 1976; ten, then twenty years after the event. Only one photo had been published of Kristján in August 1976, accompanying an exclusive interview with the *Vísir* newspaper. By then he was forty-four but looked as if he was in his fifties. Either the photographer had caught him on a bad day or the years had been unkind to him. The front page had been dominated by a large colour picture of Kristján's heavily lined face and a smaller, black-and-white one of Lára; the iconic image of her that the nation knew so well.

The photo of Lára appeared to have been taken in summer. She was wearing a dark velvet dress with short sleeves and had long dark hair. It was through this picture that she lived on, thirty years later, smiling at the nation every time the case was raked up. No doubt the impact on the readers was always the same: killing a person was terrible enough, but snuffing out the life of a young girl in the flower of her youth was unforgivable.

Yet the guilty party still walked free. And would probably never be caught.

Unless, of course . . . unless Lára was alive. Perhaps that was the most intriguing aspect of the mystery; the fact that Lára might turn up one day, safe and sound. It was a forlorn hope, but a hope nonetheless.

Whatever the truth, it was clear that Valur needed to put all his energy into getting hold of Kristján. He dialled the policeman's number: no one answered.

But work on the paper was about more than just Lára, and Valur made use of the time by contributing to the culture section. The journalists took it in turns to share their opinions of music, films, TV and books. Valur had offered to write about the TV schedule and was intending to lavish praise on *Bergerac*, the British series about the

Jersey detective who was a weekly guest on their screens. He was also planning to write a short review of a book he'd read. He didn't read much apart from the news and, when he did, it tended to be biographies, like this one. Occasionally, when he had a tight deadline and they were short of material for the paper, he commissioned Sunna to write a review of one of the numerous novels she read for her degree. She could never be persuaded to put her name to the reviews, though; not even her initials.

Valur was halfway through his piece on *Bergerac*, just searching for the right adjective to describe the leading actor, when the phone rang. He answered, giving his name, hoping against hope that it would be Kristján, finally responding to his messages.

'Hello . . .' A woman's voice, he thought, though the connection was poor, her voice faint, as though she was calling from the countryside or even from abroad. 'Is that the Valur who's been writing about . . .' A pause; crackling on the line. 'About Lára.'

'That's right,' he said.

He'd had a few calls of this type since the articles started coming out; minor tip-offs of little importance, as well as a fair number of bizarre conversations during which it quickly became clear that the caller was an attention-seeker and didn't really have anything to say. Yet he had a sudden gut instinct that this call didn't fall into either of those categories.

'I just wanted a word with you about Lára. I . . .' Again she broke off, and he waited patiently. He was sure it wasn't the fault of the connection: the woman was having second thoughts, trying to make up her mind how much to share with him.

'Yes, of course,' he said at last, in an effort to prompt her. 'I'm still working on the series of pieces about her.' Then he added, he didn't know why: 'A tragic business.'

'Yes,' she replied. He thought he heard a car drive past, as if she was standing in the street. Perhaps she was calling him from a phone box because she wanted to remain anonymous. That in itself was interesting.

'I want to help you, Valur. It's been a long time and the girl deserves better.'

This was unexpected. He waited, listening hard. Again, he heard the whoosh of a passing car.

'Is she alive?' he asked eventually, feeling his heart beat faster as he said it. He wished the call was being recorded.

'No, she's not alive,' the woman said flatly. Her calm assertion completely threw Valur. He felt strangely as if someone close to him had died. Of course, he'd never really believed that Lára was alive, but somewhere at the back of his mind he must have allowed himself to hope. He was convinced that the woman was telling the truth, though he had no idea why, and of course he couldn't be sure.

'How do you know that?' he asked, then immediately regretted it. He didn't want to frighten her off by being too pushy. Not straight away. He might never hear from her again, never manage to track her down.

She was silent for a long moment, then said: 'It doesn't matter. I just know she was killed.' She continued, as if talking to herself rather than to him: 'On the Saturday evening. Not the Friday evening.'

'What?'

'She was killed, I know that for certain,' she repeated.

He was scribbling frantically to get it all down. *Not alive. Killed. On Sat evening. Not Fri evening.*

'Could you tell me your name?'

'No. Or . . .' Another pause. 'You can call me Júlía.'

'OK. What can I do for you, Júlía?' he asked warily.

'I want you to help me with something, Valur,' she replied. 'I want the girl to be buried in consecrated ground, or, well . . . to have a proper burial.'

Valur's heart was racing now, but as usual he did his best to take the conversation down verbatim.

'How can I help you with that?' he asked carefully. 'Do you know where the body is?'

Silence.

Then: 'Yes, I do. I know only too well. But you'll have to promise me something.'

It was his turn to hesitate, then answer reluctantly: 'Er, yes . . . ?'

'The matter ends there.'

'What?'

'If I tell you where she is, Valur, you can write about it, but you're not to investigate it any further.'

'What do you mean?'

'Thirty years is too long. She needs to be at peace.'

Valur began to have his doubts. Was the woman telling him the truth, or was she some kind of fantasist? Was the whole thing a figment of her imagination?

'How do I know you're not lying to me?' he asked, instantly regretting the choice of words.

'Because I . . .' She faltered. 'Because I know where she is. I want her to be found. But I don't want to be mixed up in the case – I just want it all to end.'

'You know the police won't see it like that, Júlía . . . Even if I don't write another word about it.'

'I . . . Promise me you'll think about it. Lára needs to find peace after all these years. I can't . . . can't . . .'

'Yes, we can agree on that,' he said, keeping his voice level.

'You'll hear from me again.'

'How can I get hold of you?'

But she had hung up.

On his way home from work, Valur had dropped by Óttar's offices but had no more success getting an interview than he had before. Once he reached home, he had rung Sunna and told her about his conversation with the woman calling herself Júlía. They'd discussed it back and forth, until in the end Valur had decided to give Dagbjartur a call, late though it was.

For reasons he couldn't explain, Valur believed the woman. For one thing, it was clear that she hadn't given him her real name and that might be an indication that she had been telling the truth. She was linked to the case somehow but wanted to keep her distance.

'Are you serious?' had been Dagbjartur's reaction after Valur had relayed the gist of the phone conversation.

'Yes. It was a little odd . . .'

'A little odd? Hell, we could be sitting on a major story here, Valur. The scoop of the year. Did you let her off the hook?'

'Let . . . ? No, not exactly . . . I'm sure she'll ring back.'

'Are you quite certain about that?'

'Absolutely,' Valur replied confidently, though really he was far from sure.

'Right, you look into it, but we need to be absolutely sure that our sources stand up to scrutiny.'

'Yes, of course . . .'

'You get straight on to this first thing on Monday morning, Valur. But for Christ's sake, keep it under your hat. We can't afford for any of our competitors to get hold of it.'

'Of course, I won't say a word,' Valur assured Dagbjartur, keeping quiet about his conversation with Sunna.

'You'll see, we're going to make a big noise about this; shake up the summer recess. We're going to ramp up the tension . . . This is definitely going to trump any two-hundredth anniversary bullshit.' Dagbjartur laughed gleefully, said goodbye and rang off.

Valur stood, unmoving, by the telephone table, then carefully replaced the receiver.

Make a big noise about this, ramp up the tension . . . What on earth did Dagbjartur have in mind?

1986

14 August

Ólöf Blöndal was worried. But then Ólöf existed in a permanent state of anxiety. She was worried about saying the wrong thing, about letting something slip that she shouldn't. She was worried about cooking the wrong food. About dressing inappropriately. She was filled with anxiety every time she had to drive to the shops, picturing herself getting stuck in the snow, or having an accident, or running out of petrol. And what if the car broke down?

At this moment Ólöf was worried because she'd bought a chicken, only to discover too late that they had run out of Aromat seasoning. Óttar always liked his chicken cooked the same way, in a cream sauce, heavily seasoned with Aromat. It was a dish they had first eaten in Norway, the winter they spent in Bergen. Aromat was absolutely essential; without it, the dish would be a completely different recipe.

Ólöf stood at a loss in the kitchen of the house she

shared with Óttar. They had sold their home in Reykjavík
several years ago and moved into this new, much larger
place in the upmarket suburb of Gardabær. The kitchen
units were dark brown and white, the table and worktops
covered in Formica. The surfaces were crowded with
knick-knacks, including countless cockerels of every
imaginable size and shape, which Ólöf had been collect-
ing ever since her grandmother had brought her one as a
souvenir from Spain in the early 1950s. Now everyone
gave her cockerels – her friends, her children, and Óttar
too – until the kitchen almost resembled a henhouse.
Apart from that, their house was like any other detached
suburban home, if unusually large, but then Óttar didn't
know the meaning of moderation. At first it had been her
money he splashed around, her family's inherited wealth.
But it hadn't taken him long to make a name for himself
as a lawyer, acquiring powerful friends and clients. After
qualifying, he had proved adroit at angling for cases,
exploiting Ólöf's family connections to set up a busy
legal practice, and this had allowed them to build their
first detached house while still comparatively young. She
missed the old place; she didn't feel at home in the suburbs. Really, though, she couldn't complain. It was just a
pity that Óttar was always so tired and on edge.

In the early 1950s they'd got the idea of spending their
summers on the island of Videy, in an old property that
had long been in the Blöndal family. The legal practice
would run itself, Óttar had said airily; he'd never been one
to worry about money. But that experiment had come to
an abrupt end after the summer of 1956.

Ólöf snapped out of her reverie, back to the present. Maybe she'd have time to dash to the shop and buy the right seasoning. She could feel herself breaking out in a sweat over the dilemma. Why did something always have to go wrong? She made up her mind. She would hurry back out and buy some Aromat. Putting on the pastel-green coat she had recently bought herself, she ran out to the car and drove straight to the shop, where she swiftly tracked down a large container of Knorr's Aromat seasoning.

Óttar drove home from the centre of town in a distracted frame of mind. He'd had a busy day finalizing contracts, including one for a developer he did a lot of business with, involving construction sites in Reykjavík. That had now been completed, which should have been cause for celebration, but Óttar wasn't in the mood. He had just been tying up the final details at around four p.m. when his secretary had knocked on the door to tell him that there was a journalist to see him, a man called Valur, from *Vikubladid*, who wanted to talk to him about Lára.

Óttar had been shaken, though he had been half expecting this, after seeing the front pages advertising the series of features on Lára's disappearance. The reporter responsible had already left him a message, so he shouldn't have been surprised that the man had now turned up at his offices to sniff around in person. Nevertheless, he was badly thrown. He had little time for journalists in general, regarding them as an unnecessary evil, so discussing Videy with some tabloid hack was quite out of the question.

His secretary had still been hovering, patiently awaiting orders. She was a mousy girl with light brown hair and glasses; unworthy of interest, Óttar thought, though not bad at her job. 'I don't have time to speak to him now,' he said curtly. 'I've still got a mass of paperwork to deal with.'

The secretary had nodded and left the room, only to poke her head round the door again a minute later. 'He says he'll wait. He's taken a seat in reception.'

She had withdrawn and Óttar had returned to his pile of documents, determined to out-wait the reporter.

After all, what was he supposed to say about that wretched business? Could the young man have come across new information? Might he be planning to try and speak to Ólöf? As usual, they would need to make sure that their stories matched.

At six, Óttar had finally made a discreet exit from his office, which was situated on Ármúli, in a rather faceless modern business district. By then, he had been sitting, staring out of the window for at least three quarters of an hour, his work long since finished. He had seen the reporter leave the building and hang around outside, shivering in the cold, for another ten minutes or so before eventually taking himself off. But Óttar hadn't dared to leave himself until another half an hour had passed, at which point he had made for his car, half running, his trench coat flapping around his legs, feeling like a common criminal.

When Óttar got home, the chicken in creamy Aromat sauce was in the oven and Ólöf was boiling rice to go with it. She saw that he was tired, but then she knew that he had a lot on his plate at the moment.

Óttar was from the east of Iceland, from a family of fishermen, though he had lived in Reykjavík for most of his adult life. His father had spent long periods away at sea and it had sometimes occurred to Ólöf that Óttar's mother might have had an affair. That would explain why Óttar was so unlike his brothers.

As the oldest child, Óttar had often had to protect his younger brothers and mother from his father, who used to knock them around. He'd shared the stories with Ólöf.

They had got together while still at school, and everything had been rosy for the first few years. She had backed him up in everything he wanted to do, with support from her family, sticking by him through thick and thin. She herself had few interests, and even fewer friends. But recently she had started going along to seances, finding the thought of the afterlife more appealing than the present one.

The couple ate supper alone in the dining room. Their children had long ago flown the nest.

'This chicken's tough.'

'Oh no, really? But it was in the oven for the exact time specified in the recipe.'

'Well, it's overdone. And so's the rice.'

'Oh dear, I'm so sorry about that,' Ólöf said. She thought how much she missed having the children round the table. They still liked to come home for a roast on Sundays, bringing their families, and these were Ólöf's favourite times, giving her a chance to chat and play with the grandchildren. As long as they were there, Óttar would hide his temper, pretending everything was fine.

Only Ólöf knew it wasn't fine. This had become increasingly clear to her since she'd got to know the other women at the seances in Gardabær. Their talk often turned to men, women and relationships. One of them had referred to *abusers* – and the word had stayed with Ólöf.

She thought about the word now as she watched Óttar irritably shovelling down the chicken that was as tough as old boot leather.

Of course husbands felt overworked and under pressure at times. It was only natural for them to have a short fuse. But hitting one's wife was not right.

She stole another nervous glance at Óttar.

He was finishing the food on his plate. She wondered if he was angry. Sometimes it was as if the rage boiled up inside him until he could no longer control himself. But he always apologized to her afterwards and seemed to regret losing his temper.

Óttar grunted 'thanks' and got up abruptly, knocking over his glass, which rolled off the table and smashed on the floor. Ólöf leapt to her feet to sweep up the pieces.

'Why did you have to put out those glasses?' Óttar snapped at her. 'They're far too good for everyday use. Now look what's happened!' As Ólöf came hurrying over to clear up the mess his hand smacked into her face. Tears sprang from her eyes and she raised her arms instinctively to protect herself.

There were no more blows on this occasion. Óttar

merely swore at her, then stormed out of the dining room, slamming the door behind him. On the evenings when he was in a bad temper, he would retreat to his study to brood. She sat there for a while, weeping a little from pain and fear, though she was relieved that the explosion hadn't been any worse this time. Then she got a grip on herself and began sweeping up the shards of glass and clearing away the food. An hour later, the tidying up done, Ólöf sat at the kitchen table, smoking a cigarette before bed. As usual on Thursdays, there was no television broadcast, so she had the radio on. A programme was beginning about Reykjavík, viewed through the eyes of its poets.

Ólöf wasn't listening. She was thinking about the last seance she had attended. The psychic had been a grey-haired man with spectacles who seemed to have easy access to the afterlife. Lots of the women present recognized their mothers and fathers, dead relatives or friends coming through. There were messages asking people to take care of their health and look after themselves, or sending loving greetings. It reminded Ólöf of the *Patients' Requests* programme on the radio. She hadn't received any visitations herself yet, but then she was as self-effacing at the seances as she was everywhere else, almost blending into the background in her pastel-green coat, beige scarf and pale lipstick. Unless she had received a message during that last seance? A girl with dark eyes had come through, complaining that she couldn't find peace. None of the other women had recognized her as anyone they knew.

Ólöf had shivered. Surely Lára couldn't be trying to contact her through the psychic?

She had been such a pretty girl. Sweet-natured, conscientious and easy company.

Ólöf remembered the policeman who had come looking for her. He had suspected something, she could tell, yet he had never put her and Óttar under any pressure.

I can't find peace.

The psychic's words echoed in Ólöf's head. All of a sudden, the word *abuser* popped into her mind again. Stubbing out her cigarette, she hurried upstairs to be sure she would be asleep by the time Óttar eventually came to bed.

Grant me peace.

1986

15 August

The city was bathed in brilliant sunshine – not that Valur felt he was in the city at this moment. It was more like the countryside out here. When he got out of the taxi, he was immediately struck by the birdsong, which was so much more noticeable here than where he lived, in the centre of town. It was the first time Valur had set foot in Grafarvogur, the new suburb that had started to rise in the wake of the city elections four years previously. There were half-completed houses scattered across the landscape, interspersed with empty lots. It was clear to anyone that construction was already well under way.

The taxi driver had had the greatest difficulty not just finding the address but working out how to cross the arm of the sea that separated the new area from the rest of the city. The planned bridge had yet to be built. In the end, he had deposited Valur in completely the wrong place, but, after wandering about for a bit, Valur had blundered on to the right street by chance.

In contrast to many of the other buildings Valur had seen, the house belonging to the detective, Kristján Kristjánsson, appeared to be complete. It was an attractive, single-storey prefab with a garage and a Lada Sport parked in the drive. The handful of young poplars in the garden wouldn't provide much shelter as yet, but that would change in time.

Valur hadn't announced his visit any more than he had the previous day when he had tried to catch Óttar at work. The secretary had refused to let him into the office, and Valur was still disappointed by his failure to speak to the lawyer. At this rate he would have to resort to doorstepping him at home, as he was doing now with Kristján. At least that way, even if he didn't get to speak to Óttar, he might be able to have a word with Ólöf. He felt obliged to do this for the next front page, though the couple were unlikely to have anything new to say.

There was no chance of passing inconspicuously through the empty, exposed streets of Grafarvogur. An older man was already standing outside the house, sparing Valur the need to knock on the door. Valur recognized Kristján instantly from the photos, although he had aged visibly in the intervening years. The detective was neatly dressed in grey trousers, a white shirt and a tie, in spite of the mild weather. He cut a tall, commanding figure, like so many policemen Valur had encountered in his job. His expression was neutral; he seemed neither surprised nor angry – nor pleased, for that matter.

'You must be Valur,' he said mildly.

Valur nodded.

'I've seen pictures of you in the papers. And it hasn't escaped my attention that you've been trying to get hold of me.'

'Yes, that's right. You haven't answered my messages, so I decided—'

'Normally I wouldn't put up with this sort of behaviour. At the very least, a man's home should be sacred, don't you agree?' Kristján said, his tone veering between that of a policeman and a priest. 'But you seem fairly harmless. I trust you won't go quoting me without my permission?'

Valur hesitated, then said: 'No, of course not. I won't write anything without your permission.' He felt a twinge of frustration that Kristján had set this condition. He'd been hoping to squeeze several good paragraphs out of this visit.

'I'm aware of the stuff you've been writing,' Kristján said. 'One can hardly avoid it. But I get the impression you write about Lára with respect, from a genuine interest in finding out what happened. Am I correct?'

It was becoming clear to Valur that Kristján wasn't going to invite him in.

'Yes, though I'm not getting my hopes up that I'll be able to solve the mystery. And the last thing I want to do is turn it into a sensationalist tabloid news story. But, you never know – now that the case is in the public eye again, someone might be prompted to come forward with information they've been sitting on.' Valur's thoughts flew to the woman who had called herself Júlía.

'I see. Well, let's hope so. But you know, Valur, I've become reconciled to the idea that this case will never be solved. Some cases are like that. It's not the only one I'll be taking with me to the grave, so to speak. Not that I'm on my way there any time soon.' For the first time in the conversation, Kristján's lips twitched in a smile.

'Do you have a clear memory of that day on Videy when you—?'

Kristján cut him off. 'Look, Valur, I have no intention of commenting further on this case. I've chewed over it endlessly with journalists. Far more than I should have done. I've too often said yes to interviews, giving way to pressure, against my better judgement. But I'm in my fifties now, I've just moved into a new house in a brand-new area – I've reached the point in my life where, although I'm still working, I'd also appreciate the chance to spend more time with my wife and slow down a bit. The last thing I want is to find myself caught up in the middle of a media circus on account of a thirty-year-old case. I hope you can understand that.'

Valur nodded reluctantly. He wanted to protest that Kristján should be thinking about the missing girl rather than himself, but he bit his tongue. The policeman seemed rocklike in his resolve: Valur couldn't see any chance of him budging.

'Yes, I understand, of course . . .' After a moment's pause, Valur added diffidently: 'Could I maybe ask for your advice, off the record, if necessary? Just to help me get my head round the details . . .'

'Like I said,' Kristján repeated patiently, 'I'd rather not spend too much time thinking about the investigation. It's ancient history now and one shouldn't dwell on the past. I don't want to be remembered solely for this case – one I failed to solve.'

'No, of course not.' Valur was conscious, even as he said it, that this was wishful thinking on the policeman's part. As Kristján must be well aware.

The detective held out his hand: 'It was nice meeting you, Valur. Good luck with everything. And now I need to get on. We're holding a barbecue party in our street later today and there's a lot to do.'

'Right, have fun, and thanks for talking to me.'

Valur stood there at a loss. It had dawned on him that he would probably have to walk miles to the nearest shop or petrol station to find a phone to call a taxi. He'd been expecting this trip to pay off; that he'd manage to get the detective talking. The Lára case had so clearly overshadowed Kristján's whole career that it struck Valur as odd that the detective didn't want to discuss it, not even off the record.

'Don't you have a car?' Kristján called, though the answer must have been blindingly obvious. There was no vehicle parked in front of any the houses in the street that had so far been completed, apart from the Lada Sport that was presumably Kristján's.

'No, I came by cab, actually.'

'Shall I call you a taxi, then, or were you planning to trek back to the city centre on foot? That's where all those newspaper offices are located, isn't it?'

Kristján's tone sounded slightly more friendly, as if he felt a grudging sympathy for the stranded reporter.

'Yes, our offices are in the centre, on Kárastígur. And, yes, thanks, I'd be very grateful. It's a long way to the nearest shop or—'

'You can say that again. Come in. The phone's in the hall, and you're welcome to use it.'

Valur accepted the invitation. Indoors there was still a fair amount of work to be done. Peering into the living room, he saw that a parquet floor was in the process of being laid. There were boxes of unopened parquet bricks and tiles in the porch, a layer of dust over everything and tools lying on the floor. Valur felt tired at the thought of so much physical labour. Personally, he was happier sitting at a typewriter or out chasing news or chatting over coffee to people who had interesting stories to tell. He experienced another twinge of frustration at the thought that Kristján had more than enough to tell but was refusing to say a word.

Valur phoned for a cab, then asked casually – it would have been crazy not to seize the chance that had landed in his lap: 'Kristján, was there by any chance a woman called Júlía linked to the Videy case?'

'What?' The question seemed to take the detective by surprise. 'Júlía?'

At least he hadn't lost his rag at being asked yet another question about Lára.

'Yes. Júlía. An older woman, I think – these days, I mean. Obviously, she'd have been thirty years younger at the time.'

Kristján frowned thoughtfully.

'I think I can answer that with a pretty definite no. By the way, this is strictly off the record. I've been through the files so many times, thought about the inquiry so often that I can remember every single person who had a connection to Lára's disappearance. And there was no Júlía among them. I don't even remember her having a friend with that name, and we spoke to all, or nearly all, of her friends.'

'This woman sounded older than that. I'm guessing she'd have been an adult at the time of Lára's disappearance.'

'May I ask who this Júlía is?' Without warning, Kristján had slipped into the role of questioner. Valur had succeeded in piquing his curiosity. He felt quite proud of the fact.

'She phoned me. I don't know anything else about her as she wouldn't give me her full name. For all I know, she may not even be called Júlía.' Although Valur was aware that he was breaking his promise to Dagbjartur not to discuss the phone call, he reasoned that Kristján was unlikely to blab about it.

'Right, I see. But aren't people always calling up journalists – attention-seekers and the like?'

'You know, I got the feeling that wasn't true in this case. She was nervous and came across as genuine. In fact, she said very little and gave me almost no information about herself.'

'So what did she say?'

Valur had jotted it down almost word for word, but

his notes were back at the office. 'If I remember right, she said something about Lára needing to be buried in consecrated ground. It was like she knew what had happened to her.'

'Consecrated ground. Well. Well, now.' Kristján had turned pale. He went into the living room and lowered himself on to a kitchen stool, which was almost the only item of furniture in there. Valur slipped in after him. Finally, they were getting somewhere.

'Yes, I'm pretty sure those were the words she used,' Valur said, after a little silence had developed.

'Of course, you know this means Lára's dead.' Kristján's voice gave nothing away, as if he were merely reading out a police report. He seemed so deep in thought that Valur didn't like to disturb him.

Finally, the detective continued, speaking as if to himself: 'I've always clung to the hope that she was alive. That one fine day I'd get to meet her. Shake her by the hand, give her a hug, and hear the whole sorry tale.'

'Kristján, do you have any idea who this woman could be?'

The policeman looked up, seeming finally to notice that Valur was standing in the living room of his newly built home. He shook his head. 'I'm afraid I haven't a clue.'

'If she's for real, this Júlía, we can assume that Lára's remains are out there somewhere, just waiting to be found – or it wouldn't be possible to move them to consecrated ground.'

'Yes, right,' Kristján replied, frowning.

'Which means she can't be at the bottom of the sea.'

'Quite.' Kristján seemed winded, as if he had just lost someone close to him, not a girl he'd never known, who'd been missing for three decades.

'Do you remember anywhere in particular that you searched?' Valur asked. 'Does anything occur to you?'

Kristján took his time about answering this. 'On Videy, you mean? Among the buildings on the island?'

'Not necessarily. For all we know, Lára may have left the island.'

'Yes, that was always the headache – not knowing. Naturally, we combed the island from end to end, as I expect you've read.'

Valur had indeed. He'd gone through all the main newspapers in the archives, following the developments in the case. As time went on, the whole country had been caught up in the drama of the girl's disappearance. And always that same photo of Lára, her expression mysterious, as though she were hiding some terrible secret. And perhaps she had been.

Valur had also tried to dig up more recent news reports about the case. One that particularly stuck in his memory was the 1976 front-page interview with Kristján in *Vísir*, because the detective had spoken so candidly about the investigation. After that, he must have decided to withdraw from the limelight, because Valur hadn't come across any further interviews with him.

'Yes, you launched a particularly comprehensive search there, didn't you, with a large group of volunteers?'

'Yes. She wasn't on the island. I'm still convinced that she got back to the mainland somehow. It's always possible to find someone willing to take you on their boat. I once had to hitch a lift with a fisherman and—' Abruptly Kristján broke off. 'Here I was, planning to organize the street barbecue for this evening – we try to carry on life as normal, although the area's not really finished yet. Still, that'll sort itself out in due course.' He sighed heavily. 'Not that I imagine I'll be in the mood for a party now, to be honest. I won't be able to stop thinking about Lára. The poor girl.'

'It's awful, I know. But time's on our side. Someone who wasn't willing to speak out in 1956 is apparently prepared to provide us with a lead now.'

'Yes, I hope so. You should . . .' Kristján hesitated.

Valur waited patiently. He was in no hurry and could sense that something remained unsaid. It would take the taxi a good while to navigate to Grafarvogur, then find its way to this half-completed street.

'This is just speculation,' Kristján went on, apparently choosing his words carefully. 'But I was wondering if it might be worth your while to have a word with a man called Högni Eyfjörd.'

'What?' Although Valur had heard what Kristján said, he was momentarily confused. Why would the detective suddenly take it into his head to mention the name of a prominent property developer? Högni Eyfjörd was a well-connected man with a finger in every important pie, but he generally avoided the media spotlight. Despite going to great lengths to disguise his age, he must be somewhat older than Kristján. Valur remembered encountering Högni once at the groundbreaking ceremony for

one of his construction projects. Valur had been transfixed
by the bad dye-job on Högni's hair.

'Högni Eyfjörd – I assume you've heard of him?'
Kristján said.

'Yes, naturally, I know who he is. You're referring to
the developer?'

'That's right.' Kristján's gaze flickered around evasively.
'Your taxi is on its way, isn't it?'

'Yes, it should be here soon. Though it's a bit confusing trying to navigate around this area.'

Kristján smiled awkwardly.

'Why Högni?' Valur pressed him.

'Well . . .'

'Do you think he's linked to Lára somehow?'

'No, please don't misunderstand me. His name did
crop up at the time, but keep that to yourself. Don't bring
my name into it. I shouldn't be giving you information
like this . . . from . . . from the old files. But, the thing is,
I'd like to help you. This news – that Lára's probably been
dead all along – it's unsettling, you understand? Though I
suppose deep down I've always known.'

'I understand,' Valur answered gently. 'What, er, context did Högni's name crop up in?'

'Context?' Kristján's mind appeared to be working,
considering what he should say. 'Apparently he'd visited
Videy a few weeks earlier. On a Saturday evening.'

'Do you know why?'

Kristján paused. 'I can't really say any more, Valur. It
didn't lead to anything, that's all I can reveal. But maybe
you'll find the information helpful.' He shrugged, but

plainly there must have been more to it than casual gossip. The detective must suspect that Högni Eyfjörd was implicated somehow in Lára's disappearance.

'Well, many thanks for the tip,' Valur said. 'I appreciate your help and I promise I won't mention your name in connection with this. But are you sure there's nothing else you want to say, just in general, that I could quote you on?'

'I'm too old, Valur. I can't face yet another interview, yet another photo, yet another reminder that I failed to get justice for that girl.'

'Could I leave you my phone number, just in case something comes back to you later?'

'Certainly. Go ahead. And could I maybe ask a favour of you in return?'

'Sure. What is it?'

'Could you let me know if you make any headway? If you get any closer to finding out what happened to Lára. You can ring me any time of the day or night, if it's about that. I've done my best for thirty years. I think about Lára every day. I've been over all the loose ends, again and again. But I've run out of energy. Perhaps what the investigation needs is fresh blood, a fresh pair of eyes – a young man like you. You can write your number here, on the phone book. My home number's listed, if you look under "Kristján Kristjánsson, bookbinder". It's my hobby – has been for several years now, since I gave up mountaineering.' He paused, then added: 'It sounds to me as if your taxi's arrived.'

1986

15 August

Högni Eyfjörd was singing as he got dressed. He knotted his tie in the mirror, his mood still buoyant from yesterday's choir practice. Looking good mattered a lot to him. His image was what he liked to think of as well groomed but original, and he kept a close eye on what the main fashion moguls were importing into Iceland these days. He tended to favour clothes aimed at the youth market, but then, to Högni, age was relative. He was confident that he could stand comparison with much younger men.

> Let mine be thine, and live with me forever;
> Mankind's sorrows will afflict thee never.

Högni was a member of the Langholt Church choir. Although the church itself had only been consecrated a few years previously, the choir had been going considerably longer. Högni adored singing and relished the social

97

life it provided. They'd just started rehearsals again following the summer break and had stuck to the lighter end of their repertoire, sending traditional Icelandic songs echoing around the church. 'A Rare Evening' was a favourite of Högni's – something about the unbridled passion of Halldór Laxness's lyrics, combined with the poignantly beautiful melody, seemed to speak to him personally.

> Her shining eyes and fond replies
> Will leave him never,
> Until he dies and buried lies
> Alone forever.

Högni let out a sigh. The reference to dying and lying buried had reminded him of Finnur. His friend's end had come so shockingly fast. Högni had bumped into him in town only a few days before Finnur got his diagnosis. As soon as he heard the news, Högni had visited Finnur at his office, where his friend had put a brave face on things, talking in terms of temporary sick leave. His nephew would hold the fort while he was undergoing chemo. 'Then we'll see what he's made of,' Finnur had added, clearly sceptical about his nephew's fitness for the role. Högni had read regret in every line of his face. But Finnur had seemed optimistic that his treatment would have the desired effect and that he'd soon be able to return home to Thórdís and his business.

Not long after that, the news got around: an exploratory operation had revealed that Finnur's cancer had spread much further than the doctors had hoped. All that remained was a slow death. But, in the event, his death hadn't been that slow after all.

Högni took care over the knot on his tie, a double Windsor, which went particularly well with the Italian collar on his shirt – the latest trend, so he was told. He took advantage of a special service provided by a gentlemen's outfitters, which sent an employee to him at work with samples that he could try on at his leisure, before buying some and sending the rest back. Today's outfit consisted of grey cotton-and-wool-mix trousers and a dark-blue blazer with gold buttons. Noticing a few grey strands in his carefully blow-dried hair, which he regularly treated with Grecian 2000, he tucked them out of sight. At least he still had a magnificent head of hair, he thought, with no sign of the incipient baldness that was affecting his friends.

As part of his image, he had dropped his patronymic and used his middle name, Eyfjörd, instead, though he'd had a struggle persuading the National Registry to accept this, thanks to Iceland's conservative naming laws, which insisted on patronymics rather than the creation of new family names.

He splashed his cheeks with the usual generous helping of aftershave. His complexion was brown, verging on orange, giving the impression that he spent a lot of time in the sun, though of course he didn't really have the leisure for that. Being a property developer was a demanding business. But someone had tipped him off about these Orobronze tanning pills, which turned your skin a lovely colour from the inside. Högni had started taking them several months ago and was extremely satisfied with the results.

He pulled on his shoes – a pair of shiny, black slip-ons – and took one last affirmatory glance in the mirror. He'd recently moved into a bachelor flat on Ofanleiti, in a luxury apartment block designed for affluent types who had reached the age when their thoughts turned to downsizing. Högni had furnished the place himself, with the emphasis on light shades and chrome. The floor was carpeted in white throughout, there was a three-piece suite of pale leather, the television was the largest model money could buy, the bed was huge, with a barred chrome headboard, and there were mirror tiles in all the rooms, creating a light, airy effect.

His own firm had been involved in the Ofanleiti development and it was a good marketing ploy to claim that he built such high-quality flats that he wouldn't want to live anywhere else. This wasn't the sole reason, though. Fridrika Halldórs, his latest girlfriend and a familiar face to Icelandic TV audiences, had thrown him out of their flat on Efstasund, having finally lost patience with his constant womanizing and partying. They had a four-year-old son together, the youngest of Högni's three kids by different mothers.

His eldest, Tómas Eyfjörd, the son of Högni's childhood sweetheart, María, was in his early thirties. The polar opposite of his father, Tómas worked for a publishing company and wrote poetry in his spare time. He didn't have a girlfriend. In fact, he'd recently informed his father that he was gay. Högni had taken the news badly and they hadn't spoken since.

Högni had been head over heels in love with Anna, the mother of his daughter, Dýrleif Önnudóttir Eyfjörd, but their ways had eventually parted and Anna had gone on to stand as an MP for the Women's Party. They had little contact these days, though Dýrleif visited him at Christmas and on birthdays – mainly to have a go at him about his shortcomings, he felt.

When he first met Fridrika, she'd recently returned to Iceland after studying graphic design abroad. They'd got to know each other through the advertising agency where she had been working on the design of a new image and logo for his company, Eyfjörd Development Ltd. Fridrika was a cheerful, outgoing type who set great store by dressing up in the latest fashions, like him, and not long after they met she had got a job as a TV presenter on the state channel. When they moved into a large flat together, many people believed Högni Eyfjörd had finally met his match. But, for Högni, life was all about having the best, whether it was furniture, holidays or women, and so he could never be sure that the woman he was with was definitely the best on the market.

He was subject to moments of regret about losing Fridrika, though. Apparently she was going to be one of the main hosts on the new private TV station that was due to start broadcasting shortly. He'd have enjoyed attending those parties. Fridrika had recently done an interview for a glossy magazine about 'the relationship that didn't work out', opening up about how she'd had to start practising yoga and meditation to recover from the fallout of her break-up with Högni Eyfjörd.

Högni sighed again. He wasn't getting any younger. He had to make more of an effort these days, though a single gin and tonic, a twinkle in his eye and a spot of heavy flattery was usually enough to charm the pants off any woman – if you were lucky enough to be blessed with his personal charisma. Really, he couldn't understand his former girlfriends – or his kids, for that matter. Tómas a homosexual! And Dýrleif, just like her mother, always banging on about how society should be placing more emphasis on women's experiences. And Fridrika getting into meditation and that sort of spiritual claptrap. He supposed he'd just never found the right woman.

'I'm ready to face the day and treat everything it brings as an opportunity,' Högni recited aloud. Since attending the Dale Carnegie course, he had taken to addressing everyone by name to come across as more sincere and personal. He'd also learned some motivational mantras, aimed at guaranteeing success and a happy life, which he recited morning and evening. Although Högni had no understanding of Tómas's publishing job, let alone of his poems, he did sometimes read self-help books in English about how to realize your goals and ensure that you came out on top.

He drove straight to the company's headquarters by Tjörnin, the picturesque little lake in the centre of Reykjavík's old town. Currently, his biggest project was the construction of an estate in the new suburb of Grafarvogur, thanks to the lucrative contract his firm had secured with Reykjavík City Council. Eyfjörd Development Ltd had also been a key player in the development of Reykjavík's new city centre out at Kringlan. The success of the business had been due in no small part to his skill in keeping Páll Jóhannesson on side. It was so convenient having a friend on the city council. Högni smirked a little at the thought of Páll. Always so staid and set in his ways. He and Gunnlaug were so conventional, with their perfect home, their perfect children and their perfect life. But that didn't stop the man from being a crashing bore. He lived for nothing but politics and power.

Still, Högni couldn't deny that his connection to Páll had come in useful. Of course, Eyfjörd Development Ltd had deserved to be assigned those building sites on its own merits, but that didn't alter the fact that Högni's dealings with Páll had speeded up what would otherwise have been a more protracted process. And there was absolutely nothing dodgy about that. Really, all that red tape was far too cumbersome and merely got in the way of entrepreneurs like him, hindering them from building things up fast in the interests of the local population. Particularly as one knock-on effect of the regulations was that no one could build anything for themselves these days; there were far too many forms to fill out and permits to apply for, and so on. All this made it undeniably handy to be able to pick up the phone to Páll whenever a bunch of petty bureaucrats were blocking the progress of exciting new projects with their slavishly rule-bound attitudes. His dealings with Páll left no paper trail; all their conversations were conducted over the phone or in person, and if there was anyone he could trust to be careful with sensitive information, it was Páll. He was the most reticent individual Högni had ever met, and, counterintuitive though it sounded, this seemed to be the key to his success in politics. Needless to say, Högni had contributed generously to Páll's election fund.

Högni's next big dream was to build on Geldinganes, a large headland on the Reykjavík coastline, attached to the mainland by a narrow spit. It would be the ideal site for a tasteful, exclusive shorefront development. But there were the usual voices on the Left opposing the idea and whining about untouched beaches and public access. Public access! The mere thought made Högni snort aloud.

The development would have a superb view of Videy, of course – for those with sufficiently deep pockets.

Högni shivered involuntarily at the thought of Videy. That girl sometimes haunted him at night, following him into his dreams, or rather his nightmares.

And now some hack on Dagbjartur's trashy rag was trying to exploit the story. But the public's interest would fade in the end, as it always did.

Högni had never discussed the incident on Videy with his friends, not since that fateful evening. Yet somehow it never went away. The story kept resurfacing at regular intervals, the girl's large, dark eyes gazing out at the Icelandic public from the same old newspaper photo.

He parked in the private space, marked with his licence number, R69878, then adjusted the rear-view mirror to give his appearance a quick check before he went out to face the world.

Högni tucked his grey hairs out of sight again, grinned at himself, then got out of his car and walked with a confident stride to the entrance of his company offices, ready to tackle the day's challenges. He needed to convince the world that it was time to build on Geldinganes and that he was the right man to do it. 'I treat everything the day brings as an opportunity,' he muttered under his breath, before heading inside.

Valur knew that Högni Eyfjörd's company HQ was based in one of the beautiful old Norwegian-style houses by the lake. The developer's purchase of the property had been leaked to the press at the time as the price he'd shelled out for it had been considered extortionate. Attractive though the building was, detached houses in the old city centre were out of fashion. Valur had noticed that these days the well-off tended to prefer large modern properties in the suburbs or in the greater Reykjavík area.

Valur certainly didn't belong to this group himself. Journalists were paid peanuts and it wasn't as if he came from a moneyed background. His parents still lived in the northern town of Húsavík, where he and Sunna had grown up with loads of freedom, in the heart of nature. Life in Húsavík had been pleasant enough, but that hadn't stopped him and Sunna jumping at the first opportunity to move south to the capital. Valur was happy with both Reykjavík and his job; Dagbjartur was a fair boss and money wasn't everything. Life as a reporter was full of interest, even excitement on occasion, and Valur had resolved to take things one day at a time. He was young enough not to have many worries about the future. For now, he was content with the little flat he rented on Laugateigur, a leafy street not far from the big Laugardalur swimming pool. Later, when he was a bit older, maybe he would end up in one of those pretty wooden houses in the old city centre, acquiring it at a knock-down price because everyone else was queuing up to live in the desirable suburb of Gardabær. He pictured himself and Margrét – the girl he was seeing – shacked up together in a traditional house with large windows and a nice little garden for when the weather was good.

Granted, probably not here on pricey Tjarnargata, but somewhere in the vicinity.

The sun was shining brightly, lighting up the colourful roofs around the lake and lending an almost fairytale air to the scene, which could look very different on Reykjavík's frequent grey, overcast days.

Valur stood still for a moment, gazing out over the gleaming waters of the lake, before approaching Högni's offices. The door was locked, but next to it was an elaborate doorbell with the name of the company, Eyfjörd Development Ltd, engraved on a brass plaque beneath. Valur pressed the bell and waited.

After a short interval the door was opened by a middle-aged woman, dressed from head to toe in white, her eyes hidden behind thick glasses. She gave Valur a pleasant smile. 'Good morning?' The words contained both a greeting and a question: *What business do you have here?*

'Good morning. I'm Valur, from the *Vikubladid* newspaper. I'd like a word with Högni.'

'Do you have an appointment?'

Valur shook his head.

'Högni doesn't normally receive journalists unless the appointment's been agreed in advance. Why don't I have a word with him, then get back to you with a date?'

Valur was just searching for the right way to refuse this offer when the man himself came down the stairs, suntanned, as usual, and sporting a dark-blue blazer, apparently on his way out. He paused by the short-sighted receptionist: 'I'm going to a meeting, dear. I'm not sure if I'll come back to the office afterwards.'

As Högni passed, he threw a brief glance at Valur, his blank expression registering a complete lack of interest.

Valur, seeing his chance, backed out on to the steps then started down them after Högni.

'Excuse me, you're Högni Eyfjörd, aren't you?' he asked.

Högni stopped and looked round, surprised: 'Yes. And you are?'

'My name's Valur, I'm a journalist—'

Högni's face abruptly darkened. 'Ah, Dagbjartur's boy. Of course, now I recognize you. I have to say you look a lot better in your byline photo than you do in the flesh.'

Valur didn't let this rudeness put him off his stride. It went with the territory. 'We've met once before, a year or so ago – you probably won't remember me, but it was—'

'No, I don't remember you. I meet a lot of people. Speaking of which, I'm on my way to a meeting right now.'

'Can I ask you a quick question about Videy?'

'What?'

'Videy.'

'I'm afraid not. You'll have to make an appointment.'

Högni was about to walk off, but Valur persevered.

'I understand you were a frequent visitor when Óttar and Ólöf lived there.' OK, this wasn't exactly how Kristján had put it, but Valur was hoping to provoke a response.

'Who told you that?' Högni snapped. 'That's a pack of lies. I—'

'So you don't know them?'

'Of course I know them – that's no secret. Óttar and I are friends; we were at school together.'

'So you never visited him on the island when he was living there?'

'Sure, there's nothing wrong with visiting friends.'

'Did you go there often?'

'Frankly, I can't see how that's any of your business.' Högni was seething now. Valur guessed that a man of his sort wouldn't take an ambush like this lying down. He would be straight on the phone to Dagbjartur to give him an earful about his brash young reporter. But Dagbjartur would stand by his staff, Valur had no worries on that score.

'I understand you were there shortly before Lára went missing?'

'Lára?' It was plain from Högni's expression that he knew perfectly well who she was.

'The girl who vanished – the one who was working as Óttar's maid.'

'That was decades ago.'

'Thirty years ago, almost to the day.'

'Look, I didn't even know the girl, and I have no idea why you're harassing me about this.'

'Were you there in August 1956?'

'How the hell am I supposed to remember that? Anyway, I'm going to be late for that meeting.' Högni stormed off.

'Thanks for the chat,' Valur called after him. 'I'll be writing about it in next Thursday's paper. And, while I'm at it, I'll be informing our readers where Lára is.'

Högni stopped short and looked round. 'No one bloody well knows where the girl is.'

'I have a source. All will be revealed next week. It's time Lára got a proper burial. I expect the entire paper will be devoted to the story. A photo of her. And one of you, of course. Could I maybe take a new picture of you now? If not, I'm sure we've got an old one we could use.'

'You're not taking any bloody photos. And don't you dare write a word about me. If you do, I'll sue you and I'll sue your paper for everything you've got. I'll bankrupt you.'

'That's a great quote, thanks. Incidentally, since I don't own anything, it wouldn't make any difference to me.'

'I'm warning you, boy! You're not publishing a word about me.'

'Luckily, that's not up to you. But I'd be willing to sit down with you some time this week to hear your side of the story. You know the sort of thing: how often you visited the island, your reasons for going there . . . You must have met Lára, as she was on Videy all summer. Do you remember her?'

'My side? There is no "my side" of the story. I didn't know Lára, and I had nothing to do with that business. For all I know, she's alive and kicking, probably living abroad somewhere.'

'Lára's dead, and you'll find out on Thursday what happened to her – assuming you don't already know.'

1986

16 August

Margrét had worked on the paper the previous summer but left unexpectedly at the end of July. 'Too much testosterone in that place for my taste,' she'd told Valur.

They had got on well when they worked together, but it wasn't until they met at a nightclub the following spring that something clicked. At twenty-one, she was a few years younger than Valur and currently doing a degree in politics at the University of Iceland. They were taking things slowly, meeting up every so often, and so far he was keeping the fact largely to himself. He'd told Sunna, but not his parents. Not yet. There was plenty of time for that later. Nevertheless, he had a good feeling about this girl; they got on well and he always looked forward eagerly to their meetings.

'Are you going downtown on Monday for the celebrations?' Margrét asked now. It was Saturday, and they were having lunch at Hornid, celebrating over pizza and

Coke the fact that it was three months since their first date.

'Yes, I feel I ought to go along. Try the cake, see the fireworks. How about you?'

'Oh, I'm worried it's going to be a bit of a flop. Expectations are so high.'

Although she had done a good job at the paper, they rarely discussed his work, not directly anyway, sticking instead to politics in general, or art and culture. Sometimes he suspected that she didn't even read the paper any more.

She had grown up in Gardabær with conservative parents and *Vikubladid* wasn't the sort of rag that would be read in a home like that, or so Valur imagined. He wondered if she'd applied to do a summer job on the paper as a warning to her parents not to take it for granted that she would follow in their footsteps.

Valur couldn't avoid the sneaking suspicion that her relationship with him might just be the flip side of the same coin, a silent rebellion which would never last. He hoped to God it wasn't true.

'Should we maybe meet down by the lake on Monday evening?' he asked.

'How romantic,' she said with a smile. 'Good idea. Down by the lake it is – at eight p.m.?'

'It's a date.' He returned her smile. 'What about this weekend? Do you feel like going into town later as well?'

'I'm afraid I've promised to babysit my sister's kids this evening and tomorrow,' Margrét replied, and Valur felt a stab of disappointment.

But then she added, warmly: 'We'll make up for it on Monday, though. And what do you say to renting a video later in the week and having a cosy night in?'

The weather was unusually balmy for August, but Valur supposed he would have to stay glued to his desk most of the day in case the mysterious Júlía rang again. There was too much at stake for him to throw away this chance. His big scoop. Or his first big scoop – hopefully the first of many.

He lingered in the sunshine outside the office for a minute or two, holding his face up to the sun, aware that every fine day in August could be the last.

To his surprise, when he got in, one of his colleagues was already there. Baldur had worked as a hack far longer than Valur; he was almost as old as their editor and his career had spanned any number of jobs. Sometimes Valur got the feeling that Baldur had worked on practically every newspaper in the country.

'Well I never, what are you doing here?' Baldur asked.

Valur didn't really deserve this barb, as it wasn't that rare for him to show his face in the office at the weekend, but it was true that he preferred to work from home outside normal office hours. He wasn't going to waste his time explaining this to Baldur, though. Besides, he suspected there was a hint of envy there: his colleague's nose had been put out of joint by the success of Valur's articles about Lára. Clearly, Baldur thought Valur's rise up the ladder at *Vikubladid* had been a tad too mercurial over the last month or so.

'Got a piece to finish,' Valur replied curtly. 'What about you? Plenty to do?'

'Yet another article about Lára, I suppose.' Baldur had a knack of coming out with these comments in a neutral tone. He would have made a good politician, as it was impossible to tell what he was really thinking.

'No, there's not much left to tie up there. Actually, I've started on something new,' Valur lied, amusing himself by imagining what was going through Baldur's head.

He sat down at his desk, his eyes straying automatically to the phone, as if that would make it ring. Chances were that the woman would never call back. That there had been nothing to it, after all. He tried to concentrate on the job at hand, leafing through the papers on his desk. In reality, he didn't have anything urgent to do, but he had to fake being busy as long as Baldur was in the office.

'Any phone calls for me earlier?' he asked.

Baldur looked round. 'Hm? Were you expecting one?'

'Sort of.'

'No, no calls, but there's an envelope for you around here somewhere.'

'An envelope?'

'Yes, it was lying on the floor under the letterbox when I arrived. I thought maybe it had been delivered yesterday.'

Valur tried not to appear too interested. He hadn't been expecting an envelope, but the message could only be from one person. Surely?

'Oh, where is it?'

'Didn't I put it on your desk?'

Baldur glanced back at his own desk. 'Oh, no, here it is.'

He strolled over to Valur with the envelope and stood there, waiting for him to open it.

'Thanks,' Valur said, but made no move to open it until Baldur was sitting down again.

Then he carefully lifted the flap and drew out a sheet of white paper which had nothing on it but a name:

ARNFRÍDUR LEIFSDÓTTIR

He looked back at the envelope. It was definitely addressed to him.

Arnfrídur Leifsdóttir?

A woman's name. He didn't recognize it.

Could it be a message from Júlía? Was that really all she'd sent? Or could it be linked to a completely different story?

He put the note back in the envelope, then noticed that on the back someone had printed: *Júlía*.

So it *was* from her! Perhaps the fact she'd chosen to send him this note meant she wasn't planning to phone him again. But at least it seemed that she still wanted to put him on the trail.

Feeling elated, he got to his feet and reached for his notebook, only to remember belatedly that he'd lent it to Sunna. He'd have to add this clue to his notes later. For now, he slipped the envelope into his trusty satchel.

'I'm off, Baldur,' he said, loudly and clearly.

'Already? That was short but sweet.'

'I forgot my notebook at home,' Valur lied.

'Anything interesting in the envelope?' Baldur asked casually.

'In the envelope? Oh no, just a receipt.'

*

Valur was generally the level-headed type who didn't let himself get carried away, but this envelope constituted a major breakthrough. He had a hunch that he'd just been handed the chance to write himself into Icelandic journalistic history. Some reporters waited their entire careers for a chance like this – like poor Baldur, for example, who had toiled away in mediocrity for one party mouthpiece after another, though usually for the left-of-centre papers, without ever making his mark. And now here was Valur, sitting on the scoop of the year. With any luck.

When he got home, he rang Sunna, but she didn't answer. She was never home, he thought, always up at the university or drinking coffee at Café Mokka or out partying with her friends. But she had to come home some time. He toyed with the idea of walking over to Hlídar and lying in wait outside her flat. He needed that notebook, damn it! His head was whirling with ideas and he urgently wanted to refresh his memory of names, facts and telephone numbers so he could start re-interviewing all the people involved. One of the names he'd noted down, he remembered, was Finnur Stephensen, the owner of a wholesale company. Valur had established that Finnur had been a childhood friend of Óttar's, and that they had stayed in touch over the years. Logically, that meant they must have been friends when Óttar was living on Videy. But before Valur had got round to knocking on Finnur's door in the hope of getting some background information on Óttar, he had read in the papers that Finnur was dead. So that particular line of inquiry had fizzled out. Which made it all the more important to get to Óttar and Ólöf, as he simply had to talk to them for the next article.

Even more pressing was the need to find out who Arnfrídur Leifsdóttir was – and Júlía too, of course.

In one of those unpredictable changes of weather so typical of the Icelandic climate, the skies had clouded over and it had started to drizzle. So much for the idea of going round to Sunna's on the off-chance of catching her in. The obvious next step was to trawl through the telephone directory searching for women called Arnfrídur, but this would require patience, as the Icelandic phone book was arranged by community and he would have to comb through the alphabetical lists of names in one village after another. Feeling too excited to focus on that right now, he went into the hall and looked up Dagbjartur's number in the telephone directory. He couldn't remember it off the top of his head as he wasn't used to ringing his boss at home. Then he picked up the telephone receiver, trying to control his excitement by taking slow breaths in and out, and started dialling.

'Valur, my lad, what's up?'

'I've got news.'

Valur would have preferred to do this sitting face to face with his editor, to get the expected pat on the head in person, but a phone call would have to do this time.

'News? About?'

'About the Lára case.'

'Well, well, well,' Dagbjartur replied. 'Out with it, then. I'm all ears.' His deep voice growing confidential, he added: 'Now, Valur, you'll see – we're really going to shift some papers!'

'You're telling me.' Although Valur had no direct financial interest in the success of the paper, he was always eager to help increase sales or the number of subscriptions. He wanted to feel he was earning his keep. And one day, sooner rather than later, he would pluck up the courage to ask for a raise.

'Anyway, spit it out, what's happened?' The editor was growing impatient.

'I got a message, in an envelope.'

'What?'

'An anonymous note, sort of. From Júlía, the woman who rang me.'

'And what did she have to say?'

'She sent me a name.'

'A name? What name?'

'Arnfrídur Leifsdóttir.'

'Arnfrídur? Who's she?'

'I haven't a clue, but I'm going to find out.'

There was a momentary silence at the other end. Valur could hear Dagbjartur sucking on his pipe. Then the editor said: 'Now you're talking. But bear with me here, I'm just thinking . . .'

'Yes . . . ?' Valur waited expectantly for the praise.

But Dagbjartur wasn't the type to dole it out. With him, praise often consisted of not being told off. 'I'm thinking . . .' he said again. 'Shouldn't we stoke up the tension a bit, eh?'

'How do you mean? To shift more papers?'

Valur often had trouble following Dagbjartur's logic, and this time was no exception. Perhaps it was the man's political instincts that Valur could never quite get a handle on.

'Sure. By all means, let's shift more papers,' he repeated, to fill the pause.

'Yes, you know what? I think this is what we'll do. You're going to solve that mystery for me, but for God's sake, don't blab about your source – or the tip-offs. We're going to keep this under our hats, Valur. That's absolutely vital now you're really getting somewhere.' After a moment he added, in a tone of faint wonder: 'Who would have believed it?'

Valur sighed. Apparently, his editor had had no more faith in him than that. But he'd show him he meant business; now he was really going to earn Dagbjartur's trust.

1986

17 August

Valur had been too wired to sleep properly after his phone call to Dagbjartur and was still feeling restless on Sunday morning, unable to settle to anything. He stared distract-edly out of the window. Children were playing in the street; the sunshine flashed off the houses opposite. Valur longed to be out there too. The colours and light of August had always had a special appeal for him. That last gasp of summer, when the evenings had just begun to draw in; the sense that autumn and the first night frosts were waiting in the wings . . .

Although he wasn't Reykjavík born and bred, Valur felt at home in the city, revelling in the sheer variety it had to offer. He pictured himself strolling through the streets of the centre, postponing work on his article for a few hours, despite the pressure. The thought brought a rueful grin to his lips because he always left things until the last min-ute. As a teenager, he used to loathe Sunday evenings as they meant sitting at the living-room table in Húsavík, surrounded by homework, while Sunna lolled in front of their black-and-white TV, having finished hers hours before.

Not that Valur found the Sunday-evening offerings on the state channel exactly gripping. They invariably consisted of grim Swedish dramas about the trials of divorced couples, featuring drunken men and overworked women. Or worthy interviews with Icelandic artists about how fried eggs were supposed to symbolize breasts in their work, or some such pretentious crap. Valur had a clear memory of sitting with a pile of maths exercises, watching over Sunna's shoulder as she solemnly drank it all in. But then Sunna had always been the cultured one, while he himself preferred American shows full of swearing and people being mown down by a hail of bullets. He hoped the new private TV station, which was intended to give the state channel a run for its money, would offer more of that kind of fare. He'd been considering buying a VCR to make up for the dearth of entertainment on TV, but his wages only stretched so far and there were too many other temptations to spend them on.

He drank a cup of coffee, then jumped in the shower, trying to shake off the old dread associated with Sundays. He would take the bus down to the newspaper offices and check if any further phone calls or messages had come in about the Lára case. After that, he would go for a leg-stretch around town. Loving, as he did, the old streets with their wooden houses clad in colourfully painted corrugated iron, Valur was highly critical of the 'new city centre' that was currently under construction. A high-rise office block, known as Commercial House, had already been built on the Kringlan site out by Miklabraut, the city's main traffic artery, and a shopping centre was now being developed to replace the historic heart of Reykjavík. And this wasn't the only major innovation in the works. Valur, who was no fan of modern architecture, had recently written a report about plans for the construction of a new city hall on the shores of the lake, which filled him with dismay. Today's architects seemed devoid of the earlier generation's aesthetic sense. If Valur had his way, they would carry on building in wood.

Valur disembarked at the bus station on Hlemmur Square, noticing that town was already filling up with people out to see and be seen, although the shops were shut on Sundays. First, he headed up the hill to the *Vikubladid* offices on Kárastígur. Finding nobody in, he lingered briefly to go through the papers on his desk, then decided to go down to Austurstræti to distract himself with a bit of window-shopping.

He made a beeline for Karnabær to see the latest fashions. As he was standing there, contemplating a red-checked shirt in the window, he felt someone slap him on the back.

'Hey, what's up?'

Valur turned to see Gunnar, an old mate from Húsavík, who was doing a theology degree at the university. A genuinely nice guy, with ginger hair and a smile always crinkling the corners of his eyes.

'How's tricks? Are you run off your feet at the *Washington Post*?'

Valur grinned. 'Run off my feet, yeah. The news just keeps coming.'

'I see you're writing about the Lára case. Reckon you'll crack it? Reykjavík's very own Columbo?'

Valur groaned. 'I don't know, but I can't stop obsessing about it. It was so unbelievably sudden. She just vanished into thin air. I mean, how does someone disappear like that? It's not like she wandered off and died of exposure on Videy . . .'

Gunnar was regarding him with affection. 'Couldn't she simply have walked into the sea, Valur? Decided to end it all? Leave this vale of tears?'

'What, taking her bags with her? All her luggage? You don't bother packing a suitcase if you're going to kill yourself, do you? And there's another thing, Gunnar. I spoke to Kristján, the detective who was in charge of the case, and I reckon he's holding something back. In fact, I'm not convinced she ever left the island.'

Valur stopped himself before he blurted out the information he'd received from Júlía. He was keeping that up his sleeve for the next article.

Gunnar studied him for a moment, his face grave now, then nodded.

'It would be great if you could find her. Otherwise it'll only continue to weigh on the nation's soul.'

Valur shrugged. 'You never know. But it's not easy to solve a thirty-year-old case. Anyway, what about you? Are you anywhere near finishing your degree?'

Gunnar smiled. 'We're probably talking another thirty years of hard graft. No, only joking. I'm working on my final dissertation but not getting anywhere fast. It's about Jesus's words in the Sermon on the Mount: "Judge not, that ye be not judged."'

Valur nodded slowly. He had an odd sensation that the words were intended for him. That he should ask himself whether it was really his job to go digging up old sins.

'Well, I need to get a move on,' Gunnar said. 'Tomorrow us theology students are required to attend a service for the city's two-hundredth anniversary. I'm to assist at the cathedral, which is where I'm heading now. Apparently the services will be packed out with politicians – God help us, is all I can say!'

By evening, Valur had mulled over various titles for his article without being satisfied with any of them.

He'd also worked out a plan for the coming week. On Tuesday he'd go over to the island in search of detail to pad out his article. At the very least, he'd be able to bring the place vividly to life for his readers. So far, the most sensational material he had was the information from Júlía that Lára had been killed on the Saturday evening. He'd describe it as an anonymous tip-off. With any luck, he'd be able to reveal the significance of Arnfrídur Leifsdóttir too. And his clash with Högni Eyfjörd would add a dash of spice.

Valur fried some mince he had in the fridge and boiled spaghetti to go with it, then sat down in front of his battered old TV set to watch the eight o'clock news. The headlines announced that they would be covering the Arnarflug airline's operational problems, the mooted economic boycott of South Africa, the chess match between Karpov and Kasparov, the government's presentation of a share in the island of Videy to the City of Reykjavík for its two-hundredth anniversary – and new developments in the Lára case.

Valur exploded out of his chair and turned up the volume. When the newsreader got to the final item, he stared intently into the cameras as he reported:

> The television newsdesk's sources have confirmed that fresh information about the disappearance of Lára Marteinsdóttir will be revealed in this Thursday's issue of *Vikubladid*. In recent weeks the journalist Valur Róbertsson has been re-examining the case in a series of features about Lára, who vanished without trace from Videy, aged fifteen, in 1956. There is a real possibility that the mystery of Lára's fate could be solved this week, thanks to new information received by *Vikubladid*. We were unable to contact Valur Róbertsson for comment.

Valur's jaw dropped. What the hell? Where had this news come from? And how in God's name was he supposed to live up to this claim? It's not like he actually had any answers. He began to pace nervously around his cramped living room, rubbing his hands.

We were unable to contact Valur Róbertsson . . . If only he'd stayed longer at the office, the TV people could have got hold of him and he would have had a chance to refute the story.

Who could have leaked it? Surely his old mate Gunnar

wouldn't have blabbed? No. Besides, the newsdesk would have had no reason to consider him a reliable source. In fact, no one was in a position to report on the status of the investigation apart from Valur's colleagues at the paper, and then only the editor actually knew anything.

Valur rushed into the hall. His hands were trembling as he dialled Dagbjartur's number and there was an acid churning in his stomach as he listened to the phone ringing, waiting for the editor to pick up.

'Dagbjartur.'

'Oh, hello, it's Valur here. Have you seen the news?'

'Yes, I was watching.'

'Did you catch the bit about the paper and the Lára story? The claim that there would be a big reveal this week?'

'I certainly did.'

Valur thought Dagbjartur sounded remarkably relaxed about the whole thing.

'But it's not true!' he exclaimed, his voice rising. 'Even though I got the tip-off from that woman, I haven't a clue where it will lead. I was planning to go to Videy this week . . .'

'But Valur, my lad, you did say you thought there was a story in this . . .'

'Yes, a story, an article – but that doesn't mean I've cracked the case.'

'Well, it'll make people sit up and take notice, won't it?'

'Have you any idea where they got the information from?'

'What information?'

In the background, Valur could hear a hubbub of noise, including the shrill sound of children's voices – Dagbjartur's grandchildren, presumably. His television was turned up loud as well, but the editor didn't raise his voice. Anyone would have thought he was competing in the Icelandic championships in low blood pressure.

Valur was a little disconcerted by this reaction. He himself was sweating in panic at the thought of the massive pressure he'd just been put under.

'The fact they're expecting a scoop this week,' he said breathlessly. 'The whole thing's so tied up with my name now – everyone recognizes my face, and now they all think I'm sitting on some kind of revelation. Who could have told the TV news that?'

'It's excellent for business, Valur. Everyone will be desperate to read about Lára and our sales will go through the roof. You'll attract some well-deserved attention and there's a chance we might be in the black at the beginning of next month. I can't see any downsides.'

'Was it you who leaked this to the newsdesk?'

'If it was, would that be so bad?' Dagbjartur was almost whinnying with pleasure by now. He seemed to regard the whole thing as a big joke.

'So, in other words, it *was* you?' Valur croaked.

'Look, my lad, the paper lurches on from week to week, teetering on the verge of bankruptcy,' Dagbjartur said. Valur had the feeling this was an exaggeration; he'd never been aware of any particular cashflow problems or savings being made. 'I'm fighting to keep us afloat,' the editor continued. 'Your investigation has been great for business – it's resulted in better sales, but there's always room for improvement. Mark my words, this evening's news will have *Vikubladid* flying off the shelves, regardless of whether you actually solve the mystery. Don't ever forget that this is a business; we have to sell papers if we're to get any news out there. Just be grateful – it'll put you and the paper in the spotlight, and I have every confidence that you'll come up with the goods. After all, it's a proper challenge for you – to write something that will live up to the public's expectations.'

Dagbjartur's pleasure in the way things were unfolding was only too evident.

Valur cleared his throat. 'Yes, OK, sure. I suppose it can't be helped, then. Goodbye, Dagbjartur.'

'Goodbye, Valur, my lad.' The editor rang off.

Dagbjartur's wife, Laufey, gave him an inquiring look after he'd hung up.

'Is something wrong, dear?'

'No, that was just Valur from the paper, in a bit of a stew about the news report. Nothing to worry about.'

'That's hardly surprising, dear. It's a lot of pressure for a young man to cope with.'

Dagbjartur didn't answer, and Laufey went into the kitchen to make tea. Her husband lived for that paper; it was all he talked about from morning to night. He'd been a lot more fun when they first met – he'd had more hair too – but somehow their marriage had lasted. In the last few years, though, Dagbjartur had occupied less and less of her thoughts. Instead, she was focused on yoga, aerobics and her grandchildren, and she had little patience with hearing about her husband's hassles with the paper.

She could hear him now, talking to their grandchildren in the other room. Adjusting the scrunchie she was wearing in her hair, she waited for the water to boil.

Valur went back into the living room and dropped on to the sofa with a groan.

He would really have to knuckle down if he was going to 'live up to the public's expectations', as Dagbjartur had put it.

A fine mess he'd got himself into. He just hoped Júlía would get back in touch . . . And he mustn't forget the note in the envelope: maybe he could track down this Arnfríður Leifsdóttir, whoever she was. Yes, there were several leads he could follow up. It wasn't beyond the realms of possibility that he'd be able to turn the situation to his advantage.

He looked outside. The sun was setting, its pink glow reflected in the windows of the houses opposite. All of a sudden he felt a rush of optimism: he wasn't going to be beaten by this.

He got to his feet. What he needed now was another good, long walk to clear his head.

He'd work something out.

1986

18 August

Valur had come into the *Vikubladid* offices early that Monday morning, still reeling from the fallout of the Sunday evening news. Dagbjartur hadn't arrived yet, but the other reporters were trickling in and having their first coffee of the day. Valur threw a greeting to the team. While he was preoccupied with his own article, the others were mostly focused on the city's anniversary celebrations, which were due to kick off at noon. Some were going to take the afternoon off; others were on duty to cover the festivities. So many companies had given their staff the day off that there was a real holiday atmosphere in town.

Baldur had been sent over to Videy on Sunday to attend the ceremonial presentation of the mansion and church to the City of Reykjavík. Valur cursed himself for not having offered to cover this story himself. It would have been the perfect opportunity to have a nose around and get a feel for the atmosphere on the island.

'Valur!' It was his colleague, Sverrir. '*Morgunbladid*'s asking for an interview with you . . .'

Valur met Sverrir's eye and shook his head. Sverrir took his hand from the telephone receiver and explained that, unfortunately, Valur wasn't in the office.

'That's what you get for being a star reporter,' Baldur said acidly, lighting a cigarette.

'Yeah,' Valur sat down at his desk. He needed to concentrate so he could make a start on the final article. Taking out a pen and paper, he began to write. It sometimes helped to clarify his thoughts if he wrote a rough version first before typing it out.

Lára was murdered.

Yes, that was the headline he'd go with.

A witness has come forward claiming that Lára Marteins-dóttir, aged fifteen, was murdered on the evening of Saturday, 4 August 1956.

Lára's parents contacted the police on the Monday because they hadn't received their customary phone call from their daughter that weekend and, when they'd inquired, they were told by her employers that she had unexpectedly left her job.

Lára's employers, Óttar Óskarsson and Ólöf Blöndal, who were resident on Videy at the time, told police that Lára had handed in her notice, packed her bags and left the island on the Friday.

Valur stared down at the sheet of paper, then added:

Time and place???

 If Lára was killed on the Saturday evening – could she have been in Reykjavík at the time?

 Or did she never leave Videy?

He sighed and thought back over his conversation with the woman who called herself Júlía – his notes from the phone call were somewhere among the pile of papers on his desk – then he wrote:

Lára needs a proper burial.

 Where's her body??

'Valur!' It was Sverrir again. 'This time it's the radio news wanting an interview.'

Valur looked up and shook his head. Sverrir grinned, then said into the phone that he was afraid Valur was busy with other assignments.

'So, my lad, not a minute's peace to write, eh?' Dagbjartur had turned up, the picture of calm, in a brown velvet jacket and beige shirt, freckled and contented as if he'd spent all weekend relaxing in the sun. 'How's it going?'

'Oh, fine, thanks,' Valur said with a sigh. 'I'm feeling the pressure, but I think it'll turn out OK. I'm going over to Videy tomorrow to try and inject a bit of background colour into the article. I'll do my best, anyway.'

'Sounds like a plan,' Dagbjartur said. 'By the way, if you need a break from Lára, you can always write me some copy about the city anniversary.' He snorted derisively: 'I hear they were queuing round the block to get into that technology exhibition yesterday. Tells you all you need to know about the Icelanders' mania for innovation. The mayor's been getting some pretty positive coverage off the back of the festivities. And I'll need to send someone to cover the president's official attendance as well. Honestly, the whole thing's such a circus.'

Valur smiled. 'I've got a few more things to look into here first, but after that I can go out there, see what's happening and find an angle to write about.'

'Good boy,' Dagbjartur said. 'We'll need to cover the cake and the entertainments. And someone told me there was a stampede at the post office earlier to get hold of the first-day cover of special anniversary stamps. Maybe you could work that into a story. Never forget, my lad, that journalism involves doing the small stuff too. Don't let success go to your head. You'll be popular enough with the girls if you manage to solve the Lára case – God help us!'

Dagbjartur roared with laughter at his own joke. Valur smiled and nodded, while privately thinking that there could be few jobs more tedious than coming up with a story about stamps. The things you had to do to keep your boss sweet . . . Still, Dagbjartur knew what he was doing. Leaking the news had probably been a clever ploy. It might even work, creating anticipation for Thursday's paper and simultaneously exerting the necessary pressure on Valur to finish the job.

He turned his attention back to the sheet of paper where he had been trying to summarize the main points.

Then he pulled the envelope out of his satchel. Arnfríður Leifsdóttir – who was she?

Valur grabbed the telephone directory and started running through the 'A's for Arnfríður . . . first in Reykjavík, then systematically around the country, by postcode. After trawling through for some time, he established to his satisfaction that there were only two women called Arnfríður Leifsdóttir currently living in Iceland. He wrote down their telephone numbers and addresses, then glanced unseeingly out of the window at the sea and mountains. Should he try ringing them? Just ask them straight out whether they knew anything about Lára Marteinsdóttir?

Picking up the receiver, he dialled the number of the first Arnfríður, who lived on Raudalækur in Reykjavík.

'Hello.'

'Oh, hello, is that Arnfríður Leifsdóttir?'

'Yes. Who's speaking, please?' It sounded like the voice of a woman well past middle age.

'My name's Valur and I'm a journalist on *Vikubladid*.'

There was silence on the line.

'Erm, I was wondering if you knew anything about a girl called Lára Marteinsdóttir, who vanished thirty years ago?'

'Me?' The woman seemed astonished by the question. 'What, no – are you talking about the girl on Videy?'

'Yes, that's right,' Valur said. 'I received a tip-off that you might have known her.'

'No, I didn't.' The woman was sounding increasingly annoyed with the direction this phone call was taking.

'Lára Marteinsdóttir was born in 1941,' Valur said, changing tack. 'Could she have been a contemporary of yours?'

'No, I never knew her,' Arnfrídur replied frostily. 'And if that's all, I'm ringing off now.' There was a sudden disconnection tone and Valur cursed himself for his clumsiness. The woman had obviously felt that he'd badly overstepped the mark. He would have to work out a subtler approach.

The other Arnfrídur Leifsdóttir lived in the Westman Islands, the small archipelago off the south coast of Iceland. After the previous call, Valur had to summon up his courage before he could bring himself to dial her number.

He jotted down:

All avenues closed.

And wondered, as he waited for the second Arnfrídur to pick up, whether this would make a good subheading.

'Hello.' A bright, breezy voice this time. And a considerably younger woman. Valur cleared his throat.

'Arnfrídur?'

'Yes?'

'Oh, hello. My name's Valur, I'm a journalist on *Vikubladid*. Ahem, we've received a tip-off that you – or someone with the same name as you – might have had a connection to Lára Marteinsdóttir, who went missing thirty years ago.'

'Lára Marteinsdóttir?' Arnfrídur echoed.

'Yes, she disappeared in 1956 and *Vikubladid* has been re-examining the circumstances.'

'Oh, OK, well, I wasn't even born then,' Arnfrídur

said, sounding neither anxious nor particularly interested. 'Lára – are you talking about the story that was on the news yesterday?'

'Yes, that's right,' Valur said. 'So, you can't think of any possible connection you might have to her?'

'I'm afraid I haven't a clue,' Arnfríður said. 'I can't think of a single thing. Why would you think I had any connection to her?'

'Like I said, we received a tip that you, or someone with your name, could have a link to the case – that's all,' Valur explained.

'I see,' Arnfríður said. 'Er, no, I'm completely in the dark. But, hey, you know, good luck and all that.'

Valur said goodbye and rang off, thinking that this cheery young woman couldn't be the one in the note. On the other hand, the reaction of the first woman had been a tad suspicious. She could be around the right age too. He could check that by ringing the National Registry. Margrét had a friend called Katrín who worked there.

He returned to the problem of Óttar and Ólöf. He had mentioned the couple briefly in the first three articles but needed more background on them. The trouble was that they hadn't made themselves available for interview.

Who would have had a reason to visit them on the island? Valur had discovered that the wholesaler Finnur Stephensen had been a schoolfriend of Óttar's, which would surely have made him a likely candidate. Then there was Högni Eyfjörd, of course, whose name Kristján had brought up in connection with the case and who had been downright hostile when Valur tried to speak to him . . .

He got to his feet and went into Dagbjartur's smoke-wreathed office.

'I'd like to get a better handle on the couple Lára was working for,' he announced.

'Fair enough,' Dagbjartur said. 'But didn't the police give them a thorough going-over at the time? What about your source, Júlía – heard any more from her? That note, for instance?'

'Yes, Arnfríður – the name in the note – I'm on her trail. It's only a question of time before I track her down.' Valur had made up his mind to speak to Margrét's friend at the National Registry. 'I'm also taking a look at Högni Eyfjörð.'

'Högni? Why him, for God's sake?'

'You're bound to receive a complaint from him.'

'So what? I trust my boys, Valur. You know that.'

'If Finnur Stephensen wasn't dead, I'd probably have had a run-in with him too. His name was on my list. All society's power blocs.' Valur laughed.

'It's shaping up to be a good paper on Thursday,' Dagbjartur said with a note of satisfaction.

'It's going to be a *hell* of a paper!'

'Record sales,' Dagbjartur continued. 'Record sales, Valur my lad. But you will have time to give me a short piece on the anniversary too, won't you? There was that item on the commemorative stamps? In fact, why don't you accompany Kiddi while he's taking photos and do a question of the week with members of the crowd while you're at it.'

Valur forced himself to smile and nod. He had the feeling that Dagbjartur was deliberately bringing him down to earth with these mundane jobs. There was only one star reporter on *Vikubladid*, and that was its owner and editor, Dagbjartur himself.

But all he said was: 'Sure, I'll find a good angle.'

1986

18 August

Councillor Páll Jóhannesson shifted uncomfortably in his pew; he wasn't at ease in this setting. He hadn't gone into politics to waste his mornings in church, though today it was unavoidable. As an elected member of the Reykjavík City Council, he couldn't afford to be absent when services were being held in all the city's churches to celebrate the two-hundredth anniversary. Although Páll was neither a churchgoer nor religious, he liked to say in interviews that he had held on to his childhood faith, as he knew that sort of thing appealed to potential voters. He shifted again. The hard wooden pews in Reykjavík's old cathedral could have done with replacing, and the vicar, a verbose, middle-aged man, did nothing to distract Páll from the fact.

Páll had gone into politics to gain influence, as he put it. He placed great importance on planning and had got himself comfortably installed in that department. At one

point he'd had hopes of scaling the heights in city politics, but that was before it had gradually come home to
him that he lacked the necessary charisma at the ballot
box. Besides, he'd already achieved everything that mattered by then. Experience and an extensive network of
contacts enabled him to get things moving, even without
a majority on the council. He was an influential figure in
his own right too. Páll was in with the right people, which
secured him a certain status within the system, a fact he
valued far more highly than popularity among the voters.
He'd chosen to remain in the shadows, politically speaking. Left or right, for him that wasn't the primary issue.

Planning was currently at the top of the agenda. The
new city centre with its large shopping mall, which was due
to open the following year, would transform Reykjavík for
coming generations. The site was the focus for further
residential developments and retail premises too, not to
mention the new Broadcasting House, which had been in
the works for years but was finally nearing completion.
Páll took enormous pleasure in these projects. He loved
meeting the building contractors and basking in their
awed respect, touring the construction sites and generally
having a say in the direction of the city's future development. He took pride in the sense of his own importance.
And he looked out for his friends, particularly Högni. In
fact, they looked out for each other.

Páll had always preferred to operate behind the scenes.
He had opted to pursue a safe path in life. His father had
been a shopkeeper and his mother a housewife, the most
ordinary people imaginable, and they had brought up

their children accordingly. The goal had always been to live in a nice house, own a car, marry a beautiful wife and have promising children; in other words, to live a decent, respectable life. He darted a furtive glance at his wife, who was sitting beside him in the pew.

Gunnlaug had been that beautiful wife once. They had met at school, where she'd been one of the most popular girls, and afterwards she had gone on to study domestic science. These days, their two children were at sixth-form college, Gunnlaug's blonde hair was turning grey and her features, which used to be so soft, had sharpened. She was dressed in a dark blue coat, accessorized with a pink scarf: 'her' colours. She had recently gone to get her colours done with the other women from her sewing circle and discovered that she was a 'spring'. As a result, she'd started investing in a lot of pink, purple and lilac clothes.

At this moment, she gave every appearance of listening attentively to the vicar. A wise man built his house on rock and it survived every storm – unlike the house that was built on sand: 'And so it is with our city,' the vicar droned. 'It is built on rock and stands firm against every storm.'

Páll's thoughts went inadvertently to the building lots by Lake Raudavatn on the eastern edge of the city, which had been such a bone of contention in the election four years ago. Planning hadn't been quite such a burning issue in the most recent elections, a fact for which he credited himself not least. He had first got himself noticed in politics for speaking out against the development of green sites. 'Protect our green areas,' had been Páll's campaign

slogan. But he knew that planning wasn't only about protecting green areas: property was the only safe investment
in Iceland, the only asset that could ride out the constant
economic fluctuations, galloping inflation and interest-
rate hikes.

Páll tuned back in to the vicar's sermon to find that he
had moved on to family values. He glanced back at Gunnlaug, whose eyes were still fixed on the vicar. When had
he realized that their marriage was no longer giving him
what he wanted? Gunnlaug used to be so sunny tempered
and quick to laugh, but one day it had dawned on him
that her laughter had dried up. She kept an exemplary
home, looked after their children, cooked a roast on Sundays, followed the news and was able to keep her end up
in conversation when she accompanied him to receptions
or performed other duties as his wife. She belonged to a
sewing circle, read books and participated in Women's
Institute activities. And on top of that she took courses,
knitted jumpers and had even created a tapestry hanging
for their wall. They had an attractively furnished summer
cabin in Skorradalur, an hour or two up the coast, and
their house on Grenimelur, in Reykjavík's affluent west
end, was a monument to good taste and quality materials.
She was a woman with two fur coats – a sure sign of
success.

Yet, in spite of it all, Páll had found himself another
woman.

Elísabet was just twenty-three, a secretary with Reykjavík City Council. She had blonde hair that she wore in
a high ponytail, and dressed in cheerful pastel shades,

usually in jackets with shoulder pads, colourful plastic belts and chunky necklaces. Her job was to answer the phone, organize all Páll's meetings and make the coffee, and she greeted everyone as if she was genuinely eager to meet them. She lived in an attic flat on Njálsgata, which she took pains to make pretty. And although she was employed in the planning department, she showed next to no interest in the subject.

Her presence had gradually come to Páll's notice; she was always so bright and bubbly, her pink lipstick seemed to light up the room and her trilling laughter was infectious.

One evening there had been a staff party in the planning department and one thing had led to another. For most of the evening he had talked to his male colleagues, but as the event drew to a close, the women had started tidying up. It would never have crossed Páll's mind to help with the clearing up at home, but he had wandered over to Elísabet and offered his services. He'd caught sight of the older women exchanging meaningful glances, but Elísabet had merely given him a bright smile and accepted his help with gratitude.

Afterwards, Páll had walked her home from Borgartún to her flat on Njálsgata, where they had made passionate love. She had dragged him up the narrow stairs and giggled as he removed her salmon-pink dress. She was young and firm-fleshed and behaved as if he satisfied her. Admittedly, he and Gunnlaug still had regular sex, but always according to the same predictable script, with her in the same kind of nightie, the lights off, never any novelty. With Elísabet, he felt young again. She gazed at him with admiration and treated him like the star of the show.

Gunnlaug Haraldsdóttir was watching the vicar. Reverend Halldór was such a bore. He never said anything he hadn't said a hundred times before. She didn't actually mind going to church; she even thought highly of the bishop, who she felt actually had something to say, a message about the importance of the spiritual life. But she was no fan of Reverend Halldór and had come along mainly in her role of supportive wife to Páll.

Gunnlaug was in her early fifties, or so she claimed, though in fact this was out by a decade. She had fallen for Páll while they were still at school. He'd been dark and handsome, and had given the impression of being a man who would never put a foot wrong in life. They'd got married while he was at university, had their two children, made themselves a beautiful home and bought a cosy summer cabin. Then Páll had gone into politics, with pretty high ambitions in the early days. He wasn't a natural politician, though, and kept a low profile, coming across more like a civil servant than an elected representative. But his job paid well and he seemed to enjoy it, poring over his planning drafts until all hours, forever at meetings with developers, a key figure in the allocation of building sites.

Gunnlaug had played her part conscientiously, baking cakes and making coffee, attending endless meetings and events, always at her husband's side, loyal and dependable.

She'd lost count of the meals she'd cooked for his child-hood friends. Sometimes their wives were included in the invitation, and Gunnlaug had the most time for Thórdís, who revelled in being the centre of attention. We're all so loyal and dependable, Gunnlaug thought. But was it reciprocated?

She was conscious of Páll beside her, straight-backed, dignified, his thoughts apparently somewhere else entirely. He was the last person to rise when the vicar invited them to receive the blessing. Páll seemed increasingly distracted these days, not just at home but when they were out in company too.

Gunnlaug had known her husband a long time. For most of their married life, their interests had lain together. She had supported him in his political ambitions, but then she was ambitious herself. She wanted to belong to the best circles, attend opening nights, go to cocktail par-ties and meet other people like them. Recently, though, she had sensed that she and Páll were drifting apart. He seemed to have no interest in anything they did. They turned up to the same places as before, he greeted all the men and enjoyed playing his role, but he'd been working late increasingly often, pleading the excuse that he was snowed under with planning applications. He paid little attention to Gunnlaug, barely noticing when she dressed up, and often answered mechanically when she spoke to him. Even meals, which had always been their special pri-vate time, since Páll enjoyed his food, had become dull and monotonous. He seemed to have so little to say for himself.

It occurred to Gunnlaug that he might have developed a wandering eye, like some of his friends; that he had started taking her for granted. Well, good luck to him. She was aware that cheating and womanizing were rife in political circles, and far from unknown among Páll's group of close friends. But she also knew that although attitudes were becoming more liberal these days, that didn't automatically mean that divorce was a good look for a man in his position. Then again, she would probably be well shot of him. He wasn't exactly stimulating company any more.

The vicar invited the congregation to sing the final hymn. Beside her, Páll opened the hymnbook and moved his lips. He wasn't the type to sing aloud. Gunnlaug looked down at her book and defiantly raised her voice.

1986

18 August

Kiddi, the photographer, was a quiet, easy-going guy of around Valur's own age, from Breidholt on the eastern edge of the city. He seemed to have no interest in anything but his camera and had already earned a reputation for his striking portraits. Politicians were his favourite subject. Not that he displayed any political leanings himself or seemed to know much about individual politicians and parties, but he had a good eye for people and a knack of capturing their personalities memorably on film. He was good-natured enough to be content with most assignments, however, even if it meant going to the post office to take pictures of stamps.

Valur asked Kiddi to hang on a minute while he made one phone call. He got straight through to the National Registry and asked to speak to Katrín, Margrét's friend. After a short wait, Katrín came to the phone. Her voice was soft but clear and he pictured her with her fine blonde hair neatly held back from her face with clips. Valur explained that he was wondering if she could possibly do a discreet search on the name Arnfrídur Leifsdóttir and compile a list for him of all the women who had been called that over the last half-century or so.

Although Katrín had done him a similar favour before, she still sighed a lot and said it would take her a while to do what he wanted. He could ring back the following day, by which time she should have the information for him. Valur thanked her profusely. He was banking on this providing a vital piece of the puzzle for Thursday's article.

Valur put the envelope and notes in his bag, which he slung over his shoulder, then hurried out of the *Viku-bladid* offices with Kiddi at his side. Their mission was to go to the central post office and interview someone about the commemorative issue of stamps, then to buttonhole some festival guests for the 'Question of the Week' column. The parade was due to depart from Hallgrímskirkja church shortly, after which there would be a programme of entertainments in the park by the lake and in the old city centre.

The visit to the post office was quickly crossed off their list. Kiddi took a photo of the woman in charge holding up an envelope bearing several stamps with the anniversary postmark of a swan forming the number 200. Valur jotted down a few sentences about the citizens of Reykjavík's extraordinary passion for stamps, under the headline:

First-day cover of commemorative stamps sells like hot cakes

By the time they emerged and set off along Austur-stræti, a large crowd was already milling in the centre and the entertainments were commencing. A line of tables had been set up in Lækjargata bearing the 200-metre-long cake.

'Right, question of the day. Let's ask people what they thought of the cake,' Valur suggested.

'Won't we have to wait for them to try it first?' Kiddi asked, then shrugged.

They walked over to the cake and positioned themselves in a likely spot. The first slice was ceremonially served to the President of the Republic, a dignified woman in a smart suit and hat, after which there was a big free-for-all as what felt like every inhabitant of Reykjavík converged on the tables, determined to get a piece of the cake. Children dodged through their parents' legs and the bakers couldn't keep up with the demand to cut slices. It didn't take Valur and Kiddi long to accost some of the cake-eating festival-goers.

So, how was the cake?

Good!

So, how was the cake?

There was a definite hint of alcohol. Was there sherry in it?

So, how was the cake?

I'm not that keen on marzipan.

Having dealt with the question of the week, Valur and Kiddi seized their chance to try a slice themselves. 'Nothing special,' Kiddi muttered. After that, they walked back up to Kárastígur together. Valur dashed off the two items, submitting all the material by four p.m.

He wanted to go back into town to soak up the atmosphere a bit more, then shoot home before meeting Margrét that evening. They were planning to rendezvous by the lake at eight, then watch the entertainments from Arnarhóll, the grassy mound above Lækjargata. Valur wondered if Margrét would come home with him afterwards, as she sometimes did. He'd never been very adroit in his relations with the opposite sex, though not from any lack of interest on his part. He always felt so awkward with girls, never sure what to talk about to make himself sound interesting, and shy when it came to making a move.

He was uncertain about how best to proceed in his relationship with Margrét, though he felt that they were on the right course. She was taking a short summer holiday before the university term started. It was unusual for students not to spend the entire summer working, but with a background like hers she could presumably afford the luxury, especially as she still lived with her parents. She was pretty, with long dark hair, and dressed a little older than her age.

Although he got butterflies in his stomach every time he saw her, he still wasn't sure what the future would hold. Perhaps that was just his natural insecurity. He envied his sister, Sunna, who seemed able to make anyone, male or female, fall for her without so much as lifting a finger. Valur wasn't like that.

He weaved his way through the sea of humanity. There were people everywhere, though most were now streaming away from the centre, heading home to grab some supper before the evening entertainments began. Normally the only time one ever saw Reykjavík this packed was on Saturday nights, around three in the morning, when the city's nightclubs emptied and the streets would be filled with a drunken, heaving throng. But today's crowd was much better behaved, being made up largely of families with children. Valur wandered around for a while until it dawned on him that he'd forgotten his satchel at the newspaper offices. So back he went to Kárastígur to fetch it, before walking down to Skúlagata, where he hoped to be able to get on a bus.

As he walked, his mind returned to his article.

Could Arnfríður be the key to the riddle? If so, which of the two women was the Arnfríður he wanted?

And what did he know about the couple, Óttar and Ólöf? For instance, could just anybody go and set up home on Viðey if they felt like it? Maybe it would be a good idea to have a nose around in the city archives.

Did Lára die on the island?

Júlía had effectively told him two things: one, that Lára had been murdered on the Saturday evening, and, two, that her death was connected in some way to a woman called Arnfríður Leifsdóttir.

Valur had reached the bus stop. It was extremely busy, as the centre had been closed to private cars over the holiday. A bus was bearing down on them at considerable speed. Assuming it would be packed, Valur wormed his way closer to the kerb, determined not to miss out on a place. He wanted to have a shower and change into fresh clothes for his date with Margrét. There was something romantic about the thought of sharing this historic day with her.

His earlier stress forgotten, he was filled with eager anticipation and cautious optimism about the future.

At that moment he felt a violent shove from behind. Losing his balance, he hurtled forward into the road and found himself staring for a split second into the horrified eyes of the bus driver.

PART TWO

1986

Sunna had been doing her best to ignore the two-hundredth-anniversary celebrations, but in practice there was no avoiding them. All anyone could talk about was the holiday – and the subject of Videy seemed inescapable too. Last night's TV news had included a report about the mayor's visit to the island for the ceremonial transfer of ownership from the state to the City of Reykjavík. But a slight shadow had been cast on the story by the big news in the same bulletin that later that week Valur was planning to solve the mystery of the girl who had vanished on Videy. This had come as a bombshell to Sunna. She had tried ringing her brother repeatedly, without success.

The bastard, he hadn't said a word to her.

Was it really possible that he'd found Lára? Like the notorious Geirfinnur case, Lára's story was a cause célèbre, and the nation would be breathlessly following every update, eager for revelations about the girl's fate.

The Icelanders couldn't get enough of crime stories, Sunna thought. She remembered how she and Valur had got together every Tuesday without fail for six weeks last winter to catch all the episodes of the new British TV series about Inspector Dalgliesh, called *Cover Her Face*. The whole time it was on, their circle of friends had been obsessed with trying to guess the identity of the murderer. Towards the end of the series, Sunna had remarked to Valur that she could see herself writing a crime story one day. *Yeah, right*, Valur had said scornfully. *Like anyone would want to read a detective story set in Iceland. But I promise to solve some real crimes for you in the paper.*

On the Monday of the anniversary, Sunna stayed in until after lunch, working on her dissertation, the radio playing quietly in the background. As a rule, she listened to Radio 2, which broadcast lighter programmes and contemporary music, but she couldn't wait for more choice on the airwaves. At the moment, the only other option if you wanted to listen to rock or pop was the American Forces Radio, broadcasting in English from the NATO base at Keflavík. It was high time there was an Icelandic alternative.

God, she was bored of all the fuss over the city anniversary. It was even dominating the schedules on Radio 2. The final straw came when they started broadcasting live from the city centre at two p.m. The only way to escape the wall-to-wall media coverage – media frenzy, more like – Sunna decided, was to take one of the special free buses into town and try the famous, record-breaking birthday cake for herself. But when she got there the throng was so large that Sunna was quite taken aback.

As she wandered around, she bumped into various friends, acquaintances and relatives, but no one had time to stop and chat. The crowds of people milling around aimlessly in the streets felt like Icelandic National Day times ten. She'd been hoping to run into Valur at some point, but the chances of finding one person in that seething multitude were virtually zero. Still, in spite of herself, she gradually became infected by the atmosphere. It was a historic day, after all, and fun to experience it first-hand. The happiness radiating from the faces of her fellow citizens – and no doubt plenty of visitors from the countryside too – made it hard not to get caught up in the high spirits.

As the afternoon wore on, it hardly seemed worth going home. The sun was shining and the temperature was mild by Icelandic standards. The cake had tasted OK too, though she'd had to fight her way through the crowd to secure her slice. There weren't many people Sunna looked up to as a role model, but one of those was the president, Vigdís Finnbogadóttir, the first woman in the world to be democratically elected head of state, so she was pleased to catch sight of her in person. She would have liked to shake her by the hand, but of course there had been no chance of that.

In the end, Sunna found herself a spot on the slopes of Arnarhóll, the green mound in the centre of town, crowned with the statue of Iceland's first settler, Ingólfur Arnarson. It was lucky that she had dressed up warmly, as it soon got chilly once she'd stopped moving. From this vantage point, she watched the festival programme, the speeches and entertainments, not all of which were to her taste. The symphony orchestra and the excerpt from a play weren't her kind of thing at all, but she did enjoy the songs about Reykjavík, even some of the cheesier offerings, though she'd never have admitted as much to her friends. In hindsight, maybe she'd have done better to meet up with the girls, but it was too late now. She'd been so insistent that this holiday was only for kids and pensioners. She missed Valur's company. It would have been a lot more fun with him at her side, huddled up together against the increasingly cold breeze, to comment on and poke fun at the amusements on offer. If only she had managed to get through to him this morning and arranged to meet up. No doubt he was out there now, with his girlfriend. She supposed, gloomily, that it was inevitable she and her brother would drift apart as time went on, especially if he'd found himself a partner.

The mayor brought the proceedings to a close with a speech, which was followed by a magnificent firework display. The autumn darkness had infiltrated the light Icelandic summer nights almost without anyone noticing, until the rockets lit up a sky that was unmistakably dim. The occasion felt like a cross between the 17 June National Day and New Year's Eve.

Although Sunna had a long wait in the cold at the bus stop, she felt enveloped in an odd sense of peace, in spite of her shivers. It had ended up being an enjoyable day, after all, giving the lie to her negativity that morning.

Having finally managed to bag a seat on a packed bus, she warmed up on the ride. The short walk home from the stop was pleasant too. There were still lots of people about in her area, making their way home from the fireworks, and she was reminded once again of New Year's Eve, especially in her childhood, when she and Valur used to be allowed to stay up late with their parents. There was something magical about midnight at that age, and at this moment she felt like a child again.

She would ring Valur when she got home. No one would have gone to bed yet, tonight of all nights, and she was longing to hear his news. Find out what the deal was with Lára, get to share in his excitement about Thursday, when the next issue of the paper was due out. Today, the media spotlight had been on the mayor and the president, but Sunna suspected that by the end of the week her brother Valur would be the star of the show, especially if he really did succeed in finding out what had happened to the missing girl.

As she approached the house where she lived in the district known as Hlídar, on the lower slopes of Öskjuhlíd hill, she noticed that the lights were on upstairs in Kamilla's flat. That was very unusual, but then of course everything was different tonight. The world seemed a little brighter and more beautiful, in spite of the returning darkness. Her cynicism abandoned, Sunna had allowed herself to be genuinely moved by the anniversary celebrations in the world's most northerly capital, charmed by the artless enjoyment of its inhabitants. Now though, her mind was full of thoughts of bed, and she couldn't wait to curl up under her duvet and drift off to sleep, grateful that, against all expectations, the usual tensions had been set aside for one day. Tomorrow everything would go back to normal: work on her dissertation, news of political squabbles, and the usual controversies about whaling and planning issues.

She rummaged around in her bag for the keys, worried for a moment that she had lost them, though as always she found them in the end. But when she opened the door, she was brought up short by a totally unexpected sight: Kamilla, sitting wide awake on the stairs, as if waiting for her. Startled, Sunna froze for a moment in the doorway. The stairs were a communal area: Kamilla, who owned the house, was simultaneously Sunna's neighbour and landlady. The arrangement worked well. There were a good twenty years between them but Kamilla wasn't too fussed about the occasional party on the ground floor, though she herself was very much the quiet homebody.

'Kamilla . . .' Sunna only just stopped herself from asking: *What on earth are you doing here?*

The question wasn't really justified, given that it was Kamilla's house.

'Sunna, I was waiting for you,' Kamilla said, her voice even softer than usual.

'What? For me?'

'Would you come upstairs for a minute – there's hot coffee in the pot.'

The invitation sounded so innocent that Sunna nodded

automatically, though in fact there was nothing normal about drinking coffee in the early hours of the morning with a neighbour who never had guests and was rarely awake after midnight.

Sunna followed Kamilla upstairs to her flat, where her landlady invited her to take a seat in the sitting room, before vanishing into the kitchen and eventually re-appearing with a steaming mug.

'The thing is, Sunna, the police were here earlier, wanting to talk to you. I promised to let them know when you got home.'

'What?'

Sunna felt suddenly as if she had walked into a trap, though that was absurd. Apart from being a bit behind with her dissertation, she hadn't done anything wrong.

'They're on their way over. Let's just wait for them to get here.'

'You know, I have absolutely no idea what's going on,' Sunna said, cradling her mug. It didn't even occur to her to take a sip.

'Let's just wait for them.'

This was probably the longest conversation she'd had with Kamilla since signing the rental agreement. She liked the woman fine, Kamilla was a model landlady, but they simply didn't have anything in common.

Sunna rose abruptly to her feet, spilling coffee on her clothes. She put down the mug: 'It's no good – I can't wait. Please can you explain what's going on? I mean . . . have I done something wrong?'

She could feel herself breaking out in a sweat as her agitation intensified. She couldn't stay here another minute.

Kamilla stood up too and laid a hand on her shoulder. 'Just sit down. You haven't done anything wrong. But I'd rather the police gave you the news.'

'News? What news?'

Sunna's heart was racing now. She felt as if all the oxygen was being sucked out of the room.

'I honestly think we ought to wait for them, Sunna. I just don't know what to say.'

Only now did Sunna take in the fact that Kamilla was as agitated as she was. Clearly, she didn't want to be in this situation either. Sunna dropped into her chair again, realizing that she wouldn't be any better off waiting alone downstairs.

'Is my father all right? And my mother? Has something happened?'

Kamilla hesitated: 'Yes, they're ... They're all right, but ... Really, you just need to wait. You see, I ... I don't think they'd want me to discuss it with you.'

'You can't do this to me,' Sunna cried, her voice rising desperately. 'You've got to ... you've got to tell me. I can't handle this ...' She was close to breaking point now and could feel the tears starting to trickle down her cheeks.

But Kamilla didn't answer and the silence between them became ever more deafening.

Valur? Surely he's OK?

She hadn't heard from him, hadn't been able to get

hold of him, though normally he was never far away. He was so reliable, always there when she needed him. Of course nothing had happened to her big brother. Valur had always taken care of her. Always been there for her. Even when she'd hung around him and his friends in her teens, he'd never seemed to mind. His little sister had always come first with him. She'd known that, sensing that she was more important to him than his mates, more perhaps even than their parents.

Maybe his girlfriend would know where he was? Sunna immediately dismissed the thought.

She and Valur had sometimes been like ships at sea, far from shore, adrift without a compass, but they'd always had each other. It was Valur who had advised her to study comparative literature, who'd encouraged her, and she in turn had watched with pride as he became a successful journalist. And now it seemed he was on the verge of uncovering one of the biggest secrets of the last half-century.

Of course he was all right.

Nevertheless, her feeling of disquiet grew until she was certain something had happened to him. She could sense it, and the longer the silence drew out, the more convinced she became that she was right. Old memories rose, unbidden, to her mind. She tried in vain to push them away, her heart pounding, a ringing noise in her ears. She thought she might be going to faint.

She got to her feet again, unable to sit still.

'I'm going downstairs, I can't stand this any longer, I'm going.'

Kamilla nodded. 'It's up to you, Sunna. I . . .'

In that instant the doorbell rang.

'They're here,' Kamilla said quietly, and went into the hall, where she spoke into the intercom, then opened the door to the landing.

Sunna closed her eyes, as if that could change anything, as if she could make herself disappear and so put off hearing the bad news.

'Sunna?'

A man's voice, kind. She opened her eyes again. In front of her stood two policemen, both past middle age.

She nodded.

'It's about your brother, Valur.'

She couldn't speak.

'He was involved in an accident earlier this evening, a traffic accident.'

She stared blankly at the policeman who was speaking for both of them. A traffic accident? She couldn't make sense of it. Most people had been on foot today and Valur didn't own a car, didn't even have a driving licence. Perhaps they'd got the wrong person? She felt a stirring of hope.

'I'm terribly sorry to have to tell you, Sunna, but your brother – he died in the accident.'

And with that, her world collapsed. In one fell swoop, everything had changed, and she knew that she would never forget this moment for as long as she lived.

Knees trembling, she stood there, stunned, unable to move, unable even to stammer out a word. She felt utterly defenceless, alone in the world.

'I understand you live in the flat downstairs?'

'Yes,' she whispered.

'Alone?'

'Yes.'

'Would you like us to drive you to your parents' house? Wouldn't that be better for you, and for them as well?'

'They . . . they live in Húsavík,' she replied in a strangled voice.

'I see. Is there anywhere else you can stay? With a friend? Or a family member?'

'My mother . . . my mother's sister, I mean . . . lives in Árbær. I . . . maybe I can . . .'

'We'll take you there.'

'What happened?' she asked suddenly, getting a grip on herself.

The policeman seemed momentarily lost for an answer, though the question was hardly an unexpected one.

'The accident . . . Valur doesn't have a driver's licence.'

'He wasn't driving, he was on foot. He was crossing the road, and . . .' The policeman paused, as if reluctant to go on. And perhaps she wasn't ready to hear the gory details just yet.

She stood there, staring at him. She had to know more, even though it was probably a bad idea.

'He was hit by a bus,' the policeman said, after a heavy pause.

Sunna felt as if she'd been punched in the gut. This was the last thing she'd been expecting, and now she wished she could take her question back, wipe out this information. Or, rather, wipe out this day in its entirety, rewind it like a videotape, go back in time, see Valur and tell him – for God's sake – to stay at home.

She stood there in shocked silence.

'Shall we get going, Sunna?' the policeman asked kindly.

Dumbly, she nodded.

1986

19 August

Sunna had barely slept since getting the news.

Her parents were driving down but, as Húsavík was on the other side of the country, it would take them around eight hours to reach Reykjavík. As the day wore on, Sunna began to find the atmosphere in her aunt's house so oppressive that she just had to get out of there for a while.

She couldn't spend another minute lying in the guest-room, her thoughts circling endlessly back to Valur. A vicar had come round that morning, but Sunna hadn't wanted to talk to him. It wouldn't have changed anything. Valur was gone, with no explanation, but then how could something so incomprehensible be explained? It was simply a cruel irony of fate that he had been the wrong man in the wrong place.

Half the time she was in denial, refusing to face up to the truth, convinced it must be a dream, a mistake; the

169

rest of the time she was torn between grief and impotent rage. Eventually, desperate for some fresh air, she slipped out of the back door without a word to her aunt.

Outside it was an incongruously normal day at the tail end of summer. Although it was late afternoon by the time she left the house, the weather was still relatively mild. She kept expecting to bump into Valur around every corner, behind the next house, the next car, in that quiet suburban street. She wandered around aimlessly for a while, since anything was better than being trapped indoors, her mind held prisoner by the four walls.

Out here, she could kid herself that nothing had happened, that she could run to the shop, put a ten-krónur piece in the payphone and call her brother. And he would answer and laugh with her at the whole stupid misunderstanding.

She hadn't cried since last night in the police car. Instead, she fought back her tears whenever they threatened to spill over, as tears were too tangible a confirmation of the bitter truth. Sunna wasn't going to let herself be broken by this, that was unthinkable, but at this moment she couldn't bear to look so much as a minute into the future. All she knew for sure was that she wasn't going to meekly accept this. Instinct told Sunna that she had a role to play in what was happening.

The police hadn't shown their faces again. After Sunna had lain awake most of the night, frustrated that they'd given her so little information, she'd phoned them at lunchtime but had come away from the call having learned nothing new.

Now, almost before she realized what she was doing, she'd found her way to the nearest bus stop and was waiting to catch the next bus into town.

The world outside the windows looked drab and colourless as the bus made its infuriatingly slow progress from the eastern suburb of Árbær, down Ártúnsbrekka hill, heading for the centre. She was fretting in her impatience to reach the police station. She wasn't going to let them get away with evasive answers this time: she would insist on clarity. Her brother was dead and she knew next to nothing about the circumstances. Somewhere, among all the powerful emotions churning away inside her, she was troubled by the thought of that news report on Sunday evening; the claim that Valur was about to uncover one of the biggest secrets of the last half-century. An idea had taken root in Sunna's mind, born perhaps of grief or distress, that her brother's death had been no accident; that someone had wanted to prevent him from revealing the truth.

During the bus ride she rehearsed what she was going to say to the police, how she was going to ask – no, insist – that they fill her in on every last detail of the incident. She wouldn't take no for an answer – she owed Valur that. He had always been so doggedly determined, so single-minded in pursuit of the facts; that's what had made him such a good journalist. And she knew that she could be equally tenacious when she wanted to, despite having chosen a less confrontational path in life.

When the bus finally pulled into Hlemmur Square half an hour later, she jumped off, noticing that the temperature had dropped in the interim. Dusk had crept insidiously over the city during her slow journey.

On entering the police station, she was greeted by a uniformed officer who appeared to be close to retirement.

'I need to speak to the person in charge of investigating Valur Róbertsson's death.' As she spoke, she was overtaken by a violent tremor that made her voice shake. 'Right now, please,' she added.

The man took his time about answering. 'May I ask what connection you have to the deceased?'

'Valur's my brother – he was my brother – and I need to speak to someone.' Her voice came out high and thin.

'Of course,' he said, his tone immediately warmer. 'Let me look into it.'

He disappeared and returned almost at once.

'It's being taken care of. Please take a seat for a minute.' His voice was kind and Sunna got the impression that he meant what he said.

Nevertheless, the minutes ticked by – she wasn't sure how long she had been waiting – before another officer finally appeared. This man was around fifty, at a guess, with thinning hair.

'Sunna? Sorry to keep you waiting. My name's Bjarni and I'm working on the incident today. Would you come with me?'

She followed him through a door and up the stairs, all the way to the second floor, where they entered a small meeting room.

'Coffee?'

She nodded.

'We're still trying to piece together what happened. I'm sorry we haven't managed to come over and talk to you and your family today, but I wanted to get a clear picture of the circumstances first.' He filled a mug with coffee and handed it to her. 'To be honest, we're in two minds.'

'What do you mean?' she asked.

'In two minds about whether to deal with the incident here or pass it on to CID.'

'What are you saying?'

Though the coffee was only lukewarm, it helped to calm her nerves and give her a small boost of energy.

'Well, in layman's terms, it means we're not entirely satisfied that it was an accident.'

Sunna's hand jerked, almost spilling her coffee. 'We've hardly been told anything,' she said, her voice sounding steadier now that the fit of trembling had passed. 'Where did it happen? All we were told was that it was a traffic accident, and that . . .' She broke off and heaved in a deep breath before she could go on. 'That he'd been hit by a bus. Was he waiting at a bus stop? Valur didn't have a driving licence.'

She didn't know why she felt compelled to stress this fact, for the second time in twenty-four hours. As she said it, she was ambushed by a random memory of a day by the sea, a bitterly cold day in spring. She and her brother were standing, gazing at the horizon, and Valur said: *I'm going to learn to sail.* The announcement had stayed in her mind because it had been so unexpected. They came from a long line of landlubbers and Valur had never shown any interest in the sea before. She'd asked in reply if he was planning to become a fisherman, and he'd laughed: *I don't know the first thing about fishing.* He just wanted to be able to sail, to see the world, to feel the swell beneath his feet. He'd been an adventurous soul. Doubtless that's why he'd become a reporter; always searching, forever on the lookout for news.

'On Skúlagata,' the policeman said, breaking into her reverie. 'We believe he was waiting for a bus. The town centre was more or less closed to normal traffic yesterday, as I'm sure you know. The only way to get around was by public transport. But the vehicle that hit him wasn't stopping there; it was travelling fast, and we think – well, we're fairly confident – that your brother would have died instantly. Which is something of a blessing, in the circumstances.'

She didn't know whether to laugh or cry or scream. *A blessing, in the circumstances . . .* Her brother was dead, for Christ's sake! But she suppressed the impulse and sat there listening in stony silence.

'I gather you were in town yourself yesterday, is that right?' Bjarni asked.

She nodded.

'There were a lot of people about, as you know. A large crowd, to say the least. And there was a big crush at the bus stop. That's part of the reason why we don't have a clear picture of what happened. Not yet, anyway. We believe we've now spoken to the majority, if not all of the witnesses. Unfortunately, no one seems to have been paying any particular attention to Valur: they were talking to their friends or keeping an eye out for the bus or reading the paper, and so on. The first they knew about it, he'd fallen in front of the passing bus. According to the driver, it happened so quickly there was no time to react. He slammed on his brakes, of course, but it was too late. Which brings me to the, er, difficult bit . . .'

He paused and looked at her.

'Before I go on, Sunna, I want you to stop me if this is getting too much for you. We're doing everything in our power to find out what happened to your brother, but we're very aware of the need to show consideration to his family.'

'I have to know,' Sunna said, her voice finally recovering its strength.

'All right, then. The situation is that there was a young woman on the bus who is claiming that your brother was pushed into the road.'

Sunna let out a gasp.

'She's fairly confident, but she didn't see who did it. Of course, it will be difficult to establish the exact sequence of events, given the number of people at the bus stop – it all happened so fast, you see. But hopefully this will help to explain why we've delayed coming to see you and your family. We're trying to find out if there's any truth to her claim. Because it seems incomprehensible that a passer-by would push a young man to his death like that.'

'Valur was investigating that story . . .' Sunna blurted out.

The policeman nodded. 'Yes, we're aware of that. It seems a bit improbable, though—'

'It doesn't seem improbable to me,' Sunna said vehemently. Finally, here was a theory that might work, might add up. Of course Valur hadn't thrown himself in front of a bus – the very idea was crazy. Although the policeman hadn't raised the possibility with her, it must have been discussed at the station.

'At any rate, I believe this deserves to be taken seriously,' Bjarni said. 'We've contacted CID. You do realize that, if it's true, we'll have a murder investigation on our hands, but for goodness' sake don't breathe a word about that outside this room for now. We can't afford to have wild press speculation getting in the way of the inquiry.'

'Do you know what exactly Valur's big revelation about Lára was going to be?' Sunna asked.

'No, I'm afraid not.' Again, Bjarni was silent for a moment or two, as if mulling over how much he ought to share with her. 'Naturally, we've talked to his editor, Dagbjartur. He was deeply shocked . . .'

'Have you spoken to Valur's girlfriend?' Sunna interrupted.

The policeman couldn't conceal his surprise. 'Did he have a girlfriend?'

'Her name's Margrét. They haven't been together that long.' It occurred to Sunna that if the police weren't aware of her existence, this must mean that Margrét hadn't heard the news yet. Because she hadn't told her and their parents hadn't known about the relationship. Valur hadn't got round to telling them, perhaps putting it off because he knew they'd only grumble about Margrét's connection to the 'bloody Conservatives'.

'Well, that's news to me,' Bjarni said. 'We'd better go round and see her straight away.'

'Do you suppose she was with him at the time?'

'I find that highly unlikely. If she was, she'd have made herself known to us or the ambulance crew at the scene. You don't by any chance have her full name and address?'

'Her name's Margrét Thorarensen. She's the daughter of Jökull Thorarensen.'

'The former Minister of Justice?'

'That's the one.'

'I see. Right, well, we'll contact her. It wouldn't do for her to read about it in the papers.'

'Do you think Valur's death could be linked to Lára?'

His answer was a long time coming.

'I just don't know. But it sounds implausible, Sunna, very implausible.'

'Did he have his satchel with him?' she asked.

'His satchel?' The policeman frowned.

'Mum and Dad gave it to him – a brown leather case. It was a present when he got his first job as a journalist. He was never parted from it.'

'Now you come to mention it, I don't think he did. No, I don't believe he had a bag of any sort with him. But of course things were chaotic on Skúlagata when it happened. Someone could have picked it up by mistake, or . . .'

Sunna could tell from his expression that he didn't believe what he was saying. Of course no one would have taken a dead man's satchel by mistake. Its removal from the scene could only have been deliberate. Which lent even further support to the theory that his death had been no accident.

'A brown case, you say?'

'Made of leather, a bit battered. A typical reporter's bag, I suppose.'

'I see.' But it was obvious that the policeman had no idea what a typical reporter's bag looked like.

'I may have a photo of it in one of my albums at home. It's possible.'

'That would help. We'll search his flat and check if it's there.'

It was then that she remembered the notebook.

How the hell had she managed to forget that?

She'd stuffed it in with all the dog-eared books in her university backpack, then been so busy over the weekend that it had completely slipped her mind. She hadn't even opened it, let alone leafed through it in search of fresh inspiration, as she'd promised her brother. Well, she could make up for that now, even if it was far too late.

At least she knew now how she was going to make it through the rest of the day. She would go straight home and dig out the notebook, but she'd keep its existence to herself, just while she was trying to plot the course of Valur's investigation and work out if he'd really been on the trail of a killer. Unlikely though it was that the crucial information would be found in the book, she could at least make an effort to tackle the case, following in her brother's footsteps, and see if she could come to any conclusions.

This task might provide her with the very incentive she needed to get out of bed tomorrow morning, to keep going – one step at a time – for Valur's sake.

Yes, the first step would be to go home, not directly to her aunt's place but with a detour to her own flat in Hlídar. But there was no way she could bring herself to take a bus there. In fact, it was a mystery to her how she'd managed to catch the bus into town from Árbær earlier. She shuddered at the thought of getting into what might be the very vehicle that had been responsible for her brother's death.

'I don't think I can cope with any more just now,' she said abruptly. 'I'm so tired all of a sudden.'

'That's perfectly understandable,' Bjarni said. 'You need to rest, Sunna. You should be with your family.'

'Is there any chance I could get a lift home?' Although she phrased it as a question, the look she gave him made it clear that she wasn't going to take no for an answer.

'Of course. It's the least we can do,' he said.

1986

20 *August*

Sunna had visited her brother at the newspaper offices on Kárastígur but had never felt particularly at home there. There was much about it that didn't appeal to her – the bohemian lifestyle with its heavy smoking and drinking, the casualness and unpunctuality, and, more than anything, the fact that it was such a man's world, with all the attendant chest-beating. No wonder Margrét had quit.

They'd always given her a friendly reception at *Viku-bladid*, though, perhaps because her brother had been well liked and clearly had a bright future as a reporter. This time, when she put her head round the door on the first floor, the clattering of typewriters abruptly ceased and silence fell on the office. There were three journalists in there: Baldur, Steingrímur and the editor himself, Dagbjartur.

'Sunna.' Baldur was the first on his feet. He'd often

worked closely with Valur and taught him various tricks of the trade, yet Sunna had always been a bit wary of him. 'I'm so sorry for your loss,' he said now. 'It's absolutely shocking news, a terrible tragedy.' He came over and gave her a hug.

'Thanks,' she said awkwardly.

Steingrímur and Dagbjartur followed Baldur's example, each giving Sunna a bear-hug and trying to express their sympathy. She found the whole thing extremely uncomfortable.

Two days had passed since Valur's death, which had been reported in that morning's news with the simple statement that he had been killed in an accident. So far, she hadn't heard any theories being aired publicly to suggest that there was anything suspicious about the circumstances. But in her own mind she was convinced that Valur's death had been murder and she'd spent the last twenty-four hours poring over his notebook, searching in vain for any clue that might explain why he'd been killed.

'I'm just here to collect his things,' she explained.

'Yes, of course, of course,' Baldur said. 'Is there anything I can help you with?'

Shaking her head, she made straight for her brother's desk.

It was a total mess, as usual. For all his cleverness, he'd been dreadfully disorganized. She opened her university backpack and began shovelling in papers, scribbled memos and notepads, some of them work related, others clearly just shopping lists or receipts. There were also several old notebooks that Valur had already filled. He tended to have only one on the go at a time, cramming every page with his semi-illegible handwriting, before moving on to the next. She worked quickly, eager to keep her visit short as she couldn't let herself think too much about Valur when other people were present. Breaking down in tears in front of his former colleagues would be so humiliating. Focusing on Valur's notebook had given her the strength to get through the last day or two, but she'd had to put it down whenever she was overtaken by one of her frequent bouts of weeping. Just then, she spotted his press pass on the corner of the desk and slipped it into her bag with a faint smile, as a souvenir of her favourite human being.

And there was his mug, which he'd borrowed from home when he first started work here. It was still half full of cold coffee, so Sunna took it into the kitchen to rinse it out.

'Sunna.'

A tap on her shoulder made her start and almost drop the mug in the sink. Breaking it would have been the final straw.

Turning her head, she saw Baldur behind her.

'Sorry, I didn't mean to startle you.'

He was standing far too close.

'It's OK, no problem. I'm just leaving.'

'I only wanted to ask, about that envelope, whether you—?'

'Envelope?'

'Yes, the envelope that was delivered to Valur shortly

before he died . . .' He paused as if embarrassed at having bluntly said the word 'died'. 'Sorry, I meant . . . sorry, but about the envelope, someone left it . . .'

'When?'

'On Saturday, as far as I can remember, or . . . yes, it was definitely on Saturday.'

Sunna began edging sideways so she could continue the conversation without Baldur breathing down her neck.

'Was that unusual?' she asked.

'Well, it did make me wonder. Because, you know, he was working on the Lára story and it's not every day we get an anonymous tip-off through the letterbox. Sadly, our job isn't like in the old movies.' He corrected himself: 'Though if anyone belonged in that world it was Valur. He reminded me of one of those ace reporters in a Hollywood film – the character Cary Grant would play. All he was missing was the hat. He was a natural at this game.'

Sunna couldn't tell whether this praise was genuine or whether Baldur simply meant to be kind, but, either way, it worked. She felt faintly comforted.

'Do you have any idea what was inside the envelope?' she asked.

Baldur shook his head. 'Sadly, no. I asked, but Valur was cagey. And since I haven't seen it anywhere on his desk, I assume he must have taken it with him. His name was on the front, in elegant handwriting, belonging to an older man or woman, I'd guess. Not many people write like that nowadays.'

Sunna hadn't noticed anything resembling this on the

desk, but she would go through Valur's papers more systematically later. The more likely answer was that he had
put the envelope in his good old satchel; that was the
logical conclusion, because it's where he'd kept anything
of significance. And now the satchel was missing.

Margrét answered the door of her parents' house, a handsome detached villa in the upmarket suburb of Gardabær.
Her eyes were red and puffy from weeping.

'Thanks for coming round,' she said to Sunna. 'Do
come in. My parents are out. I made them go to work
as I couldn't cope with them hanging over me all the
time.' Margrét forced a watery smile. 'Can I offer you
anything?'

'No, thanks.'

Inside, the house couldn't have been more different
from Sunna's family home in Húsavík. All the furnish-
ings, including the paintings on the walls, made it clear to
visitors that the owners were not exactly short of money.
Margrét's parents were both lawyers and ran their own
legal practice these days, though her father was best
known for having done a term in office as the Minister of
Justice.

'How are you doing?' Margrét asked, once they were
sitting down.

Sunna shrugged. What was she supposed to say? Margrét could multiply her own suffering by ten, or a hundred,
if she wanted the answer.

'I just can't believe he's gone,' she replied eventually, to
say something. She hadn't met Margrét that often; in fact,

she'd never really understood what Valur had seen in her. Perhaps in a sense they'd both been rebelling against their backgrounds, Margrét by hooking up with a penniless journalist on a weekly paper, Valur with a girl who had everything and would never vote for anyone but the Conservatives, like her mummy and daddy. Still, what did Sunna know? Maybe opposites getting together was the key to happiness. But the answer was probably more straightforward. Margrét was quite simply Valur's type: dark-haired, with a mysterious look in her eyes; the kind of girl Cary Grant would have ended up with in one of those classic newsroom movies that Baldur had talked about.

'Have the police been round to see you too?' Sunna asked.

'Only to break the news. Not since then. Why do you ask?'

Sunna came straight to the point. 'The thing is,' she said, breaking her promise to Bjarni, the officer in charge of the case, 'we believe someone pushed Valur in front of that bus.'

She had rarely seen anyone look so blindsided.

'What?' Margrét asked, aghast. 'What are you saying?'

'You weren't with him at the time, were you?' Sunna asked with studied casualness.

'*With* him?'

'When it happened.'

'No, of course not. He was alone. On his way to meet me, I think, or maybe he was going home first, because we'd arranged to meet by the lake at eight, and the buses were driving round and round the area, so he must just have decided to . . .' Margrét faltered.

'I see.'

'Did you really say he was pushed?'

Margrét didn't seem offended by Sunna's question about her whereabouts, or to have taken it as an indirect accusation that she might have something to hide – or might not have been telling the whole truth.

'Yes, according to the police.'

'But that's unbelievable.'

Sunna was silent.

'It's unbelievable,' Margrét repeated. 'Who would have done it? And why?'

'We don't know, but it goes without saying that it must be linked to Lára somehow.'

'Lára? You mean the girl he was writing about?'

'His satchel is missing too.' Again, Sunna reminded herself not to mention the existence of the notebook. 'I believe he must have got uncomfortably close to a dangerous secret of some kind.'

Margrét shook her head incredulously. 'I don't know much about the Lára story. I'm too young to remember the case. Of course, I read some of Valur's articles, but we didn't really discuss it. In fact, we didn't talk much about his job at the paper – you know how it is. I wasn't particularly keen to hear about the office after my experience of working there.'

'I'll be straight with you,' Sunna said. 'I was wondering if you might be able to help me.'

'Me? How?'

'With the Lára case.'

'But I know nothing about—'

'I'm going to find out what happened, Margrét. Someone pushed my brother in front of that bus—'

'We can't be sure of that . . .'

'Will you help me?'

'Yes, I suppose so,' Margrét said hesitantly, her voice a little high and strained, as if she was close to tears. Perhaps Sunna had been too hard on her. She reminded herself that she wasn't the only one who was grieving for Valur and that other people might prefer to deal with their loss in a different way from her.

'I've been looking through his note . . . his notes,' Sunna said, narrowly avoiding letting slip that she was in possession of his notebook. 'I went to the office and fetched his stuff. And I've re-read all his articles about Lára. But he must have got his hands on some new evidence as well, something that would have blown the case wide open.'

'So what are you planning to do?'

'Investigate the story, of course. Continue his work, since he can't do it himself.'

Margrét's expression suggested that she thought this was crazy, and perhaps she was right. But Sunna had to keep herself busy, and right now what comforted her most was the thought of continuing Valur's work from where he had left off. She felt as if she was caught in the middle of a storm, struggling through a blizzard, and that there was nothing to do but plough on until the wind died down or she reached a safe haven. But at the same time, she was suffering from a grief so great that she couldn't begin to find words for it, couldn't even cry any more, as Margrét had evidently been doing. She felt so inexpressibly proud of her brother, of the extraordinary amount he had achieved in his short career, that she was determined to keep his name alive, and wasn't the best way to do that to solve the mystery of Lára's disappearance? She could write one final article in *Vikubladid*, under both their names, Valur and Sunna. A collaboration reaching beyond the grave, allowing them to work together, this one time . . .

'OK.' Margrét interrupted Sunna's musings. 'Why not, I suppose . . .'

'You know the basic facts of the case, don't you?'

'Yes, sure. Lára went missing on Videy in 1956. Couldn't she have deliberately drowned herself?'

Sunna didn't bother to answer that. 'She was working there as a maid, yes, for a middle-aged couple called Óttar Óskarsson and Ólöf Blöndal. They're still alive. He's a lawyer, like your parents.'

'Óttar and Ólöf, yes, I know them. Friends of Daddy's. I sometimes think all these lawyers are friends. We've often had them round to dinner.'

'Small world.'

Margrét smiled.

'Look,' Sunna went on. 'I really need to speak to them, so I was wondering if you could get in touch with them for me and maybe even come with me to meet them?'

'Why? Because of Lára?'

'Yes.'

Margrét wavered. 'Wouldn't that be a bit weird, Sunna? You can't imagine they'd want to talk about it – after all this time? They're decent people, though I wouldn't exactly describe them as a barrel of laughs. But I'm sure they wouldn't hurt a fly.'

'I know it's an awkward thing to ask you to arrange, but we've got to do it for Valur,' Sunna replied impatiently. She mustn't let Margrét get on her nerves – this girl born with a silver spoon in her mouth, who'd never had to do anything awkward in her life.

'Well, it's just that I don't have much contact with them myself, even though Óttar's an old schoolfriend of my parents . . .'

'It was only an idea,' Sunna said, relenting a little. 'For Valur's sake,' she repeated.

'Yes, all right, I'll help. No problem.' Though it was plain that Margrét didn't relish the thought. The longer they spoke, the harder Sunna was finding it to understand what had brought Valur and this girl together – it was difficult to imagine a more mismatched couple.

Nevertheless, she smiled. 'Thanks, Margrét. It would be brilliant if you could invite them round for coffee or something, then I could have a proper chat to them.'

'Of course.'

'So.' Sunna changed the subject. 'You and Valur were planning to meet up? On Monday?'

'Yes. In the evening. We were going to watch the open-air concert together, but he never turned up and I just assumed we'd missed each other or something. These things happen. But then I couldn't get hold of

him on the phone when I got home, or the next day . . .
And . . .'

Sunna suddenly couldn't cope with hearing any more
about Valur. She was hit by a wave of grief so devastating
that she had to end the conversation.

'I think I'd better be going,' she said, trying to stop her
voice from betraying her. 'Thanks for agreeing to see me,
and thanks for the help. Do you think we might be able to
have coffee with Óttar and Ólöf as soon as the funeral's
out of the way?'

'Er, yes, I expect so.'

Sunna forced herself to smile, then said goodbye.

1986

25 August

Sunna had borrowed a car, an old Skoda, from a friend, for the drive north to Húsavík. It was on the other side of the country from Reykjavík, and flying was expensive Besides, she needed time to herself to think. The funeral was scheduled for one o'clock on Tuesday, so she drove up on the Monday. It was a beautiful late summer's day, the grass clothing the landscape was still green, the birch scrub thick with leaves, though the fresh colours had faded and matured.

She left the city, heading north towards the long, slumbering hulk of Mount Esja, through the farming district of Mosfell, which was fast developing into an urban centre. Then on, skirting the foothills of the mountain, round the Kjalarnes peninsula into the long road around Hvalfjördur. She drove slowly, partly to savour the beauty of the fjord, but mostly because her mind was preoccupied with working through what had happened.

What possible reason could anyone have had to push Valur to his death like that? It had to be linked to the Lára case. Valur didn't have any enemies. He hadn't fallen out with anyone in his private life. No, this had to be connected to his job. He must have uncovered some secret that couldn't bear the light of day. And surely that could only be about Lára? It had to be significant that the TV news had announced a big reveal was imminent, that he might even have solved the old mystery.

The Skoda steadily ate up the miles. It was nearing midday when Sunna drove into the picturesque little west coast town of Borgarnes, so she stopped at the Stadarskáli service station for lunch – burger with chips and cocktail sauce – a mixture of ketchup and mayonnaise that the Icelanders claimed as their own – real comfort food, which helped to lift her mood a little.

Long hours later, having crossed seemingly endless expanses of moor and mountain, Sunna finally reached the Adaldalur valley, the last stretch before home. As the evening sun cast its enchanted glow over the wide bay of Skjálfandi, touching the snow-capped mountains with pink, she felt overwhelmed by an almost palpable sense of grief and loss. This was the countryside where she and Valur had grown up, where they had played together, gone to school, messed around, shared secrets, clubbed together to buy their parents Christmas presents at the Co-op, picked blueberries, gone in search of adventure and discussed their future dreams. That chapter in her life was now irrevocably closed: Valur was gone for ever.

After the greyness of Reykjavík, the little town of

Húsavík had never looked lovelier, the colourful fishing boats in the harbour, the wooden houses on the docks, the distinctive, Swiss-chalet-style church and the burnt-orange and green slopes of the mountain, all luminous in the rays of the setting sun.

She dreaded seeing her parents so much that she remained sitting in the car outside the house for a while, delaying the inevitable. But in the end, she composed her features, got out, taking her small sports bag, and walked up the neatly tended path to the unassuming white 1950s building, a bit shabby now but infinitely familiar and dear to her. It was past nine in the evening but she was met by the unmistakable aroma of coffee and baking when she opened the door.

'Hi,' Sunna called.

'Hello, Sunna, love.' Her father came to meet her, looking oddly shrunken in his woollen sleeveless pullover and shirt, no longer his normal, well-fed, contented self, but subdued and withdrawn. He took her in his arms. Her mother followed on his heels, a short, bustling woman who had always run her family and her home in exemplary fashion. She too gathered Sunna into a tight, loving embrace, the grief starkly etched in every line of her face.

Her parents had only spent two nights in Reykjavík before hurrying back up north to prepare for the funeral. Seeing them again now, Sunna was hit even harder by the feeling that no one should ever have to lose their child.

They spent a quiet evening. Her mother served coffee with those old favourites: Ritz crackers, prawn salad and a raisin sponge cake. Sunna ate as much as she could, then went upstairs to her old room. There was her bed, neatly made, her desk and the white lace curtains her mother had made for her, at her special request, the year Sunna was confirmed. She let out a deep sigh. She had left home at sixteen to go to college in Akureyri, the nearest big town – only a year older than Lára had been when she went to work on Videy.

Lára's room had probably looked something like this.

1986

26 August

Sunna slept surprisingly soundly in her old bed and was woken by the sun shining mercilessly through the flimsy curtains. She smiled as she remembered her mother pointing out to her at the time the folly of the arrangement. But Sunna had been a romantic teenager and pictured the white lace fluttering in the breeze as she sat by the window, gazing moonily out to sea . . .

Reykjavík had cured her of all romanticism.

She and her parents arrived at the church just after noon. The pride of the little town, it was an unusually picturesque building dating back to the beginning of the century, made of wood imported from Norway, its white walls decorated with red trim, contrasting with its green roof and steeple. In the lead-up to her confirmation, Sunna had attended services there and received instruction in Christian values and customs. She had been a believer in those days, conscientiously saying her prayers every evening, fearful that something bad might happen to her loved ones. And now, despite all her prayers, the worst had happened.

They sat at the front. Sunna, aware that Margrét was planning to attend, had decided to invite her to sit with them. She arrived at half past twelve and accepted the invitation, though she evidently felt terribly awkward to be meeting Valur's parents, who might one day have become her in-laws, for the first time in these circumstances.

By twenty to, the church had filled up. Sunna scanned the faces of the congregation and spotted two of Valur's colleagues from the paper, Dagbjartur and Baldur. Schoolfriends from Húsavík were also present, including Gunnar, who was studying theology in Reykjavík but had travelled up specially. She used to have a crush on him when she was ten. He gave her a warm smile and she started, realizing that she'd been staring at him.

It was a beautiful ceremony, though Sunna felt her hackles rising when the vicar, a middle-aged man known for his pleasant manner, took the words of Ecclesiastes, 'To everything there is a season,' as the subject of his sermon. She clenched her fists. Valur's time had not come: someone had taken time into their own hands and murdered her brother, and she had no intention of letting that crime go unsolved, like Lára's disappearance.

The vicar traced the main events of Valur's life, then referred back to Ecclesiastes. 'His time came all too soon. But now let us put our faith in God and commit our sorrow into his hands.' Before Sunna knew it, the service was over and Valur's schoolfriends, led by Gunnar, were approaching the coffin to carry it away. It was crowded and hot in the church, and the pallbearers were red in the face, their eyes visibly wet, as they made their slow way past the front pew, Chopin's 'Funeral March' resounding in the nave. Sunna felt the tears pouring down her cheeks.

Once the coffin had been carried out to the hearse, Sunna and her parents drove to the cemetery for the committal. Meanwhile, the other mourners walked over to the hotel where the reception was to be held. By the time the family joined them, people had started helping themselves to coffee, pancakes and slices of *braudterta*, a sort of multi-layered sandwich, coated in a thick layer of mayonnaise and decorated with thinly sliced rounds of cucumber. Sunna looked round at the mourners. Although her place should probably have been at her parents' side, she was desperate to seize this chance to talk to people, to find out anything that could shed light on who had murdered her brother. The very thought made her stomach churn. Pushing aside her plate with its slice of *braudterta*, she smiled at her parents and got to her feet.

She began by making a beeline for Gunnar, who was sitting with a group of Valur's schoolfriends from Húsavík.

'Hello, nice to see you,' she said, a little awkwardly.

'You too, Sunna.' Gunnar, who had never suffered from social awkwardness, rose and gave her an affectionate hug. 'It was so shockingly sudden,' he said. 'Such a bizarre accident. You know, I bumped into Valur, er, it must have been on the Saturday before. We chatted briefly about the Lára articles. I got the feeling then that he knew much more than he was letting on. But I don't suppose we'll ever find out what he'd discovered.'

'It wasn't an accident,' Sunna blurted out before she could stop herself.

Gunnar sounded surprised. 'What do you mean? I thought Valur was hit by a bus?'

'Yes, but someone pushed him ... Someone who didn't want him to publish what he'd found out about the Lára case.' As she said it, Sunna realized she sounded like a madwoman.

Gunnar regarded her thoughtfully but didn't contradict her. Instead, he nodded slowly, then asked in a level voice: 'Have you told the police about your suspicions?'

'We've discussed it,' she said warily.

'Then you can be sure they'll look into it,' Gunnar said, his brow furrowed with concern. 'We should have faith in the police and the justice system.'

'Huh, that didn't exactly work out well for Lára,' Sunna said flatly.

Gunnar was studying her gravely, but she got the impression he was listening. She smiled at him. 'Did he say anything to you that day?'

Gunnar furrowed his brow again as he thought. 'I remember him saying that Lára might never have left Videy. I suggested she might have drowned herself, but he obviously thought a crime had been committed, and I gathered from what he said that he believed it had happened on the island.'

Sunna nodded, then caught sight of Dagbjartur and Baldur getting up from the table in another part of the room. Saying a quick goodbye to Gunnar, she hurried over to intercept them.

'Hello,' she said, holding out a hand to Dagbjartur.

'Hello, Sunna dear. This is so awful.' Dagbjartur had gone to the effort of squeezing himself into his best suit, which looked as if it had been bought years ago and was now far too tight. He had even donned a green-striped tie, though normally he never wore anything round his neck.

Sunna said in a rush: 'I'm genuinely afraid that Valur may have been murdered over the Lára story. That someone who didn't want any new information to get out was responsible for pushing him into the road. There were witnesses who got the impression he was pushed . . .'

Dagbjartur was looking at her with a pained expression on his face. 'My heart goes out to you and your parents.' Clearly, he didn't believe her.

Sunna gulped, feeling her stress levels rising, conscious of a desperate need to convince the world that she was right. 'What if Lára was murdered too?' she persisted, her voice strained with emotion. 'And Valur discovered the fact? Someone may have seen the news and realized they had to stop him from writing that final article.'

Dagbjartur was frowning with concern. 'Sunna, I don't know how to say this . . . It was me who leaked the information to the TV newsdesk that there was about to be a revelation in the Lára case. I was just doing my bit to try and sell more papers, as *Vikubladid* is always on the verge of going under. Valur's series about Lára was the only thing keeping us afloat, to be honest. But, oh God, if it led to this . . . I can't bear to think about it.'

Sunna felt knocked sideways. Although on one level she understood what could have motivated the editor to act in that way, she was filled with rage at the thought that the whole tragedy could have been averted.

But Dagbjartur hadn't finished. 'I didn't know exactly what he was planning to write – I doubt any of us on the paper did. Had he let you into his confidence, by any chance?'

Sunna shook her head and sighed. 'No, I hadn't heard from him, I . . .'

'I'm so very sorry. I do hope things will become clearer in time,' Dagbjartur answered kindly, then said goodbye. She saw him pausing to pay his respects to her parents before he left the hotel with Baldur in tow.

Sunna spent the night after the funeral in her old bedroom again. Her mother and father agreed that the service had been beautiful and that the reception had gone off very well. They asked especially after Gunnar, and Sunna got the impression they hoped she might be interested in him. She thought perhaps she should invite him to coffee when she got back to Reykjavík.

Early the next morning she set off back to town. Her parents walked her to the car, where they hugged and kissed. She felt an unbearable wave of sadness as she saw them in the rear-view mirror, growing ever smaller as they watched her drive away.

The journey back to Reykjavík passed without mishap, although there was always a risk of a puncture on Iceland's rough gravel roads, particularly at the end of

summer, when the surface had worn thin and the car jud-
dered over the frequent ridges and furrows. When Sunna
reached Skagafjördur, the sun even put in an appearance,
flashing off the blue waters of the fjord.

As she covered the long miles, her mind revolved
ceaselessly round the twin mysteries of Lára's disappearance and Valur's 'accident'. She was more determined
than ever now to throw herself into investigating the
events when she got back to town. She would read Valur's
notebook from cover to cover.

She was going to find out the truth if it was the last
thing she did.

1986

29 *August*

Afterwards, Sunna found she could only remember fragments of the funeral. They had a dreamlike, nightmarish quality; unreal, yet at the same time so horribly, uncompromisingly real.

She had hoped that in the hour of parting she would be able to reconcile herself to what had happened and say her final farewell to Valur, but she had failed. She was so far from being able to do that. If anything, she felt as if Valur were closer to her than ever before, as if they had made a pact to find Lára and get to the bottom of what had happened to her.

That was why she was sitting at the desk in her little flat, leafing through his notebook, jotting down facts and ideas. She'd re-read Valur's articles until she knew some sentences by heart – her brother had always had an ear for a good turn of phrase. She had also spent hours at the National Library on Hverfisgata, borrowing back issues of the newspapers and combing through them in the grand setting of the old reading room, at a heavy wooden desk covered in green leather, in a similarly heavy chair. She felt at home in these surroundings, remembering the times when she and Valur had sat there side by side, doing their respective research. The reading room, in fact the whole building, had been one of Valur's favourite places, as he had often mentioned to her, so it was hardly surprising if she had a powerful sense of his presence as she sat at the desk, turning the pages of the thirty-year-old newspapers.

By now she felt she had a good grasp of the background to the case. The notebook had turned out to contain a variety of useful information and possibly even some clues. Her studies would just have to take a back seat for a while; her dissertation on Elías Mar could wait. It made no difference in the great scheme of things whether Sunna graduated this term or next spring. It wasn't as if the world would end — not again. That had already happened.

One name in the notebook presented a bit of a puzzle: Gréta Grímsdóttir. There was a woman by that name in the telephone directory but so far Sunna hadn't managed to reach her.

In the margin of one page, Sunna noticed that Valur had scribbled another name that didn't seem to have a direct link to Lára: *Finnur Stephensen*. It sounded vaguely familiar. She ran the name by her mother, who said there was a well-known wholesale company called F. Stephensen Ltd, and Sunna realized that was why the name had rung a bell.

It was one of the biggest wholesalers in the country, which suggested that the owner must be a very wealthy man. Sunna had jotted down two numbers from the phone book, one for the company itself, the other for a man listed as 'Finnur Stephensen, wholesaler', whose address was on Laugarásvegur. That figured, Sunna thought to herself, as it was an affluent street of detached houses.

Going into the hall, she sat down in the wicker chair by the phone and dialled the wholesaler's home number. 'Nothing ventured, nothing gained,' she told herself.

The phone rang and rang, but just as she thought it was going to ring out, someone answered. Not Finnur himself but a female voice; an older woman, by the sound.

'Yes, hello? Hello? Who is it?' The connection was so poor that the voice seemed almost to come echoing down the line from another dimension.

'Hello,' Sunna said tentatively. 'My name's Sunna Róbertsdóttir. I'm trying to get hold of Finnur Stephensen. I hope I haven't got the wrong number.'

'No, dear, this is the right number.' The woman paused for so long that Sunna was beginning to think the connection had been lost, then went on: 'But Finnur is dead.'

Sunna was badly thrown by this. She couldn't immediately work out why. It felt as if she'd hit a brick wall at the very beginning of her investigation.

But almost immediately she was struck by another thought: suppose this wasn't a coincidence? If someone had pushed Valur in front of a bus, surely they could have murdered Finnur as well? All in order to hide their tracks?

She realized she was leaping to rather wild conclusions but she couldn't shake off the idea.

'Oh, I am sorry,' Sunna said. 'Please excuse the intrusion and ... My condolences,' she added, though she didn't know if it was the wholesaler's widow she was talking to.

'No need to apologize. And thank you.'

'Do you mind my asking when he died?'

'Very recently – at the beginning of the month.'

Again, Sunna felt a creeping suspicion: could it all be connected somehow?

'Did you know Finnur?' the woman asked, unexpectedly.

'What? Oh, no, I'd never met him. I was only hoping to have a quick word with him.'

'What about?'

Sunna hesitated for a moment, wondering if she was doing the right thing, then decided to tell the truth. 'It's in connection with an article my brother was working on. He died very suddenly and I want to try and finish it with him . . . *for* him, I mean.'

'I'm so sorry to hear that. How awful. My condolences, Sunna. What was his name?'

'Valur.'

'Valur, oh. Again, I'm so sorry for your loss. What was his article about?'

'About a young girl called Lára who went missing. You may remember the case?'

'We all remember it, dear – at least everyone of my generation. And you say you were hoping to speak to my late husband about something to do with this?'

'Well, my brother had made a note of his name – but I have no idea why.'

'No. How strange.'

'Could I possibly – do say no if you'd rather not – but could I possibly meet you for coffee some time?'

'Of course you can, Sunna. My life's pretty uneventful these days; time seems to pass so slowly that I'd be grateful for the company. And I imagine you might be feeling the same?'

'You could say that,' Sunna replied.

'Why don't we put it in the diary that you'll drop by next week – on Monday afternoon, perhaps, at coffeetime? I assume you have the address, since you found my number?'

'Yes, I do,' Sunna replied.

'Good. By the way, my name's Thórdís. I look forward to meeting you.'

Later that day, Sunna paid a visit to Valur's newspaper offices. As far as she was concerned, *Vikubladid* would always be *his* paper. She did have some business to conduct there, but, if she was honest, the real reason was that she was missing Valur and she still felt an almost tangible sense of his presence at the Kárastígur office.

She hadn't shared Valur's fascination with the world of journalism before but was beginning to get an inkling of what it was that had attracted him: the buzz, the pressure, the heady excitement.

When she entered the office, she was almost hit by a wall of adrenaline. The air was thick with smoke, a phone was ringing, there was a clacking and pinging of typewriters and Dagbjartur was yelling at Baldur, who was yelling back: 'It just won't be ready!'

'Then there won't be a bloody paper. We're not publishing a load of blank pages!'

They both looked round when she walked in.

'Sunna.' It was Dagbjartur who spoke, his voice switching in an instant from bellowing at Baldur to a tone of gentle solicitude. 'Such a beautiful service.'

'Very beautiful,' Baldur chipped in.

'Excuse the raised voices,' Dagbjartur continued. 'Just the usual pressures. Is there something we can do for you?'

'I was wondering if I could have a very quick word.'

Dagbjartur showed her into his cramped office, which was like a scene from a film: the chaotic mess of papers, mugs, ashtrays, even an old reporter's cap hanging on a peg – perhaps as a prop, unless Dagbjartur wore it to hide his bald head.

'How are you, Sunna? How are you coping?'

'I don't know. Hanging in there, I suppose.'

'You could say the same about us, though of course it's much harder for you – that goes without saying.'

'Dagbjartur, I . . .' She chose her words carefully: 'I want to finish Valur's article.'

'Finish his article?'

'Write the final piece in the series, I mean. To provide closure. One last article, under both our names.'

The editor leaned back in his chair, mulling it over. 'Hmm, why not? Yes, why not? Valur always spoke very highly of you, Sunna. He said you were much cleverer than him. Maybe you ought to consider doing this for a living . . .'

'Oh no, I didn't mean that . . .'

'You're doing a degree in Icelandic, aren't you? That's a good grounding for a journalist . . .'

'Comparative literature, actually.'

'Same sort of thing.'

'All I really meant is that I want to finish this one thing for him . . .'

'Of course you can. There's no rush – take all the time you need. We'll always have room for one more article by Valur. And Sunna . . . if you're looking for work, I'd be very willing to give you a try-out here at the paper.' After a moment he added: 'It's what Valur would have wanted.'

1986

1 September

Sunna sat at the kitchen table in her flat in Hlídar, drinking fruit tea. She'd bought it from a café that had recently opened in a little building tucked away behind Laugavegur high street. It was a novelty, in a country with a strong coffee culture like Iceland, to have a place where you could enjoy a cup of tea and toast. To Sunna, these moments were precious, the sweet fragrance helping to distract her mind briefly from brooding on her loss, and she regularly bought packets of exotic tea in an attempt to re-create the experience at home. But today she had work to do. She took another sip of tea, then opened the notebook with a sense of purpose.

Valur had never been a very organized thinker, she reflected as she flipped through the pages. Names and dates stood out, along with speculative comments and the odd sentence here and there. She noticed the name of the original detective on the case, Kristján Kristjánsson, and an address in Grafarvogur – were people living out there already?

Beside the name, Valur had written: *Why didn't the police investigate the Viðey end more thoroughly?*

Óttar and Ólöf's names were there too, of course, along with a lot of scrappy jottings that Sunna could make little sense of, though she did manage to decipher the comment that it was proving so difficult to get hold of Óttar that maybe Valur ought to focus on Ólöf instead. Then, in the margin, was the name of the wholesaler, Finnur Stephensen, crossed out. Next to this, Sunna thought she could make out: *schoolfriend*. Or something like that.

She had an invitation to go round for coffee with Finnur's widow, Thórdís, later that afternoon. But first, after finishing her tea, Sunna headed for Hverfisgata and the National Library. She'd begun taking the bus again, in spite of the bad associations, forced by simple necessity.

At the information desk, she encountered a fusty librarian with horn-rimmed glasses and a grey beard, the type who'd always charge the maximum fine if you were late returning a book.

'I'm looking for news about Finnur Stephensen,' Sunna said. 'He died at the beginning of August.'

The man regarded her with an expression of weary surprise. 'Then you'll find him in the obituaries, of course. That's where we keep the dead.'

'Ah, yes, of course . . .'

Then he added, rather grudgingly: 'But there was also an

item on the funeral, if I remember right. In *Morgunbladid*. You'll have to find it yourself, though. Just fill in a form. But don't request too many papers at once – I can't be expected to lug around a whole year's worth of issues.'

Sunna smiled awkwardly. 'Thanks. Right, I'll fill in a form.'

The obituaries went on at length about Finnur's life but didn't seem to contain anything that might shed light on the Lára case. Among the contributors was Óttar, who had written a piece recalling their long friendship that had begun at school. So when Valur had written 'schoolfriend' in his notes, clearly he'd been referring to the fact that Finnur had been a schoolfriend of Óttar's. As she read the obituaries, it dawned on Sunna that the Thórdís she had an appointment with that afternoon was none other than Thórdís Alexandersdóttir, the actress. Sunna remembered her from countless TV plays and comedies.

Later, she came across an item covering the funeral, on page four of *Morgunbladid*.

Finnur Stephensen laid to rest.

The first two pallbearers, who were visible in the accompanying photo, were named in the caption as:

City councillor Páll Jóhannesson and the property developer, Högni Eyfjörd.

Perhaps she should try talking to them too. It couldn't do any harm.

She glanced back at the paper carrying the obituaries. Sure enough, Páll Jóhannesson had written a piece about Finnur as well, describing him as a very honest, upright man, and quoting from a poem. But there was no sign of an obituary by Högni.

Sunna returned the papers and bestowed a bright smile on the librarian. She could have sworn the corners of his mouth twitched reluctantly in return.

Her next port of call was Thórdís's house, but, as she was waiting at the bus stop, she began to get cold feet. The woman had recently lost her husband. Sunna, who was finding it hard enough to cope with her own grief, realized she probably wasn't in the best position to offer sympathy and a listening ear. No one ever talked about feelings in her family, so she'd had no practice.

Obeying an impulse, she walked over to a nearby telephone box. It had occurred to her that Gunnar, who she'd bumped into at Valur's funeral, was a theology student. Maybe he would know the right sort of thing to say to Thórdís. Sunna found his name in the directory – he lived on Reynimelur in the west end – dialled his number and let it ring.

'Hello, Gunnar Gunnarsson speaking.' His voice was as mellow as ever, perfect for a would-be vicar.

'Hi, Gunnar, it's Sunna here,' she said, belatedly deciding that this was an idiotic idea.

'Oh, hi,' Gunnar said, sounding very friendly.

'I, um, well, actually, there's something I need a bit of help with.'

'Of course, it would be my pleasure,' Gunnar said. 'I could do with a break from my dissertation.'

Sunna asked him to meet her at Café Mokka and he arrived half an hour later, wearing a blue waist-length jacket and jeans. A little too trendy for a vicar, Sunna thought, though she knew it would be hard to find anyone better at talking to a grieving widow than this nice young man who positively radiated warmth and decency.

But when she explained what she wanted him to do, Gunnar wasn't at all happy.

'Sunna, this is a job for the police. What are you doing with that notebook? It might contain vital evidence for the investigation.'

'The police aren't doing anything,' Sunna retorted scornfully, then fixed an imploring gaze on him. 'There's nothing earth-shattering in there, just names and vague speculation. All I want is to see if Finnur's widow can explain why his name turns up in the notebook,' she said, though she thought she already knew the answer to this: Finnur and Óttar had been friends; there was no more to it than that.

In the end, Gunnar gave in to her pleading and drove her over to Laugarásvegur. It was past three o'clock, which was near enough to coffee time.

Sunna raised the impressive knocker, glancing, as she did so, at the imposing lions that stood on plinths either side of the drive. Gunnar shifted from foot to foot behind her, muttering that Thórdís probably wasn't home, which was just as well, since this was a crazy idea. Sunna ignored his warnings. The door opened.

Thórdís Alexandersdóttir was dressed in black from head to toe, in a smart suit. When she saw Sunna, her face split in a warm smile.

'You must be Sunna. And you are . . . ?'

'Gunnar Gunnarsson. A friend of Sunna's,' he replied – a little flustered, Sunna thought, which didn't happen often.

He was quick to recover his composure. 'I'd like to offer you my condolences on the loss of your husband,' he said. 'I understand that you and Sunna had arranged to meet today. I do hope you don't mind my coming along.'

Thórdís regarded them both for a moment. Sunna darted a quick look at Gunnar and saw that he was wearing his politest expression.

Then Thórdís's gaze locked with Sunna's for an instant, before she said: 'Do come in.'

The house was expensively but tastefully furnished – if one ignored the plaster lions outside. It was evident that the owners had travelled widely and brought back exotic objects as souvenirs of their trips. The walls were hung with paintings by the Icelandic masters but also by younger, upcoming artists who Sunna could barely put a name to. The bookcases revealed an eclectic collection too, though perhaps rather more conventional, featuring the kind of titles the social elite felt they ought to own, rather than the books they actually read.

'I was so sorry to hear about your brother,' Thórdís began. 'Dreadfully sorry.'

'Thanks,' Sunna replied in a small voice.

'You mentioned that he had written something about us, mentioning Finnur by name? Or both of us?'

'Only Finnur. Did you know him? Valur, I mean?'

Thórdís shook her head, rather theatrically, Sunna thought.

'No, I'm afraid I didn't know your brother, Sunna.'

The thought flashed through Sunna's mind that Thórdís could be Júlía, the woman who had rung Valur.

'Was your husband by any chance acquainted with Lára?'

'No, he wasn't.'

'What about you?'

'No . . .'

'But you do know Óttar and Ólöf, the couple Lára worked for on Videy?'

'Óttar and Finnur were friends. They'd known each other almost all their lives.'

At this point, to Sunna's annoyance, Gunnar intervened: 'We're aware that this must be a very difficult time for you, we—'

'You needn't worry about me,' Thórdís cut him short. 'I remember the Lára case, like everyone in Iceland. As I said, my husband and I didn't know her. Have you spoken to Óttar?'

'Not yet.' Sunna paused, then decided to go for it: 'I believe Valur was murdered – because of Lára.'

Thórdís looked visibly shaken. 'That . . . no, I can't believe it, no . . .'

'He was pushed in front of a bus,' Sunna insisted.

Thórdís stiffened with shock. 'Oh my God. Why hasn't this been reported on the news?'

Next moment, she was on her feet.

'I'm sorry, but I can't help you. And I really am

dreadfully sorry about your brother,' she repeated. She was staring at Sunna rather wildly, as if cracks were developing in her mask.

Slightly taken aback by her reaction, Sunna and Gunnar both stood up and followed her out to the hall.

Gunnar shook Thórdís's hand in parting. 'Thank you for taking the time to speak to us. If you happen to remember anything later on, you'll find us both in the phone book: Gunnar Gunnarsson, theology student, and Sunna Róbertsdóttir.'

Thórdís gave him a smile, then took Sunna's hand. 'Good luck, dear,' she said in a tremulous voice and closed the door behind them.

They stood outside the house, momentarily at a loss. Although the sun was shining, there was a chilly wind blowing down the street.

'She knows more than she's letting on,' Sunna said with conviction.

'I don't think she does. Let's just leave it.'

Sunna sighed. She liked Gunnar, but she decided it would be better to talk to Óttar and Ólöf without him. It might be worth paying a visit to the two pallbearers, Páll and Högni, as well.

'You know, I think I'll leave it for the moment and concentrate on my dissertation,' Sunna said, smiling disingenuously, while inwardly she remained dead set on uncovering the truth.

1986

3 September

'You must be Sunna.'

It was Margrét's father, Jökull, who answered the door. She was so familiar with the former Minister of Justice from seeing him in the press over the years that this felt almost like stepping into the evening news on TV; all that was missing was the newsreader.

From Jökull's brusque tone and unsmiling demeanour, Sunna gathered that she wasn't welcome. All the more credit to Margrét, then. It had taken a while, but somehow, in the face of her parents' disapproval, she had managed to twist their arms into setting up this meeting with Óttar and Ólöf. Sunna knew from Valur's notebook that all his attempts to approach the couple had been unsuccessful. She felt a little smug that she'd had the brainwave of using Margrét to bring about the interview, succeeding where her brother had failed.

'Yes, I'm Sunna,' she said, taking off her shoes, according

to Icelandic custom. Peering into the sitting room, she saw that the guests had indeed arrived.

'We don't have long, as we have a dinner engagement,' Jökull said, lowering his voice. 'I'm not quite sure what the point of all this is, but Margrét begged me to provide you with an opportunity to talk to Óttar and Ólöf. Just to be clear, though, they're friends of ours and I won't put up with any funny business.'

Sunna was privately amused to hear the honourable cabinet minister, or rather ex-minister, using a term like 'funny business'.

'No funny business,' she agreed, suppressing a grin.

'Óttar, Ólöf,' Jökull said then, in a louder voice. 'This is Sunna, who's so keen to meet you. As I mentioned, she's the sister of the reporter Valur Róbertsson, who recently passed away. I've explained to her that we don't have much time as we're on our way to a dinner party, but she'd just like a quick word with you about the story Valur was working on for that . . . er, that weekly paper.' Such was the contempt in his voice that he might as well have said 'that trashy rag'.

Óttar rose to his feet and extended a hand.

'My condolences.'

'Thank you.'

Sunna had found an old photo of Óttar in the Icelandic Bar Association's list of registered lawyers, but he had aged since then; his iron-grey hair was receding at the temples and his eyes were weary. On the other hand, his dress sense obviously hadn't changed since the 1950s, judging by the grey double-breasted

suit, bow tie and the silk handkerchief in his breast
pocket.

In contrast, the woman beside him – Ólöf, presumably –
was utterly nondescript, with her thin, lank hair and
matching beige jacket and skirt. Yet in spite of this she
radiated displeasure. The couple were seated side by side
on the light-coloured sofa, drinks on the table in front of
them: his looked like a gin and tonic with a slice of lemon;
hers was something pink in a wine glass – kir royale, perhaps. Jökull and his wife, Nanna, were nursing glasses
too, but they made no move to offer Sunna a drink. Margrét was sitting in the corner, well out of the firing line,
on an antique chair with an embroidered central panel. A
grandfather clock ticked ponderously beside her, and
there was a lingering smell of cigarette smoke in the air,
although the ashtrays were empty. The floor was carpeted
in a pale-coloured deep pile and the curtains were of
wine-red velvet.

Óttar spoke again: 'As you can imagine, we've discussed Lára's disappearance endlessly over the years, and
we came to a decision a long time ago not to make any
further public comment on the tragedy. She was in our
care when she went missing. But we've never got any
answers to what happened to her, never really recovered
from the incident – not entirely. It's a tragedy for a young
girl in the prime of life to disappear like that. But at some
point you have to draw a line under the whole thing and,
as I said, we did that a long time ago. We have no explanation for what happened and . . . well, to be frank, I am
sceptical about the claim that your brother had discovered

anything conclusive. To be completely honest, I don't believe the mystery will ever be solved. Not now, so long after the event.'

'I have complete faith in my brother's—'

This time Óttar cut across her without ceremony: 'Sunna, I can quite understand that you had faith in your brother. I can also understand that you desperately *want* to believe that he'd found Lára. But, take it from me, that's preposterous. I've lived with this case for far too long. I'm older and more experienced than you, I've been a practising lawyer for nearly forty years, and I know when people are bluffing and when they're telling the truth. Trust me, that television news story was almost certainly a bluff. I know old Dagbjartur and his tricks. He'd go to any lengths to sell his paper. He's always been like that. Anyway, having said all that, how can we possibly help you?'

He sat down again. The smile he gave her was kindly enough, but Sunna wasn't fooled: she could sense the coldness behind it. Óttar would have made a good politician, like Margrét's father. For a moment Sunna had even believed – almost believed – that he genuinely wanted to help her.

She floundered around for something to say, then drew out Valur's notebook, in which she had written down some questions for the couple.

'First, I wanted to ask if you were acquainted with a man called Finnur Stephensen, who recently passed away. He had a wholesale . . .'

Óttar answered this, while his wife dropped her gaze, her face worried, seemingly unable to meet Sunna's eye.

'Finnur, yes. It was rather sudden. He had cancer, poor chap, and it was only a matter of weeks – a month or two at most. He was my age, my exact contemporary, in fact. Iceland's a small country, as I don't need to tell you: everybody knows everyone else.'

'Well, maybe that's a bit of an exaggeration,' Sunna said, 'but you did know him, in other words? You and your wife?'

Again she tried and failed to make eye contact with Ólöf.

'We were at school together, if that helps. But then I was at school with a large number of people and I can't say I'm closely acquainted with all of them. I'm not entirely sure what it is you're asking.' Óttar sniffed.

'What about you, Ólöf? Did you know Finnur?'

The woman kept her eyes lowered and didn't respond. Puzzled by her silence, Sunna fixed her with a stare, but it didn't seem to have any effect.

'When did you last see each other?' Giving up, Sunna directed the question back to Óttar.

'I don't recall, but I expect it was two or three years ago, at one of our class reunions.'

'So you were in the same class?'

'Yes, as I have already told you.' Óttar's tone had changed slightly, losing a little of its confidence.

'Actually, you said you'd been at school together. Did you go to his funeral?'

There was a brief hesitation, then Óttar replied: 'Of course I did. Wouldn't you attend the funeral of someone in your class?'

'Not necessarily all of them,' Sunna said, then put her next question: 'Did he ever visit Videy?'

'Who?'

Sunna smiled. This was a transparent attempt by Óttar to buy himself time.

'Finnur.'

'Oh, Finnur. How the hell am I supposed to know that?'

'To visit you and your wife, I meant.'

'We didn't have many visitors when we lived there. It's a bit out of the way.'

'Did he know Lára?'

'What kind of nonsense is this?' Óttar shot a look at his host.

Jökull duly intervened. 'Sunna, we invited you here, out of politeness, so you could have a quick chat with Óttar and Ólöf. I wasn't expecting you to use my house to conduct an interrogation. You're behaving as if you're investigating on behalf of the police.'

At this point, Margrét's mother, Nanna, who was wearing a pastel-coloured dress with vertical stripes, coughed. 'Sunna, it's understandable that you're distressed by your brother's death, but I can't think what you're hoping to achieve with all these questions.' She directed a cold glare first at Sunna, then at her daughter, who was keeping a low profile in the corner.

Sunna steeled herself to say: 'Valur was investigating Lára's disappearance. She vanished while she was working for Óttar and Ólöf. I have proof . . . evidence . . . linking Finnur Stephensen to Lára. And, as we've established, you and your wife were acquainted with both Lára and Finnur.'

'What evidence?' Óttar demanded in tones of outrage, very much in lawyer mode now.

'I'm afraid I can't reveal that,' Sunna said, trying to come across like a woman who was holding all the trumps. 'Valur was working on a story about it when he was murdered.'

A low cry burst from Ólöf's lips: 'Murdered?'

Sunna, watching her, saw that she was frightened.

Óttar glowered at Sunna and said, enunciating with such clarity he might have been acting in a radio drama: 'Is there any actual evidence that your brother was murdered?'

Sunna didn't flinch. 'He was pushed in front of a bus.'

Óttar didn't say anything in response to this.

'Did Finnur Stephensen ever meet Lára, to your knowledge? Did he visit you on Videy?'

'It's possible,' Óttar said. 'But it was such a long time ago, I can't be expected to remember everyone who visited us—'

Sunna interrupted. 'But just now you said that it was so out of the way that you didn't have many visitors.'

Óttar hesitated, then said: 'I don't remember Finnur coming over. But Finnur Stephensen would never have been involved in anything criminal. He was a very upright, decent man.'

'Are you acquainted with Páll Jóhannesson, from the city council?' Again, Sunna addressed her question to Óttar.

At this point Jökull rose to his feet, looking extremely

disgruntled: 'That's it. I'm drawing a line here. This is my house.' He gestured to the sitting-room door. His wife, Nanna, stood up too.

'Thanks for the chat,' Sunna said, undaunted. 'I hope you have a pleasant evening.'

Margrét emerged, almost furtively, from her corner and accompanied Sunna out of the room.

'They weren't happy about that,' Margrét said in a small voice.

'They certainly weren't,' Sunna agreed. 'And what does that tell us? Óttar knows something. Finnur has to have visited them on Videy.'

'I suppose so,' Margrét said uncomfortably. 'Daddy wasn't very pleased about this . . .'

'Thanks, Margrét,' Sunna said. She sensed that Margrét had genuinely wanted to help, and this meant a lot to her. 'I'll be in touch.'

Margrét nodded, smiling half-heartedly.

Sunna glanced over her shoulder as she walked away from the house and noticed Jökull watching her departure from the door. But what did she care? She had a bus to catch.

Dusk was falling and the streetlights had come on. Radio 2 echoed around the almost empty bus as the driver cranked up the volume.

Sunna closed her eyes and felt the tension slowly easing out of her muscles.

She'd got some excellent material for her article – *their* article. Next on the agenda, with any luck, would be a visit to the city councillor, Páll Jóhannesson.

1986

4 September

'The film's absolutely brilliant,' Margrét exclaimed. 'And so's Tom Cruise.'

They were standing in the queue for snacks during the interval at the University Cinema. Margrét had unexpectedly rung and invited Sunna along to see *Top Gun*, currently the most popular film in the country. She'd explained that she wanted them to stay in touch, and sounded as if she genuinely meant it, but Sunna had wondered if this friendly overture was also motivated by a wish to make up for her parents' rudeness. Other than this, Sunna's day had passed uneventfully, apart from managing to book an appointment to see Páll, the city councillor, though he didn't have a gap in his diary until later that month.

'Yes, it's fun,' Sunna agreed. She wasn't a regular cinemagoer, not like Valur used to be, since she was more interested in books than films. This wasn't really her sort of thing either. She'd have preferred something less action packed, like *The Color Purple*, for example, which was showing at the Austurbær Cinema.

Although Sunna didn't want to come across as unfriendly, she found herself instinctively maintaining a slight distance from Margrét. They couldn't become friends, she thought; somehow it wouldn't work. They came from such different worlds: she was a country girl, Margrét the daughter of a conservative politician from Gardabær.

'What are you doing this weekend?' Margrét asked. They were still waiting to be served. Sunna was growing impatient at having to spend so much time chatting to Margrét. Sitting in the auditorium was one thing, as you couldn't talk in there, but there was no way she was going out on the town with Margrét on Saturday night, if that's what this question was leading up to.

'I haven't got any particular plans,' she replied, realizing belatedly that this answer was far too open. 'I mean, I've set this weekend aside to work on my dissertation. I'm aiming to graduate at the end of this term, as I think I mentioned? But it's not going all that well.'

'You should go easy on yourself.'

Margrét wasn't so bad; in different circumstances, they might even have become friends. If only Valur hadn't died . . . That's how all Sunna's thoughts began and ended these days, as her life wore on in weary monotony, every day a repetition of the day before, although from a distance they might appear different.

'What about you?' Sunna asked mechanically.

'I'll probably go to Hollywood, as usual.' Hollywood was one of the biggest discos in town.

It hasn't taken her long to get over Valur, Sunna reflected sourly, though of course this was unfair. 'Oh,' she said aloud.

'I mean, not necessarily to drink or dance or anything like that. But my friends always go there and it's a way of breaking up the week. It's hard sitting alone at home the whole time, thinking about Valur, you know?'

'Yes,' Sunna replied politely.

'What can I get you?'

Without realizing it, they had reached the front of the queue.

'Just popcorn and Coke, please,' Sunna said.

'Listen, while I remember, there was a girl at Hollywood last weekend . . .' Margrét said suddenly, apparently failing to notice that the teenage boy behind the counter was waiting for her order.

'Margrét, what are you having?' Sunna prompted.

'What? Oh, just popcorn. And a Tab, if you've got it?'

The boy nodded.

Margrét turned back to Sunna: 'Yes, there was this girl – I completely forgot to tell you. She was asking about Valur.'

'Valur?' It couldn't have escaped anyone who followed the news that Valur had died in an accident. The young journalist who had 'caught the public's eye' with his articles about Lára, had suddenly been elevated to the sainthood, his picture splashed all over the papers – her big brother who no one had known from Adam before the tragedy occurred. 'What did she want to know about him?'

'Oh, it wasn't that she wanted to know anything about him. Her name's Katrín; she's a friend of mine. Valur once met her with me. The thing is, apparently he rang her recently, because she works for the National Registry.'

'What? Recently? When?' Sunna didn't budge from the counter, although she had got her popcorn and Coke.

'Before he died, she said.'

Sunna sighed in exasperation. 'When exactly?'

'Just before he died, I meant.'

'What did he want?'

Someone tapped Sunna on the shoulder and she jumped, spilling popcorn on the floor.

'Sorry, but the film's about to re-start, so could you two get out of the way?'

Sunna stumbled out of the queue and followed Margrét back into the auditorium.

'Why did Valur ring her?' she asked, once they'd retaken their seats.

'It was about some woman. He asked her to look up a name, a woman's name.'

'What name?'

'I can't remember, or maybe she didn't tell me. The music was so loud.'

'And did she?'

'What?'

'Did she look the woman up?'

'Yes, I think so, but he never rang back. You can talk to her if you like. Katrín Gudjónsdóttir, at the National Registry. It's probably best just to drop by during office

hours. Unless you feel like coming along this weekend –
she's always at Hollywood.'

'No, thanks. I'll go to her office.'

They were interrupted by a screech and blare of sound
as the film recommenced after the interval, having been
clumsily broken off mid-scene, as usual. Silence fell on
the audience, apart from the inevitable crunching of
popcorn.

1986

5 September

It was probably a waste of time, but at least it had got Sunna out of the house, and that had to count as a positive step. If Margrét hadn't told her about the girl at the National Registry, Sunna would have spent the whole of that Friday sitting in her flat, pretending to write her dissertation.

She had woken up unusually early, just after seven, eaten a bowl of Cheerios for breakfast and automatically switched on Bylgjan, 'the Wave'. In the week since the new radio station had first gone on air, Sunna hadn't listened to anything else, Radio 2 having long ago lost its shine. There was something so exciting about a new radio station, with all those fresh voices for listeners to get to know. And before long it would be fresh faces on their TV screens too. If Valur hadn't died . . . The same thoughts kept circling round and round in her head . . . He might have ended up working for Bylgjan, or as a star on the new TV 2.

The National Registry was located on the second floor of a functionalist building on Hverfisgata. Sunna turned up there just after nine and asked to speak to the friend Margrét had mentioned.

Although Katrín hadn't been expecting her, she gave her a friendly reception. Once Sunna had briefly explained who she was, Katrín invited her into a small office with a view of the autumnal street outside.

'I only met Valur once or twice, but I was so shocked to hear the news. I don't know what to say.' Her voice was warm.

'You don't need to say anything.'

'Excuse the mess, I've just moved into this deluxe space and I'm still getting settled in. I used to share an office with two other people, but I'm slowly working my way up the ladder.' She grinned.

'I see.' Sunna smiled politely. 'I just wanted to ask you about your conversation with Valur . . .'

'Yes, of course. He rang me. I was trying to remember when, and it was on the morning of the two-hundredth anniversary.'

The day he died.

Katrín went on: 'He wanted me to look up a woman's name, Arnfrídur Leifsdóttir. I don't usually do people favours like that but, you know, he was my friend's boy-friend. I'd nothing against helping out. I kept expecting him to call back, but then of course I heard . . .'

There was a moment's painful silence.

'Who was this Arnfrídur? Or was there more than one?'

'There were three: two of them alive; one died in 1940.

I wrote it all down in a note for him – that's to say, the little information I have. I know nothing about these women, but I'm sure you can find out more with a bit of detective work.'

She handed Sunna the note. 'Do you know why Valur was asking me about this woman?'

Sunna shook her head. 'I haven't a clue, but I'm grateful that you told Margrét about it.'

'I hope it'll come in useful.'

'I'm sure it will,' Sunna replied, though privately she felt as if this had set her back to square one. She had no idea what had prompted her brother to ask about this woman. Perhaps he had been pursuing a whole new angle on the case that she knew nothing about.

1986

12 September

Sunna was woken from a peaceful morning slumber by the shrilling of the phone. She hadn't been intending to have a lie-in but she had so few pressing commitments these days that she could afford the luxury.

Rubbing the sleep from her eyes, she hurried into the hall. Missed phone calls always left her feeling uneasy: she would end up wondering all day who'd been trying to reach her and whether she could have missed out on some exciting opportunity.

The week had been uneventful. Sunna had twice gone down to Tjarnargata in an attempt to intercept Högni Eyfjörd, but to no avail. Then she had slipped a letter through Lára's parents' door, in the hope that they'd agree to talk to her. She'd also tried Gréta Grímsdóttir's number again but the woman still wasn't answering.

Perhaps it was Gréta ringing now, or Lára's parents. Then it occurred to her that it might be the literary journal calling at last. Back in the summer, she had popped a short story in an envelope and sent it to the editor in the hope of getting it published one day, perhaps among the works of more established writers. Pure wishful thinking, of course: the journal must be inundated with short stories and poems by literature students; perhaps they all went straight into the editor's slush pile, or ended up in the bin without even being read. As a child she had sent stories and verses to the *Youth* magazine, which had published pretty much anything. The adult world wasn't quite so easy to crack.

Still, she allowed herself to hope, on this sunny morning, that it was the journal's editor on the line with the wonderful news that her story would be published in the next issue.

'Is that Sunna?' A man's voice.

'Yes. Who's speaking, please?'

'Sunna, this is Jökull Thorarensen, the lawyer.'

He was the last person she was expecting a call from. Funny that he should introduce himself so formally rather than simply stating that he was Margrét's father, but perhaps she should be grateful that he hadn't added that he was the former Minister of Justice as well.

'Oh, hello,' she replied warily, wondering what on earth he wanted.

'The main reason for my call is to apologize for my, er, choice of words when you visited us last week. Naturally, we were all rather upset, but I should have been more civil. It was unlike me, and I hope you didn't take it to heart. We're aware of course that you've suffered a great loss, like our daughter.'

'It's difficult for all of us, but thanks for calling.'

'It's the least I could do. By the way, how are you getting on with . . .' He paused, as if searching for the right words: '. . . with the, er, investigation?'

'I'm making progress, slowly.'

'Are you expecting to get to the bottom of it? Of course, the whole thing was extraordinary – the way the girl disappeared like that. Personally, I suspect she drowned herself and that's all there is to it.'

With all her luggage? Sunna wanted to object.

'To be honest, I have no real expectation of finding Lára,' she replied. 'But it really mattered to Valur – that's why I'm looking into it. That's all.'

'I see, fine. Good luck with that, Sunna. And good luck with your studies. I gather from Margrét that your degree is in Icelandic or literature or something of the sort?'

'That's right,' she said. She couldn't be bothered to put him straight about the difference between a degree in Icelandic and one in comparative literature.

As the day wore on, the sun went in and it started to rain. Autumn had crept up on Reykjavík, turning the first leaves yellow and the skies grey.

The flat was a tip; there was dirty washing overflowing from the laundry basket in the bathroom, since Sunna hadn't got round to going down to the basement and shoving it in the washing machine. Her dissertation consisted of piles of paper all over the coffee table, and the shabby sofa was buried in books. In the kitchen, the bread was going mouldy. She'd had little appetite recently, from grief and obsessing over the Lára case.

After turning the place upside down in search of a clean pair of knickers, she promised herself she would do a wash that evening. She surveyed the limited choice in her wardrobe, feeling dispirited. In the end, she put on an orange dress that would have been better suited to a garden party at the height of summer, then toned it down by pulling on a wine-red cardigan over the top. A matching wine-red lipstick and some mascara completed the look. She bared her teeth at her reflection in the mirror. She was on the hunt again, making yet another attempt to buttonhole Högni Eyfjörd.

Sunna paused in the narrow hall. The rain was coming down heavily now, and the most sensible option would have been a rainproof jacket and boots, but the man she was hoping to meet was a notorious womanizer: he was bound to give her a better reception if she wore high heels and a summer coat. After dithering for a while, she decided on the heels she only ever used as a last resort, having never properly mastered the art of walking in them. She was more of a trainers girl. Then she forced her arms into her light summer coat, which was a little tight over her thick woollen cardigan. She'd have to fork out for a taxi, as all this glamour would be wasted if she turned up looking like a drowned rat.

By the time they pulled into Tjarnargata, the taxi driver had concluded his analysis of the main political issues of the day. Clearly, he knew who owned the house she'd directed him to stop at.

'Going to see Högni Eyfjörd, are you?' he asked. 'Work in development, do you, dear? Or are you planning to build a house?'

'No, I don't work in that area,' she replied lightly, ignoring the bantering tone. 'But, yes, I am going to see Högni Eyfjörd.'

'Now he's got style,' the driver said. 'Got himself a younger model, I see.' He winked at Sunna. She merely smiled and handed him a banknote.

It was still raining. Sunna turned up her collar and ran up the steps of the elegant wooden house, which couldn't have been in starker contrast to the concrete boxes Högni Eyfjörd inflicted on the people of Reykjavík. Beside the front door was a brass plate with *Eyfjörd Development Ltd* engraved on it. Inside, a dignified middle-aged woman with glasses and a bun sat behind a desk, her eyebrows raised inquiringly. Her ivory twinset and the gold cross on her chest made her look as if she would be more at home working in a diocesan office than for a developer.

'Back again? Are you here to see Högni?' she asked in a mechanical voice.

Remembering the taxi driver's misconception, Sunna decided she might be able to use it to her advantage. Smiling shyly at the receptionist, she whispered: 'Is Högni in his office? I'm here on a . . . um . . . for personal reasons.'

The woman gave her a measuring look, her eyes sharp, then asked her to take a seat for a minute. She hurried upstairs, returning shortly afterwards with an invitation to Sunna to go up.

Högni Eyfjörd was sitting behind a desk in a large office with a view of the lake. He radiated vitality: sleek, tanned, his dark – obviously dyed – hair styled in the kind of windblown look favoured by male models in aftershave ads. Indeed, the wall of cologne that hit Sunna as she entered was so overpowering that she almost choked.

'Hello there. Who are you and what can I do for you?' Högni was affable, his voice as rich and resonant as that of the lead tenor in an opera. He wore his shirtsleeves rolled up, like a man with a lot of projects on the go. A carefully cultivated image, no doubt. There was a blazer with gold buttons hanging over the back of his chair.

'Hello. It's nice to meet you at last . . .' Sunna thought for a moment, then decided to lay on the flattery. 'Of course, I understand that a prominent man like you must be terribly busy with lots of important projects.' She smiled flirtatiously in the hope that this would make Högni lower his guard a little. 'My name's Sunna and I just wanted to ask you a couple of questions about your connection to Lára Marteinsdóttir, who disappeared in 1956.'

'Well, well.' Högni leaned back in his chair, a smile spreading across his face. 'Are you a journalist too?'

'Too?'

'There was another journalist asking the same question – Valur, if I've remembered his name right.'

So her brother had been here before her.

Sunna hesitated. 'I have links to *Vikubladid*, which has been covering the Lára story recently.'

'Ah, you're one of Dagbjartur's girls, are you?' He looked Sunna up and down. 'Surely he didn't send you here?'

Sunna knew she was on thin ice. 'I'm conducting an independent investigation based on *Vikubladid*'s inquiry.'

Högni wrinkled his brow, then adopted an expression that he no doubt believed was irresistibly charming. 'This is all very mysterious, young lady. I think you'd better explain yourself a bit more clearly.'

What harm could it do to tell the truth? 'Valur was my brother,' Sunna said. 'He was murdered in August because—'

'Murdered? Surely not?'

'I know you know Óttar, who Lára was working for on Videy.'

'I'm absolutely sure your brother wasn't murdered. That sort of thing simply doesn't happen in Iceland. But, yes, I do know Óttar.' Högni clasped his hands, smiling benignly at Sunna. 'We were at school together. And our paths have often crossed in connection with business. But our acquaintance has absolutely nothing to do with Lára's disappearance.'

'So you were at school with Finnur too?'

'I'm sorry?'

'Finnur Stephensen?'

'Yes, actually, not that it's relevant.' He seemed nettled.

'Did you visit Óttar on Videy when he and his wife, Ólöf, were living there?'

Högni seemed to be thinking. 'Yes, I suppose I must have popped over there at some point to see how they were doing. Though why anyone would choose to live in such primitive conditions was a mystery to me.'

'Did you meet Lára?'

'Not that I recall. And I've got a pretty good eye for the ladies, let me tell you.' He winked at Sunna as if they were in the bar at the Broadway disco, a notorious pick-up spot. But then Högni would have been perfectly at home with the kind of dinosaurs who hung out there.

Sunna, who had been prepared for exactly this kind of reaction, nevertheless found herself becoming increasingly riled by this male-chauvinist pig.

'She was working on Videy in the summer of 1956,' she persisted, pulling out a picture of Lára she had photocopied from the paper.

'No, I don't remember meeting Lára,' he repeated. 'And I can't quite work out where you're going with this conversation, young lady.'

Sunna stared at Högni, wondering what all those women saw in him. He met her gaze, without a shadow of self-doubt in his expression.

'How do you know Arnfrídur?' she asked.

Högni was looking at her attentively now. 'Who the hell is Arnfrídur?'

'Arnfrídur Leifsdóttir,' she replied, hoping she'd remembered the name right.

'Sunna, I think you've got completely the wrong man. But it was nice meeting you, all the same.'

She rose reluctantly and said goodbye in a markedly frostier tone than she'd used to greet him.

Högni merely smiled and raised a hand in parting.

Sunna went downstairs, past the stiff-backed woman with the gold cross, and outside into the cold rain.

Perhaps she was barking up the wrong tree.

Was there any point wasting time on the city councillor next week if it would only mean hitting another brick wall?

And why on earth had her brother been asking questions about a woman called Arnfríður Leifsdóttir?

Sunna was so preoccupied that she was oblivious to her surroundings until she was shocked back to the present by someone shouting practically in her ear.

'Sunna!' Gunnar had materialized at her side, panting. 'Jesus, I've been running after you halfway down Tjarnargata, calling your name. You were in another world.'

Sunna smiled. Gunnar's ginger hair was soaking wet and plastered to his head. Returning her smile, he gave her a hug. 'How are you? How are you coping? That was quite a visit we went on the other day!'

'To see Thórdís, you mean? You're telling me. And I've paid a few more visits since then,' Sunna said, though she hadn't necessarily intended to share this information with anyone.

'Have you been playing private detective again?' Gunnar asked, looking a little concerned. They were almost in the centre of town by now. 'Come on, why don't we pop into Nýja kökuhúsið?'

She let herself be persuaded and they went inside the café, out of the rain, and ordered coffee.

'I've talked to Óttar and Ólöf, Lára's employers on Videy. And Högni Eyfjörd, the developer.'

'Högni Eyfjörd? What on earth for?'

'He was a pallbearer at Finnur Stephensen's funeral, and Finnur's name was in Valur's notebook. It turns out Valur talked to Högni too. They were all at school together: Högni, Finnur and Óttar.'

'Huh, everyone knows everyone else in Iceland. It's a small country, Sunna.'

Ignoring him, Sunna went on: 'I'm trying to get hold of a woman called Gréta too – though I have no idea how she's mixed up in all this . . . And . . .' She paused briefly to catch her breath. 'And Páll Jóhannesson, who's a city councillor, I think . . . Or, I don't know . . . He was one of Finnur's pallbearers too and . . .'

She was braced for Gunnar to bring her down to earth by pointing out how little solid evidence she had to go on.

But instead he asked: 'Sunna, is there any way I can help? I've got nothing better to do, apart from writing my dissertation, and I'm not making any progress there. I never dreamed that the Gospel of St Matthew would turn out to be so complicated.'

Sunna threw up her hands. 'Oh God, don't mention dissertations – my essay on Elías Mar is lying on the sofa in complete disarray. I don't suppose I'll ever finish it now. But I have to do this . . . You know, for Valur's sake . . .'

'Just let me know, Sunna.'

'Thanks,' she said, holding his gaze for rather longer than strictly necessary.

1986

25 September

The last few days had thrown up a couple of unexpected developments.

The city councillor – or rather his secretary – had postponed his meeting with Sunna by a week. Although she had given her real name when she booked the appointment, she didn't get the impression that there was anything suspicious behind the decision. Páll Jóhannesson was probably just rushed off his feet, with little time to meet voters – or potential voters.

Then Gunnar had invited her out on a date.

That's actually what he'd said, *a date* – it sounded like something out of an American movie. She smiled at the thought. He'd suggested going to *Top Gun* and she hadn't liked to tell him that she'd already seen it. Strange though it seemed in the circumstances, some spark, old or new, had been ignited when they had coffee together, and she'd said yes – even though it meant missing the first episode of the new TV series about Inspector Dalgliesh.

The date had gone well. She felt comfortable in Gunnar's company and he had even kissed her at the end of the evening. Thinking about him in recent days had helped to distract her from brooding on Lára and Valur. She'd even found the energy to do a little work on her dissertation and to drop by the *Vikubladid* offices to sound Dagbjartur out about that job offer. He'd welcomed her warmly, saying he'd do anything for Valur's sister, and even given her a hug in parting. The job, on a trial basis, was hers if she wanted it, and she was increasingly tempted to accept.

But now, at last, the morning of Thursday 25 September had arrived, the date of her meeting with Páll Jóhannesson. Lára was back at the top of the agenda.

It was a day of brilliant sunshine, though there was an almost palpable autumnal chill in the air, and the leaves in Sunna's garden were turning red and gold.

She had always loved this time of year; to her, autumn was associated with new beginnings: a new academic year, new coat, new shoes, new faces. She had a sense that there was a real chance she could, with Gunnar's help, carry on her life without Valur, embracing the future with open arms.

She caught a bus down to Borgartún for her meeting with Páll. According to her research, he was in charge of the city planning department, which seemed to be inordinately busy at the moment. There were new suburbs proliferating all over the capital area and numerous construction projects at the consultation stage, including the new city hall, which was shaping up to be quite controversial. Páll wasn't a high-profile politician, though; Sunna doubted most inhabitants of Reykjavík were even aware of his existence.

She knew almost nothing else about him. She'd looked him up in the phone book, and, on learning that he lived in a detached house on Grenimelur in the west end, she'd taken an evening stroll in that direction, sneaking up to the house as if to drop something through the letterbox. There was a brass plaque on the door inscribed in decorative script with the names of Páll Jóhannesson and his wife, Gunnlaug Haraldsdóttir.

Sunna arrived at the Borgartún offices just before eleven, reported to reception on the ground floor and was shown upstairs to wait for her interview. The other people in the waiting room were almost exclusively men; builders, presumably, or else involved in other development projects. One by one they went in to see the city councillor, were granted a few minutes of his time, and emerged, mostly smiling.

Almost an hour had passed before Sunna's turn finally came. A young woman with blonde hair in a high ponytail came out and called: 'Sunna Róbertsdóttir to see Páll — please come this way.'

The walls of Páll's office were lined with dark bookcases containing impressive volumes with gilt lettering on the spines. The councillor himself sat behind a dark-wood desk with a few neat piles of paper on it which looked as if they had been arranged there for show. There were planning drafts spread out on a round table by the window.

The young woman took a chair in the corner of the office. She held a notepad and pen at the ready, and studied Sunna curiously.

'Take a seat,' Páll said to Sunna, indicating the chair facing him. Sunna sat down and smiled. She'd prepared the opening of this conversation but found it impossible to guess where it would end up.

'Hello. I'd like to discuss your connection to a young woman who disappeared on Videy in 1956.'

She was gratified to see the immediate impact of her words. Páll's eyes widened in horror. The young woman with the ponytail looked intrigued.

'I'm afraid you've lost me,' Páll said, clearing his throat. 'Aren't you here to discuss a planning issue . . .' He glanced again at the paper in front of him: 'Sunna?'

Without so much as blinking, Sunna persisted with her line of questioning: 'I also wanted to ask you about your association with the late Finnur Stephensen. Oh, and, by the way, the girl who disappeared was called Lára Marteinsdóttir.'

Páll shot a look at the young woman in the corner: 'Elísabet, could you fetch me a coffee while I'm dealing with this?'

The young woman, clearly put out by this development, grudgingly rose to her feet and left the room. Páll rounded on Sunna, his eyes blazing with anger.

'How dare you muscle in here during my public interview hours, asking questions like these? Are you a reporter?'

But Sunna wasn't going to let him intimidate her. 'I'm the sister of Valur Róbertsson, the late journalist who was writing about Lára's disappearance. I'm investigating the story . . .' Here she paused briefly to elaborate a little: 'I'm investigating the story in association with *Vikubladid*, Valur's old employer.'

Páll merely stared at her without saying a word.

'I know you and Finnur were acquainted,' she added. 'And I know that you both met Lára.'

At this, Páll erupted to his feet, only to sit down again almost immediately: 'Of course I knew Finnur Stephensen, but I have no idea why you should think we'd met that girl. That's an outrageous allegation.'

'Do you have any links to Videy?' Sunna asked next, fixing him with an unwavering gaze.

'Do I have any links to Videy? No, I do not,' he said angrily, his face now shiny with sweat.

'How did you and Finnur know each other?'

'We're . . . we were old schoolfriends. Finnur was a thoroughly decent, honest man.'

He fell silent again, and Sunna watched him intently. It was clear from the way he kept shifting in his chair and fiddling with the shirt cuffs protruding from the sleeves of his grey suit that he was rattled.

Judging that this was the right moment, Sunna stood up and almost spat out her final question: 'Who is Arnfrídur Leifsdóttir? Did she play some part in Lára's disappearance?'

The colour drained from Páll's face.

'This conversation is over.'

Sunna didn't wait to be told twice. The city councillor's alarm was unmistakable, so she must have got something right.

Outside, the girl with the jaunty ponytail was waiting with a cup of coffee in her hand, clearly bursting with curiosity.

Sunna glanced round and said in a loud, carrying voice, before Páll could close the door: 'You'll be seeing me again.'

1986

1 October

Sunna got up at the crack of dawn, unable to lie still a moment longer, impatient to start her day.

Marteinn, Lára's father, had got in touch with her the previous evening, agreeing to her request for a meeting with him and his wife, and suggesting a place. For a moment she'd considered taking Gunnar along but then decided it was inappropriate to bring anyone with her to their initial meeting. She would see the couple alone.

But first on the agenda was some toast with cheese and a glass of milk, the new radio station on in the background and the newspapers spread out over the kitchen table. Madonna's latest release was playing, forming a brief musical interlude between the almost constant stream of updates on the imminent – and entirely unexpected – summit meeting between President Reagan and General Secretary Gorbachev.

It had been reported the day before that the leaders of

the two world superpowers, the USA and the USSR, had agreed, with less than two weeks' notice, to hold a meeting in Iceland, and the nation had been thrown into a state of turmoil. All the hotels in the city had been booked up in the last twelve hours and now the scramble was on to find a suitable venue for the meeting itself, with the Kjarvalsstadir Art Gallery and Hotel Saga as the most likely choices.

Instead of being filled with eager anticipation, even excitement, about the leaders' visit, all Sunna could feel was sadness that Valur wasn't there to experience it. He would have loved being caught up in the middle of it all and would no doubt have got to see Reagan and Gorbachev in the flesh, maybe even had a chance to put a question to them at the press conference.

Yet again she found herself seriously considering accepting Dagbjartur's offer of a job at the paper, if only to experience the historic summit first-hand. But that could wait. She was going to devote today to Lára. Her meeting with the girl's parents might provide her with the remaining material she needed to produce a respectable article, even though she hadn't, in truth, made much more progress than Valur had.

There was no point submitting the article yet anyway, with the two world leaders dominating the news. Not that it really mattered how many people read her piece. Sunna was motivated by a desire to uncover the truth, not to be the centre of attention. Yet, in spite of that, she visualized the article about Lára, when and if she finished it, as front-page news in *Vikubladid* – in honour of Valur's memory, if nothing else. For the present, though, it was obvious that the next two issues at least would be entirely taken up with news of the summit.

'We don't give interviews any more, as you know.' Marteinn's manner was gentle; there was no irritation in his voice, only candour. 'We don't discuss Lára with strangers, as it doesn't serve any purpose. But we've made an exception for you.'

'Thank you,' Sunna said. 'I really appreciate it.'

'The fact your brother died makes the circumstances unusual. We were terribly sorry to hear the news. But I gather you're not a journalist yourself. You weren't planning to write about us, were you?'

She sighed inwardly, a little disappointed, but said: 'Not about you. I do want to finish Valur's article, but I promise not to write a word about you, if you'd rather I didn't. I just felt it was important to meet you, even if only for a quick chat.'

'We're sorry we couldn't invite you to our house, but that's another decision we made a long time ago. Because everyone wants to see her room, and we can't allow that. We had to draw the line somewhere, set some boundaries.'

Sunna nodded.

The couple were sitting facing her across a table at Café Prikid, a Reykjavík institution. It wasn't somewhere Sunna usually went, but Marteinn and Emma had assured her that the coffee was good there. Sunna had paid for three cups and they were now sitting by the window, watching the city centre waking up to a new day outside.

'This is our favourite place. We've been coming here for years,' Emma said. 'We live nearby in Grjótathorp. We've always lived in the same house: I inherited it from my parents.'

Marteinn and Emma both looked to be around seventy, perhaps a little older – Lára herself would have been forty-five today ... 'Careworn' was the adjective that sprang to mind when Sunna first saw them.

'We both used to teach, Marteinn sport and me English. I used to stand in for the maths teacher too sometimes. But our life is quieter these days. We go for a lot of walks.'

'Thank you again for—'

Marteinn interrupted before she could finish: 'We didn't mention it on the phone, but we met your brother. We don't speak to reporters, as I said, but he ambushed us here one day. I don't hold it against him. It was a bit of an unusual way of working, but that's the younger generation for you. If I'm honest, I was slightly annoyed at the time, but he struck us as a very nice young man. Didn't he?' He glanced at his wife.

Emma concurred: 'Yes, very. That's why we agreed to a meeting with you, Sunna.'

'Valur promised to find Lára. But then it wasn't the first time we'd heard that kind of talk.' Marteinn took over the conversation again. 'I was impressed with his drive, though; he seemed genuinely convinced that he'd succeed. Of course, Lára's gone, we know that, but she lives on in our memories. We may never know what happened, but I hope we'll live long enough to get some answers at least.'

'We live in hope,' Emma added.

Sunna decided this wasn't the moment to tell them about the phone call Valur had received claiming that Lára was dead and needed a proper burial in consecrated ground . . .

'Could I ask what you and Valur talked about?' she said instead.

The couple exchanged glances.

'He didn't ask many questions. He seemed reluctant to intrude on us too much, bless him,' Emma said. 'Mainly, he wanted to know whether anyone else had been on the island that summer. Of course there was no one else living there then – only the three of them: Lára, Óttar and Ólöf. I mean, if there had been another eyewitness there then surely the police – Kristján – would have questioned them?' This seemed to be directed at Marteinn rather than Sunna, and it was Marteinn who replied:

'Yes, I should think so.'

Sunna got the feeling this was a conversation they'd had many times before. 'So, in other words, you couldn't tell him much?'

'Well, we told him about Gréta,' Marteinn said.

'Gréta?'

'Gréta Grímsdóttir.'

Sunna caught her breath: the woman she had been trying in vain to get hold of. 'Just a minute, who is Gréta?' she asked, trying not to sound too excited.

'A distant cousin of mine,' Emma replied. 'She'd worked on Videy the previous summer. It was her mother who recommended us – Lára, that is . . .'

This information was followed by a lengthy pause, filled in by the hubbub of voices and clinking of cups and saucers from the other customers in the café.

Eventually Emma continued: 'Yes, she put in a good word for Lára. That's how Lára got the position. She told us that Óttar and Ólöf paid well, the job wasn't too demanding and it couldn't harm our daughter to get to know influential people like them. Ólöf's from a very good family, as I expect you're aware.'

There was no hint in what Emma said that she suspected Óttar and Ólöf of any wrongdoing. Unless it was simply too difficult for her to face up to the fact that she and her husband might have sent their daughter to work for bad people.

'She was only fifteen, as you know,' Emma continued. 'We went down to the docks with her in May – it was at the beginning of May, I remember it so well, such a beautiful summer's day and the island looking so green and pretty in the distance. I'd never been to Videy myself . . .'

'So you never visited her there?'

'No, she didn't want us to. She wanted to stand on her own two feet. Our daughter was always so independent.'

'I assume the police went over the whole thing with you in detail at the time and left no stone unturned, so to speak?'

'I suppose so,' Marteinn replied hesitantly. 'You can read all about it in the old newspapers; the main facts, more or less. She just disappeared. We didn't hear from her. She usually rang us once a week but then suddenly we were told she wasn't on Videy any more. It's still difficult for us to talk about, as I'm sure you'll understand, even after all these years. You should be able to find the information in the newspaper archives, like I said – a description of the whole thing. Obviously we went out to the island to take part in the search with our friends and family members, but it was no good.'

'I'm afraid we can't help you,' Emma added. 'Perhaps you'll manage the impossible and find out what happened and where Lára is . . . I hope so, I do hope so . . .' In spite of her words, it was plain that Emma had long ago abandoned all hope.

Sunna knew that she would at least have to try and get hold of Gréta. The woman might have something interesting to tell her.

'Anyway, I won't bother you any longer,' Sunna said. 'You can finish your coffee in peace.'

Emma gave Sunna a grateful look and said: 'It was nice meeting you. And good luck. Do you mind my asking what you do?'

'I'm a student, doing a degree in comparative literature.'

'Oh, I like the sound of that. Very good, excellent.'

Sunna pushed back her chair and rose to her feet.

'Could I maybe ask you one more question before I go?'

'Of course. We're not in any hurry.'

'Was everything significant covered in the papers? I'm just wondering if there were any details I don't know about . . . Anything my brother wouldn't have been aware of either . . . I've been going over and over his notes and I do so want to get to the bottom of this.'

'I like your optimism – it's always good to be optimistic,' Marteinn said. 'And maybe you will succeed. But I can't remember anything; the coverage was so thorough that at times I found it a bit too much.'

'The necklace, Marteinn – we could tell her about that,' Emma said.

'The necklace?' Sunna echoed.

'Yes, Lára always wore the necklace her grandmother gave her. We didn't mention it to the press. She got it after the photo was taken – the one we used when she was reported missing. The police wanted to withhold some details from the public so they could rule out any time-wasters. I don't know if there were any, but we kept the information about the necklace to ourselves. Not that it matters any more.'

'What sort of necklace was it?'

'It was never found. She would have been wearing it, I'm sure of that. It was – is – a beautiful piece of jewellery; a large filigree cross on a chain. It was an heirloom – quality work, not cheap. The dear child never took it off.'

1986

6 October

Sunna and Gunnar had been seeing more of each other, which was fine by her. He was kind, quick to smile and understood her perfectly. But what had probably tipped the balance most strongly in his favour was that he'd been a friend of Valur's.

She and Gunnar had gone out dancing at Hotel Borg on Saturday night. Then he'd dragged her along to a conference in honour of the university's seventh-fifth anniversary, which had turned out to be rather dull, if she was honest, though the company had made up for it. Gunnar was quite studious, but endearingly so.

He had suggested they go later that week to a technology exhibition at the new City Theatre, but Sunna had drawn a line at this. She couldn't imagine anything more boring than visiting an exhibition like that, surrounded by over-excited kids pressing buttons, so she had suggested it might be better for him to go on his own if he wanted to learn about the brave new world.

Gréta Grímsdóttir was still proving hard to get hold of. She wasn't answering her phone or returning Sunna's calls. As there was only one person with that name in the directory, Sunna was pretty sure she had the right person, and had tried her several times, leaving polite messages on the answerphone.

Sunna was planning to spend the day at the National Library but she thought she'd make one more attempt to contact Gréta first. To her intense irritation, she couldn't even get a dialling tone. The new Bylgjan radio station was playing in the background and, as usual these days, hordes of listeners were ringing in to take part in a phone-in quiz. Sunna had recently come across an infuriated reader's letter in *Morgunbladid* complaining that the telephone system couldn't cope with the weight of all these calls, so she guessed Bylgjan was to blame – the phone lines were simply overloaded. Clearly the Icelanders couldn't contain their excitement at the prospect of all the quiz prizes.

This wasn't the only way in which Iceland's infrastructure seemed likely to be overwhelmed at the moment. It was being reported that some three thousand people would be coming to the country in association with the Reagan–Gorbachev summit, but Reykjavík simply wasn't set up to cater for an event of this magnitude. There were loud complaints that hotels had been raising their prices to exorbitant levels and that restaurants had abandoned their old menus and introduced fancy new ones aimed at the influx of foreign visitors. It seemed that everyone was determined to get in on the action. Come to think of it, the overloaded telephone system might have something to do with the impending visit too.

In the end, neither the Kjarvalsstadir Gallery nor Hotel Saga had been chosen to host the historic meeting. Instead, the Jugendstil mansion known as Höfdi House had been deemed the most suitable venue for the occasion. Although Sunna had never been inside, she knew that the former consular residence had hosted such luminaries as Marlene Dietrich and Winston Churchill in its heyday, so why not add Reagan and Gorbachev to their number? According to the papers, Reagan would be turning up without his wife – no Nancy, in other words – but Raisa Gorbachev would be accompanying her husband.

Sunna tried Gréta's number again – still no dialling tone – and slammed the receiver down on the battered old telephone. As she did so, a loud jangling echoed around the hall. Clearly, someone had managed to get through to her.

It wasn't Gréta, though. The voice on the line was male; not Margrét's father, Jökull, this time, but just as unexpected in its way: 'Hello, is that Sunna?'

She recognized his voice before he went on to introduce himself:

'Elías Mar here.'

'Elías, nice to hear from you,' she said, loudly and clearly. It was her author.

'About our meeting a while ago. You were asking me how I came to write *Poetry in a Wild Age* and I think I was a bit stumped by some of your questions at the time. Since then, though, I've had a chance to dig through some old papers and . . . I wondered if you'd like to drop by and have a look at them? You can take them away with you, if you like, as I have very little use for them myself.'

'I'd be so grateful,' Sunna replied, perking up a little. The extra material would come in very handy for her dissertation, but it wasn't only that: it was the feeling as if a window had been opened into the past, back to those carefree days when Valur had been alive. 'When can I come round?'

'Well, whenever you like, really. Things are quiet at my end. And I might as well let you in on a secret I didn't mention the other day: I've got a new book coming out before Christmas.'

'Really? A new book?'

'Yes, a translation this time.'

'How exciting. Can you share any details about it?'

'Oh, yes, I should think so. It's another Agatha Christie translation – I think I told you I'd translated a story by her for the radio years ago. It was called *The Mysterious Affair at Styles*, such a clever plot. Mind you, I remember that when the translation was broadcast, a certain famous composer told me he thought it was beneath my dignity to read a whodunit by Agatha Christie on the radio. I said he didn't seem to have turned his nose up at conducting a few inferior pieces himself when he was working with all those prestigious orchestras abroad.'

Sunna grinned. Against all the odds, Elías had succeeded in lifting her spirits. She looked out of the window at the dim morning light and, for once, felt a burst of optimism that the clouds would soon give way to the sun.

After Elías Mar had rung off, she finally managed to get a dialling tone on the line and tried Gréta Grímsdóttir again, leaving another message on her answerphone, a little more pointed this time:

Hello Gréta. I've been trying to reach you for several weeks. It's in connection with the disappearance on Videy in 1956, which I'm investigating. My brother, Valur, was covering the story for his newspaper when he died suddenly in August. I'd really appreciate it if you could ring me and—

There was a warning bleep to indicate that she had used up all the available tape.

The moment she put the receiver down, the phone started ringing.

She was quite ready for it to be Elías Mar again, calling to say there was something he'd forgotten to tell her. As soon as she got a moment, she'd have to go round and see him in the smoke-filled flat where he created his poems and stories, and his translations of detective novels, of course. Sunna regarded these as in no way inferior to his more literary offerings, though she would never dare admit the fact to her fellow students.

'Hello? I'm trying to reach Sunna.'

This time it was a female voice that had succeeded in getting through on the overloaded phone lines, past all the radio listeners eager for prizes.

'Yes, speaking.'

'Hello, Sunna. My name's Gréta. I got your messages.'

Sunna was momentarily speechless.

'I've been on sick leave in Hveragerdi and I've only just got home. I was going to return your calls.'

'Oh, thanks for getting back to me. Yes, I wanted to ask you about Videy.'

'Oh?'

'Yes. My brother was investigating the story, the disappearance – you're familiar with that, aren't you? Lára . . . I gather she was a distant cousin of yours.'

There was a lengthy silence.

'Yes, she was,' Gréta said at last. 'Why do you ask?'

'I gather you worked there yourself, the summer before Lára went missing?'

Another silence.

'That's right. I was there in the same role as her – I was working as a maid for the same couple.'

'Could I possibly meet you, just for a quick chat?'

'Well . . . I suppose so . . . It was a long time ago, of course. Thirty years – thirty-one, actually . . . You can come and see me at work if you like, I'll be there all day . . .'

Gréta worked at the Directorate of Health, on the first floor of a building on Hlemmur Square. The approach was rather off-putting. There was a barred gate at the entrance, followed by a cold, drab stairwell, but when she reached the door of the office Sunna came face to face with a figure she recognized from television, the Director of Health himself, a distinguished-looking man with thick, black-framed glasses and greying hair. He greeted her with a friendly familiarity, as if they knew each other, though they'd never met before.

Sunna had arranged to meet Gréta at lunchtime. She didn't need to ask for her because no sooner had the director disappeared down the stairs than a middle-aged woman came down the corridor and smiled at her.

'You must be Sunna,' she said. 'The director has just gone out, so we can take a seat in his office. I have his permission to use it for meetings when necessary.'

Sunna settled herself on a reddish-brown leather sofa, an exercise book at the ready. Valur had often used tape recorders for his interviews but she didn't own one and wasn't prepared to invest in one quite yet, as she still wasn't sure if she wanted to abandon her literary studies to become a fully fledged reporter.

'As I already explained, I have very little to tell you.'

'But you did work for Óttar and Ólöf as a maid?'

'Yes, in 1955, the year before Lára vanished. For the whole summer.'

'Did it go smoothly? No incidents of any kind?'

Gréta looked away briefly, brushing the hair from her eyes, then met Sunna's gaze again. 'Nothing to speak of. Though Óttar had some friends who used to visit, and I remember that one of them was a bit . . . well . . .'

Sunna waited.

'He made me feel uncomfortable, if you know what I mean?'

'In what way?' Sunna leaned forwards, opening her

exercise book, eager to take Gréta's answer down, as the conversation had taken an interesting turn.

'Oh, it doesn't matter now. It was so long ago. You're not a journalist, are you?'

Sunna shook her head. 'I'm just trying to make sense of the story. My brother died and I still don't know why. There's a theory that someone may have pushed him in front of the bus.'

'Pushed him? Oh my goodness!' Gréta looked deeply shocked.

So far, this speculation had not been made public. Sunna had recently spoken to the detective in charge of the investigation now that it had been transferred to CID, a man called Snorri, and he had told her that the case was 'still open' but that no new evidence had come to light, no witnesses had stepped forward . . .

'I'm just trying to explore all the possible leads. And you're one of them. He didn't speak to you, did he? My brother, Valur?'

'No, I never met him. No one's ever spoken to me about it.'

'What about at the time? The police must have interviewed you?'

'When Lára vanished? No, they didn't. I was never involved.'

This fact brought Sunna up short. How rigorous or, rather, superficial had Kristján Kristjánsson's original inquiry been?

'Tell me about this man, if you can.'

'Óttar's friend, you mean? It was such a long time ago.

I was fifteen and didn't know who any of the men were –
I could hardly tell them apart. But there was one who
wouldn't leave me alone at first – it was so embarrassing –
but then he backed off for the rest of the evening.'

'Were there many of these men?'

'They met once a month, always on the first Friday
evening of the month. I do remember that. They used to
have dinner and drinks together. I was asked to serve at
the dinner when I first arrived on the island in June, but
when they came back for their July and August meet-ups,
Ólöf gave me the evening off. I sometimes wondered
whether it was because of how that man had behaved;
you know, whether Óttar was trying to avoid a scandal. So
I only met them the once, and barely even then. I just
went round topping up their drinks a few times that one
evening.'

'Can you remember who they were? Their names or
what they looked like? And how many of them there were?'

Gréta smiled. 'That's quite a lot of questions at once.'

'Sorry, I'm new to this. To be honest, I'm more at home
in a library with my nose in a book than interviewing
people.'

'I hadn't heard of any of them before and didn't bother
to memorize their names that evening. To a teenage girl
like me, they just seemed like a load of middle-aged
blokes knocking back *brennivín*. They were of no interest
to me. I doubt I'd recognize any of them today. Mind
you, I do have a feeling that the man who made me
uncomfortable had red hair, though I can't be sure; it
could just be my memory playing tricks on me.'

Sunna scribbled this down. She was starting to feel like a proper journalist, as if Valur were looking over her shoulder, showing her the way and urging her on.

'Óttar and a bunch of friends – you don't happen to remember how many there were?'

Gréta thought for a moment. 'You know, I'm just not sure. Four or five? No more than that.'

'And Ólöf wasn't there?'

'No, it was a boys' evening. She kept out of sight upstairs. And I stayed in my room – the other two times they came, I mean. But it was all quite innocent, you know? Just a sort of boys' club. I suppose they must only have been around thirty at the time.'

Quite innocent . . .

Sunna pictured Lára filling those same men's glasses. Could one of them have drunk too much and gone too far? The possibility couldn't be ruled out.

But who were they?

Óttar, obviously.

And Högni Eyfjörd, perhaps?

The late Finnur Stephensen, the wholesaler?

Páll, the city councillor?

A lawyer, a businessman, a developer, a politician . . . They'd all got themselves well established in life and maintained strong ties to each other. Was there any chance that the unbreakable bond between them had its origin in a terrible secret they all shared?

'Högni Eyfjörd, do you know who he is?'

'I've heard the name. But I can't put a face to it.'

'He's a developer.'

Gréta shrugged.

'Another name that comes to mind,' Sunna continued, 'is Finnur Stephensen, who died recently. He was a wholesaler.' Sunna could have kicked herself for not having thought to bring along any pictures of the men to show Gréta. An amateur's mistake. She could drop into the library, look up Finnur's obituaries and find a suitable picture to photocopy.

'Yes, I recognize that name too. Isn't the wholesale business called after him?'

'Yes, that's right.'

'I'm afraid I wouldn't know him by sight either.'

'What about Páll Jóhannesson, the city councillor?'

'I'm not actually familiar with the name. Is he new?'

'He's been in city politics for years but never in the front rank.'

That was precisely the problem. These were men who stayed under the radar. They were well known in their professions or in the business world but few members of the public would recognize them in the street. They operated in private. Which was understandable enough, since few people would choose to spend their lives in the media spotlight. But could their low profile be in part due to the fact that many years ago they, or one of their group, had been guilty of an appalling crime?

'Always on Fridays, you said?'

'What? Yes. It stuck in my memory because Fridays are my favourite day of the week.'

It was then that Júlía's words, relayed to her over the phone by Valur, came back to Sunna.

On the Saturday evening. Not the Friday evening.

She couldn't be sure she'd got them right, but perhaps she was getting closer to the truth now than at any time before.

Had Júlía been hinting that the group – the boys' club – had on that occasion met on a Saturday evening, rather than the usual Friday? That they had deviated from their custom for some reason? And that Saturday evening had been Lára's last one alive?

1986

7 October

The skies were ominous as Sunna paid yet another visit to the National Library on Hverfisgata. She headed straight to the reading room, found a table at the back and sat there, her mind wandering as she stared out of the tall, arched windows at the pinkish-grey morning light. The silence hung thick in the room, as usual, since the occupants were there to read or do their research. There was no sign of the fusty librarian today. Instead, there was an older woman wearing elegant glasses and her hair in a bun.

She handled the requests of readers eager to mine for treasure in the library's archives, but of course talking wasn't allowed, only whispering. So Sunna had duly whispered her request to the woman earlier that morning. She was there to have a look at *Chibaba, chibaba,* the German translation of Elías Mar's novel *Lullaby.* It had a colourful cover, featuring a young, dark-haired boy, but Sunna found she couldn't focus on the text. Her exercise book lay open in front of her but the page was blank and her pencil lay untouched on the desk. After all that had happened, she thought, what did any of this matter? What important insights could some old translation offer up? There was no room in her mind for anything but Lára and Valur. It had been a mistake to come here. She realized that she wasn't in any fit state yet to get back to normal life.

The need to find Lára: that's what got her out of bed in the mornings and helped her fall asleep at night. Not an obsession so much as a necessity, a simple survival mechanism.

That was why she had also crammed all Valur's papers into her bag – the trusty notebook and everything that had been on his desk. Of course, she had already been back and forth through the notebook, gleaning all the information she could, and some of the pages were smudged with her tears, because it was hard to pick her way through Valur's almost illegible scrawl without breaking down. She could hardly bear the thought of going through it all yet again. The papers she'd found on his desk had been little help, as they'd mainly turned out to be notes on things unconnected to Lára. Valur had been working on several assignments side by side. That's the journalist's life for you, he used to say; never a dull moment. Never any time to immerse yourself properly in any subject because of the constant distractions. Yet, in spite of this, Sunna was still considering Dagbjartur's offer. The more remote the prospect of finishing her dissertation became, the more appealing she found the idea of plunging into something new and different, of taking over the journalistic baton from Valur.

Her conversation with Gréta kept coming back to haunt her. She felt as if the bigger picture was finally beginning to open up before her eyes. The four friends on Videy . . . Something must have happened, but none of them was likely to break their silence after all these years. The secret had been well kept; the men had formed a kind of blood brotherhood, and none of them would dare to spill the beans when there was so much at stake.

She pushed her exercise book aside and carefully placed *Chibaba, chibaba* on the neighbouring desk: the reading room wasn't busy that morning. Most sensible students had no doubt taken one look at the threatening sky and opted to stay in bed. Then she picked up her bag from the floor and emptied the contents on the desk with a rustle and clatter. Glancing up quickly, she saw that the librarian was directing a disapproving glare in her direction and raising a finger to her lips. A noise like that would not be tolerated in the august surroundings of the National Library reading room.

Sunna sent her an apologetic smile across the large room. *Sorry.* Then she started trying to bring some sort of order to the mess. There were loose sheets of paper, memos and the last issue of *Vikubladid* to be published before Valur died. She'd read it at the time, especially Valur's article, of course, so the newspaper had a sentimental rather than practical value for her.

She opened it anyway, for no particular reason, inhaling the smell of printer's ink. Valur's article was past the middle, but she turned the pages slowly, drinking in the reminders of life in Reykjavík before the two-hundredth anniversary, before her life had fallen apart: an ad for a video recorder (she wasn't prepared to shell out for one, so she made do with renting a machine and tapes several times a year instead) and another for a SodaStream (she'd already got one) and news of the preparations for the city's anniversary celebrations. The prime minister commenting on the strength of the Icelandic króna and stating that devaluing the currency was out of the question. The short review of a novel, which she knew Valur had written, though he hadn't put his initials under the piece.

Life had been utterly transformed since those innocent days of a few short weeks ago: only she was left, alone in the world. Her gaze was drawn back to the window just as the heavens opened and the greyness dissolved in a violent cloudburst.

She continued turning the pages until she reached Valur's article. There was a photo of Videy and the familiar image of Lára. And then she noticed that Valur had scribbled something in the margin. She recognized his handwriting with a sudden flutter of the heart. She hadn't opened this particular copy of the paper before as it had never crossed her mind that Valur might have used it to make notes on. But after lending his notebook to her, he must have grabbed whatever was to hand during his last few days of life.

Her brother had scribbled:

Lára.
   Not alive. Killed. On Sat evening. Not Fri evening.
   Júlía?
   To be buried in consecrated ground – or to have a
proper burial.
   Knows where the body is.
   Needs to be at peace.
   Wants her to be found.
   Doesn't want to be mixed up in case.
   Wants it all to end.

Sunna read the notes again and again, poring over
every word, examining every letter to make sure she'd
deciphered Valur's handwriting correctly.
   It was probably the last message she would ever receive
from her brother.
   They were obviously the notes he had jotted down
while he was talking to Júlía on the phone. He'd told
Sunna the gist of the conversation, but there were details
here that might be significant.
   On Sat evening. Not Fri evening.
   Gréta's evidence might well have shed light on that
mystery.
   From his scrawl it was also possible to infer that Júlía
knew exactly when Lára had died – or, rather, when she
had been killed.
   Then came a line that niggled at Sunna for some reason:
   To be buried in consecrated ground – or to have a proper burial.

He must have taken down Júlía's words almost verbatim.

. . . or . . .

Why 'or'? Wasn't being buried in consecrated ground the same as receiving a proper burial?

Sunna closed her eyes, lay forward on the desk and listened to the silence around her. It was made up of so many components: the echo of the downpour outside, the rustling of books and papers on the neighbouring desks, the scraping as someone moved their chair – they were big, solid pieces of furniture – and a faint whispering somewhere. Even in a place like this, silence was illusory. There was no true silence to be had except in the grave, where Valur now lay.

The grave . . .

To be buried in consecrated ground – or to have a proper burial.

Sunna opened her eyes and read the words again.

She asked herself: *What if Lára was already lying in consecrated ground?*

Was it possible?

If she was, the sentence would make more sense.

Júlía had made a slip of the tongue when she said that Lára needed to 'be buried in consecrated ground'. Realizing that Lára was already lying in consecrated ground, she'd corrected herself to say that what she needed was a proper burial.

Did that mean Lára was lying in a churchyard somewhere?

If so, which churchyard?

It didn't take much guessing.

Could she really have been buried on Videy all along?

Sunna knew there was a churchyard there, but it was a while since she had visited the island herself. Even if it was tiny, there was no way the authorities would agree to digging up every single grave.

She returned the papers, the notebook and the copy of *Vikubladid* to her bag, almost adding the German translation of Elías Mar too – that would have been an expensive mistake, as she doubted the librarian would be amused by readers who tried to smuggle the library's treasures into their bags.

On the way out, she paused to speak to the severe-looking woman: 'Sorry,' she whispered, 'but is there anywhere here that I can look up graves?'

'I beg your pardon?'

'Graves.'

The librarian looked bewildered.

'I mean I'm looking for information about cemeteries.'

'Then why didn't you say so?'

'Is there somewhere I can look them up?'

'Information about who's buried where? Is that what you're asking?'

Sunna nodded. Having to whisper all this was proving a strain.

'No, we don't hold that kind of information,' the librarian told her curtly.

'Sorry, but do you know where I could find it, then?'

There was a pause.

'Is there one particular cemetery you want to look at?'

'The one on Videy.'

'Ah, then you want to speak to the Capital Area Cemeteries office.'

Having established where she could find this office, Sunna smiled and thanked the woman.

She hurried down the library's grand, marble staircase, feeling for a moment as though she were in some European metropolis, but the rain lashing the windows dispelled the illusion. She was still stuck in the little Arctic capital on the edge of the world.

Sunna had no idea how she should phrase her question to the people at the cemeteries office: could a young girl have been buried on Videy? Was there any way of finding out? Of digging up old graves?

If nothing else, she could at least request a list of all those buried on the island.

As she stepped outside into the teeming rain, it finally came to her:

Arnfríður Leifsdóttir. The woman Valur had asked Katrín at the National Registry to look up, without explaining why. There had been three women with that name, one of whom had died in 1940 . . . Was it possible?

'Videy cemetery, you say?'

The man studied her through his thick lenses. He was completely bald, wore a checked waistcoat, a shirt and grey trousers, and must have been nearing retirement age, if he hadn't already passed it without anyone noticing. Here he sat in his private realm, forgotten by everyone, surrounded by folders, books and files. There was an overpowering smell of coffee, but he didn't offer Sunna a cup.

'Yes, Videy.'

'We don't bury many people there these days, as I expect you know.'

'No, I didn't suppose you did.'

'I can dig out some documents about the cemetery, if you *insist*.'

'I'd be very grateful,' Sunna said, in her most dulcet tones.

'Oh, well. What exactly is it you want to know, young lady?' The man's manner was so patronizing that she wondered if perhaps he was unaccustomed to dealing with people who belonged to the land of the living.

'I need a list of the people buried there.'

'There aren't that many of them. Not compared to the big cemeteries.'

'I expect you're right.'

'I *am* right. I *do* know what I'm talking about.'

'So, do you have the names somewhere? Are they difficult to find?' Sunna asked with rising impatience, sensing that he had no intention of being hurried.

'Depends what you mean by difficult . . . but I can find the information.'

'There's one name in particular that I'm after.'

'Well, why didn't you say so right away?' the man huffed. He adjusted his glasses. 'What name is that?'

'Arnfríður Leifsdóttir. She died in 1940.'

'Arnfríður Leifsdóttir . . .' he rumbled. He frowned: 'No, I don't recognize the name, but I'll look it up. I'll be back in a minute.'

A minute had stretched into half an hour before the man finally reappeared.

'Do excuse me,' he said. 'I hadn't realized it was lunch-time. I always pop down to the canteen at midday. Well, it's not much of a canteen: cold porridge and brown cheese, but it's better than nothing, I suppose.'

'Did you find Arnfrídur?' Sunna asked, rather shortly.

'Yes, indeed. She's there all right, lying in Videy soil. Buried in 1940, as you said. Was she a relation?'

Sunna didn't answer.

Although she hadn't actually expected her conjecture to prove right, another part of her was ashamed that she hadn't worked it out before.

Once she had recovered from her initial surprise, she felt extremely smug, even proud, while simultaneously dreading the next step.

She'd found Arnfrídur Leifsdóttir. Was it possible that she'd found Lára too?

1986

8 October

Sunna slept fitfully, her mind racing, convinced that she was getting close to solving the mystery. When she finally dropped off, it was inevitable that she should dream of Valur.

How far had his investigation progressed?

Had he worked out that Arnfrídur Leifsdóttir was buried in Videy cemetery?

Almost certainly not, since Katrín from the National Registry hadn't managed to make contact with him with the results of her inquiries. And of course he hadn't actually visited the island while researching his articles. Sunna remembered scolding him at the time for this omission.

But of course the million-dollar question was: could there be something – or rather someone – else buried in the consecrated ground where Arnfrídur lay?

Sunna hardly dared to pursue this thought to its logical conclusion.

She wondered if she should talk to someone on the paper, like Dagbjartur himself or Baldur, but was hesitant to take this step. She didn't feel she knew them well enough to sit down with them over coffee and discuss the next move. They were from a different generation; too far removed from her. And she couldn't talk to her parents, as they had no idea that she was looking into Valur's story and were unlikely to give her efforts their blessing.

She tried calling Gunnar, but he didn't answer. He must be over at the university, pondering the Sermon on the Mount.

Her thoughts turned next to Margrét, no doubt partly because a band called Berlin was on the radio at that moment, playing the love song from *Top Gun*, and partly because Margrét was one of the few people Sunna had spoken to about Valur's death and the Lára investigation. She was around Sunna's age too, and although they didn't have much in common – Margrét had never even heard of Elías Mar! – they did at least share the fact that they'd both loved Valur. Sunna had the impression that Margrét was genuinely interested in helping to solve the Lára mystery, in spite of the awkward encounter with Óttar and Ólöf at her parents' house. Her father, Jökull, had at least apologized for his behaviour afterwards and Margrét had tried to make up for it by inviting Sunna to the cinema.

To Sunna's relief, Margrét answered the phone herself. She'd been afraid she might have to speak to one of her parents.

'Hi, it's Sunna here.'

'Sunna?' The surprise in Margrét's voice was plain. 'Oh, hi, how are you?'

'I'm fine.'

'It's nice to hear from you. Actually, I was going to give you a call. What do you think of the news – about Reagan and Gorbachev coming to Reykjavík?'

'Oh, you know, it's—'

'Completely wild, isn't it? Daddy reckons he'll get to meet them.'

'Really?'

'Yes, apparently he's going to be part of some reception committee or delegation or something. It's so exciting.'

'Oh, right,' Sunna said, then realized Margrét had probably been expecting a more enthusiastic reaction to the news that her father was about to meet the two most powerful men on the planet. 'Anyway, I was wondering if we could meet for a coffee?'

'Coffee? Yes, sure. Any time.'

Later that afternoon Margrét came round to Sunna's flat in Hlídar. Her visit brought it home to Sunna just how long it was since she had last received any guests; time seemed to have stood still in recent weeks, every day the same, the voices on the radio her only company. It wasn't as if she met many people outside the four walls of home either, apart from Gunnar; she'd stopped going into the university and had shelved her dissertation for now.

As if to underline how little entertaining she'd done, she had to go upstairs and knock on Kamilla's door to ask if she could borrow some sugar, and only avoided being drawn into a conversation by explaining that she had a visitor and promising that they'd catch up soon.

Margrét perched on the edge of the sofa, holding a mug of coffee with sugar and milk. She was so smartly turned out that she looked completely out of place on the shabby sofa with its threadbare cushions.

'Look, I know it was a bit weird,' Sunna said.

'I'm sorry?'

'Inviting you round for coffee out of the blue like this.'

In the background they could hear the radio host of the new afternoon show discussing Reagan and Gorbachev, like everyone else at the moment.

'Don't be silly, Sunna. It's nice – I wasn't doing anything special.'

'The thing is, I've been looking into the Lára business.'

'Oh? Any news?'

'Yes, I think so. That's why I rang. I'm not quite sure where to go from here, so I really needed to talk to someone I could trust . . .'

'Oh, I'd love to help. It would have pleased Valur, I'm sure.'

Sunna nodded.

'You haven't found her, have you? Lára, I mean?'

'Not exactly,' Sunna said hesitantly.

'Don't say you've found evidence that implicates Ólöf and Óttar?'

Sunna picked up on the sudden note of concern in Margrét's voice, suggesting that she didn't want her parents' friends to be mixed up in anything discreditable.

'I don't think so. But I can't say for sure.'

'OK. I was only curious,' Margrét said apologetically.

'No problem.' Sunna chose her next words carefully: 'Margrét, I *believe* I know where Lára is.'

Margrét looked incredulous. 'What? Where?'

'I believe she's been dead all this time.'

Margrét nodded, waiting solemnly for her to continue.

'My suspicion is that she's buried on Videy.'

'She's been on Videy all along?'

'Yes, in the churchyard. Of course, it's obvious, in hindsight. She vanished on the island, and the best place to hide is in plain sight. Have you read any Edgar Allan Poe?'

Margrét shrugged. 'No.'

Sunna shook her head impatiently, but this was hardly the moment to start lecturing her guest on her pet subject: the origin of detective stories and Edgar Allan Poe's role in the development of the genre. Instead, she cut to the chase: 'I think I even know exactly *where*: in the grave of a woman called Arnfrídur Leifsdóttir. You see, Valur was asking about her just before he . . . before he died.'

'Wow . . . that's incredible, if it turns out to be true. I mean, you may have just cracked a thirty-year-old mystery!'

'We have . . .'

'We?'

'Yes, me and Valur – we've done it together.'

'Of course.' Margrét gave an embarrassed smile. 'So what now?'

'That's what I wanted to pick your brains about. Do you think I should go to the police? Or talk to Dagbjartur and get the paper on my side? I mean, digging up a body's bound to be a legal nightmare, don't you think? Getting all the necessary permissions, and so on. And what if someone gets there first – if the news leaks out? Iceland's such a small place that it's going to be impossible to keep this secret for long . . .'

'Well, you can rest assured that I'm not going to tell anyone, Sunna.'

'I know.'

'I could ask my father, I suppose . . . You know, ask him how much hassle it would be to get permission to open up a grave, without mentioning why.'

Sunna mulled this over. She was reluctant to involve the lawyer in this, for fear he might work it out and alert his mate, Óttar. After all, Óttar and Ólöf would be in very hot water if Sunna's theory proved correct; if the girl, who'd been working as their maid, turned out to have been buried on the island. Something terrible must have happened, maybe by accident, maybe not . . . And it was high time the truth came to light.

She almost regretted her impulse to share her discovery with Margrét, but, on the other hand, it was helpful to have someone to discuss the alternatives with.

'Margrét, I've had an idea,' she said.

'Yes?'

'What if we went together, just the two of us . . . to Videy, this evening or tomorrow, and had a poke around in the graveyard ourselves?'

Margrét didn't immediately answer.

'Well . . . I definitely think we should leave Valur's

newspaper out of it,' she said eventually, with conviction. 'And maybe it's not such a good idea to ask my father either. Let's just do it ourselves, as you suggest.'

'Are you sure?'

'Yes. I don't often get a chance to step outside the comfort zone my parents have created around me, and they'd go ballistic if they knew I was even discussing doing something like this – but I want to do it. To break out. Even if it's against the law.'

'Well, I sincerely hope we won't end up in jail. We're only following a clue. It's not like we're actually going to dig up Arnfríður's coffin. Just scrape away a bit of earth and see if there's any sign that someone else could have been buried there too . . .' Sunna had a mental image of this being not so very different from a tough day's research among old manuscripts in the National Library.

'I'm up for it,' Margrét said. 'A hundred per cent. When shall we go?'

Following her conversation with Margrét, Sunna made a few phone calls and established that there were no scheduled ferry trips to the island except at weekends. The person she spoke to at the ferry office told her: 'There's not much call to visit Viðey during the week, but there's a fisherman who's been taking people out there as a sideline for several years. Would you like his name and number?'

When she got hold of the fisherman later that same evening, he said he'd be only too happy to give the girls a lift out to the island. Sunna was keen to go as late in the day as possible, to be sure their movements wouldn't attract attention. Some things were best done under cover of darkness.

'We're hoping to get some photos there at dusk, so would you be able to take us over tomorrow evening, at six, say – and maybe pick us up again around nine?'

'Yes, sure, I should be able to do that. Though I'll have to charge you a bit extra for an evening trip, you know how it is.'

'That won't be a problem,' Sunna said, confident that she could persuade Margrét to cover the cost.

After all, Margrét had to spend all that family money on something.

1986

9 October

They sat comfortably enough in the little fishing smack, eating biscuits provided by the fisherman. The sea was calm and they were making rapid progress across the sound, but the air was chilly.

'To take photos, you say?' the fisherman called from the door of his wheelhouse. 'People are always wanting to photograph the island. Is it the birds you're after? Lots of visitors seem to be interested in them.'

'Anything, really,' Sunna answered for them both. 'The scenery, the plant life, the birds . . . we're particularly keen to capture the twilight.'

'I've had this boat for ten years and done countless trips to Videy when the conditions are good. It was my father's boat before me. He often used to ferry people out there in the old days.'

'So your father must have been doing the Videy run around the time Lára went missing?'

The fisherman raised his eyebrows enquiringly.

'The girl who vanished there – in 1956.'

'Yes, I know. I've heard the story, of course. Yes, the old man would have been going strong in fifty-six.'

'The reason I ask is that my brother was researching the story of Lára's disappearance for his newspaper.'

'Is that so?'

'It would be great to have a chat with your father some time and see if he remembers the girl.'

'You're a bit late: he died several years back.'

'Oh, dear. I'm sorry to hear that. Please excuse me for asking.'

'No need to apologize.' Changing the subject, the fisherman said: 'We're nearly there. Are you sure you want to stay till nine? You'll be freezing by then. Mind you, just so you know, they generally leave the church unlocked. Its doors are always open, as they say.'

Just the sort of thing Gunnar would come out with, Sunna thought, with a private smile. Part of her wished she was sharing this adventure with him rather than Margrét – if he'd only been home when she rang. He was a sweet guy, even if he did go on about God a bit too much for her taste. Still, she could live with that. All kinds of people made a go of things, even if their interests didn't perfectly coincide.

'Maybe just till eight, then,' Margrét piped up suddenly. 'I'm sure we won't need any longer than that.'

On her lap she was hugging a large rucksack containing two small spades. The girls hadn't liked to cart any bigger tools out to the island, since even the backpack was probably enough to arouse suspicion. Sunna had noticed the fisherman eyeing it during their conversation, but luckily he hadn't asked why they had so much luggage. No doubt he was used to his passengers' eccentricities.

Once he'd moored the boat to the jetty, he gave them both a hand ashore.

The breeze blowing on the island was bitingly cold and the light was already failing. Sunna began to have second thoughts. She wondered if she should have gone straight to the police instead of mixing Margrét up in all this.

Sunna covertly studied her companion. Could she trust Margrét? She'd been suspiciously quick to agree to this crazy plan. What if Margrét knew more than she was letting on? What if she'd heard something from her parents about Óttar and Ólöf's role in the events and had come along to prevent Sunna from solving the mystery? She tried to read Margrét's expression, but the other girl was peering up the slope towards the mansion and the church.

Sunna tried to shrug off her paranoia.

Margrét was only trying to be nice, she told herself. And, of course, Sunna didn't want to involve the police at this stage. The truth was, she wanted to find out the answers for herself. If her conjecture proved right, the next step would be to contact the authorities – and to write that article for Dagbjartur. Finish Valur's work . . .

'Night owls.'

Snapping out of her thoughts, Sunna glanced round. She and Margrét were still standing on the jetty. 'I'm sorry?'

'Night owls, I said.' The fisherman was smiling at his joke as he loosened the moorings. 'I was just wondering what kind of birds you were hoping to see at this hour. Personally, I find my eyes work better in the daylight than in the dark, but each to his own. I'll be back later. Try not to get into trouble – the island's bigger than it looks.'

Without another word, he stepped into his wheelhouse and steered a course away from the jetty.

'He's obviously guessed that we—' Margrét began.

Sunna cut her off. 'He can't possibly have guessed anything, and besides, it doesn't matter. We've got to do this for Valur's sake. And Lára's too. OK?'

Margrét nodded. 'It can't hurt to take a look in the churchyard,' she said, as if trying to convince herself. 'And maybe that'll be enough. I mean, if we can't find the grave, or . . .'

'We'll do what we can, Margrét.'

Although the daylight was fading, they could still see well enough for their purposes. Sunna set off briskly up the grassy slope towards the mansion and the church, and after a pause she heard Margrét's footsteps behind her.

Struck by the loneliness and isolation, Sunna found herself wondering what might have been going through Lára's head the first time she set foot on the island to start her job as a maid. Fifteen years old – she'd been no more than a child. That had been in May, according to her parents. Her surroundings would have looked much more promising in the light nights of spring than they did now, in the autumnal gloom: Lára would have sensed more hope in the air, more optimism. Although Videy was within sight of the city, for a Reykjavík girl like Lára it must have felt like suddenly stepping into the middle of the countryside, making her feel closer to nature and at the same time strangely free. She must have been excited about getting to stand on her own two feet, earning her own wages, and making the acquaintance of a respectable couple from the higher echelons of society. Óttar and Ólöf were generally regarded as model citizens. No one would have hesitated to send their child to work for them: a respected lawyer, a woman from a prominent family . . .

Sunna felt an impulse to make a detour past their farmhouse, but it was too far out of their way, according to the map she had consulted in the National Library, and it simply wasn't their priority on this trip. Anyway, the house stood empty these days and there would be nothing there but old ghosts, the echo of the lost girl's voice.

Sunna threw a quick glance over her shoulder. Brooding on the past had sent a sudden shiver down her spine.

Margrét, seeing her look round, gave her a conspiratorial smile, and Sunna's heartbeat slowed a little in response. But she still felt oddly spooked. There was something menacing in the air, a feeling that they were walking into the unknown . . . And, to make matters worse, the friends – was that what they were now? – were heading straight for the graveyard.

They were nearing the two white-walled, black-roofed buildings, the mansion on the right with its rows of black, lightless windows that seemed suddenly sinister in the gloom, and the church on the left, looking even smaller than Sunna had remembered. But then it was ages since her last visit to Videy and the photos she'd studied recently were deceptive.

It was a pretty little building, recently restored, and there, to the left of it, as modest in scale as the church itself, was the cemetery. It shouldn't take them long to locate Arnfrídur Leifsdóttir, assuming the graves were clearly marked.

'This is quite an adventure,' Margrét said, her voice betraying nothing but high spirits. Despite her initial wobble, she didn't seem to be sharing Sunna's qualms now. It had been a sensible decision to bring her along after all. She was sunny by nature, even light-hearted. Perhaps those were the very qualities that had attracted Valur. Certainly, she didn't seem to take after her parents, those rigidly conventional lawyers from Gardabær.

There was a chance that in time she and Sunna might develop a true friendship. Wasn't that what Valur would have wanted?

'Right, let's get on with finding Arnfrídur,' Sunna said, filling her lungs with cold, fresh air to steel herself. 'Then we'll find Lára.'

'You know, Sunna, I never dreamed I'd one day be creeping out in the dusk to dig around in a graveyard. My biggest crimes up to now have been speeding and sneaking into a country swimming pool at night without paying. Aren't you usually the law-abiding type too?'

'Yup. I don't even nick library books.'

Sunna tried the door of the church and found it

unlocked, as the fisherman had said. That was a relief: they'd be able to warm up in here afterwards. Groping at the wall inside, she encountered a light switch and flicked it on. The interior sprang into view. It was tiny by modern standards, but then the congregation had probably never been large. For a moment Sunna had the sensation of stepping hundreds of years back in time. Most buildings in Iceland dated from the twentieth century, but she'd read that the church had been consecrated in the second half of the eighteenth century, which made it ancient by local standards. The wooden pews were painted blue and brown, and, attractive as they looked, were no doubt uncomfortable to sit on for any length of time. The altar, with the elaborate pulpit above it, was painted in the same colours, with the addition of green. Sunna closed her eyes. She didn't think of herself as religious and teased Gunnar when he forgot himself and started going on about Christ and God and synods and rituals. Yet she felt moved to send up a silent prayer now, for her brother and for Lára. She had a momentary sense that Lára was very close to her here. Imagination or wishful thinking? Perhaps.

'Shall we get on with it, then?' Margrét asked with a touch of impatience. She was still standing outside the church.

'Sure.' Sunna turned, switched off the lights and went back outside, closing the door softly behind her.

On the point of entering the cemetery, Sunna wavered, conscious that they were in a very grey area legally. Disturbing a grave would be hard to justify, but then, she told herself grimly, necessity broke laws . . .

They were here now and, as Margrét had said, surely it couldn't hurt to do a little poking around. Sunna paused to survey their surroundings in the uncertain light. The church and mansion stood on flat, grassy ground between two low, mound-like hills. She couldn't see any sign of movement and there was no cover in the open landscape where anyone could be hiding. Again, she reassured herself that they must be the only people on the island.

Her mind conjured up another image of Lára, this time running towards the mansion and the church, perhaps in the August twilight, with someone in pursuit, someone who meant her harm. Is that what had happened? Had the girl fled for her life, over the uneven landscape, and tripped on the tussocky ground? Had she been fleeing an attacker – male, almost certainly – and failed to get away? She wouldn't have stood a chance, as there was nowhere to run to on a small island like this. Had she taken refuge in the church, crouching between the pews? That would have achieved little, since there were no real hiding places in there.

'Right, let's get on and find the grave: Arnfrídur Leifsdóttir.' Margrét sounded determined. Clearly she was in no mood to back out now or waste time letting her imagination run away with her. Sunna was grateful for her resolve.

'Yes, there aren't that many.'

The churchyard was square, surrounded by stone walls so low they could easily step over them, and the few, scattered graves were marked by flat stones or slight hummocks in the grassy ground.

Bending down, Sunna peered at a stone. There was still just enough daylight left to manage without a torch, but it wouldn't last much longer.

Sunna had been aware that the writer, Gunnar Gunnarsson, was buried there, and it didn't take her long to stumble on his grave. She paused for a moment out of respect.

'Don't waste time hanging about by every single grave,' Margrét hissed. Despite being alone, they had both instinctively lowered their voices, perhaps out of guilt at the illicit nature of their mission.

'I found a famous author,' Sunna explained.

'We're not here to look for authors.'

Chastened, Sunna carried on scanning the inscriptions on the stones.

'Arnfrídur! Found her,' Margrét called in a slightly louder whisper. 'That didn't take long.'

Sunna felt a knot in her stomach. What now? Were they really going to dig up an old grave?

'I've got a Thermos of coffee with me,' Margrét said. 'In my backpack. Why don't we go and sit in the church and have a hot drink while we're waiting for it to get properly dark? Then we can get down to work.'

Fifteen minutes later they emerged from the church, armed this time with torches and spades. Night had fallen swiftly, so at least they would now be able to conceal their activity in the dark. The lights of Reykjavík were twinkling across the sound.

'I'll start,' Margrét said. They had agreed that it might

be best to begin by levering up the flat gravestone and digging underneath it, to avoid making a mess of the turf. Margrét eased her spade under the edge and tried in vain to shift the heavy slab.

Sunna felt her heart sinking. This was a really bad idea. 'Are you sure?' she faltered.

'We're doing it for Valur. Remember?' Margrét said, encouraging her. Suddenly, she was the driving force and Sunna the reluctant one.

Sunna nodded and set to work, helping her friend. Because that's what Margrét was, she realized. It was just the two of them now, digging up the grave of an unknown woman.

Time passed with agonizing slowness, the cold was biting and so was her conscience, but Sunna tried to ignore both. It was far harder than she'd imagined to move the stone and they were soon sweating with the effort. But she went about the task with extreme care and got the impression Margrét was doing so too. Even so, it soon became clear to Sunna that it would be impossible to hide the traces of what they had done, as the freshly disturbed soil made such a stark contrast to the grass. Which meant that if Lára was buried here, Óttar and Ólöf must have known about it. The killer would have had to bury the girl, then disguise any signs of fresh earth, re-laying the turf so professionally that none of the subsequent searchers had noticed anything untoward. No way could that have been achieved in a hurry and it was hard to imagine it being done without the knowledge of the island's only inhabitants. All the evidence seemed to point to the same conclusion – that Óttar and Ólöf had been responsible for Lára's death.

'Have you seen *The Color Purple*?'

'What?' Sunna looked up. The question was so unexpected that she was momentarily confused.

'The film. It's still on at the Austurbær Cinema.'

'Oh, no, I haven't. But then I rarely go to the cinema,' Sunna replied, then corrected herself: 'Apart from seeing *Top Gun* with you, of course.' She refrained from mentioning that she'd seen it again with Gunnar.

By directing their attention to ordinary things, Margrét had managed to dissipate the intense atmosphere and reduce some of the tension.

Sunna smiled and said: 'Maybe we should go next week.'

'I've already been. Some guy invited me – a poet. I don't know why I said yes. He told me he'd read the book. I don't think I'll bother going out with him again – poets don't do it for me. We should definitely go to a film next week, though.'

'Great.' Sunna felt a flash of resentment at Margrét's casual reference to going on a date so soon after Valur's death, but she tried to suppress it.

They relapsed into silence again and the only noise was the thudding and scraping of the spades, accompanied by the rattle of dislodged soil and their panting breaths. Sunna's thoughts returned to Ólöf and Óttar. The couple seemed so staid, and at the same time their manner had been so distant. When they met at Margrét's house, she'd felt instinctively that they were hiding something. She was frustrated now that she hadn't been more determined and gone in harder, demanding answers. Ólöf hadn't even responded to the question Sunna had put to her. Despite the suspicions aroused by her conversations with Högni and Páll, and however much she turned the problem over in her mind, Sunna always returned to the same conclusion: that Óttar must be the killer. The only snag with that theory was the fact that he didn't have red hair. According to Gréta, the man who'd made her so uncomfortable was a redhead, but it was always possible that the two incidents had been unrelated. After all, Gréta would have said if it had been her employer. Had one of the gang of friends hit on Gréta, and a completely different man been responsible for Lára's death?

'Reagan's flying in tonight,' Margrét remarked suddenly. Evidently she wasn't comfortable with silence.

'Yes, so I heard. Exciting times, eh?'

'It'll be cool to see them. I gather Daddy's meeting them tomorrow.'

'It's unbelievable. Amazing when you think about it.'

At that moment they felt the first spots of rain, and before long it was coming down heavily. Sunna was struck by the insanity of skulking around in the dark like this in the rain and wind. The whole idea was probably nonsense and all they'd get for their pains was a bout of pneumonia.

'Shall we take a break? Wait for it to stop?' she asked.

'No way,' Margrét answered, panting from the effort. 'Let's finish the job. We can shelter in the church afterwards, once we've found Lára.'

It felt as if the weather gods were punishing them for daring to go ahead with this plan. Nevertheless, Sunna carried on digging, inserting her spade tentatively, trying to show respect for the grave, while driven by a fierce need to find Lára. Her mood fluctuated between certainty that her theory was right and crippling doubts about what they were doing. At one point, her ears catching what might have been a noise in the distance, her suspicions of Margrét came flooding back: could she have blabbed about their trip? Was someone coming to stop them?

No, of course not. Sunna told herself grimly to focus and stop being so paranoid.

The darkness was all-encompassing now, stealing around them, whispering in Sunna's ear, sending a shiver down her spine. Yet she persevered, telling herself that it was too late to chicken out.

It was then that her spade struck something with a click.

She recoiled, then straightened up and took a step backwards.

'Shh,' she hushed Margrét, who immediately stopped digging. Sunna wanted absolute silence – apart from the pattering of the raindrops.

She aimed her torch into the black hole.

A bone was poking out of the wet soil. As the beam of Sunna's torch played over the grave, she spotted more bones. So there were some remains here after all. They couldn't possibly be Arnfríður's as they weren't deep enough and there was no sign of a coffin. Sunna moved closer again, knelt down and, asking Margrét to shine her torch into the hole, began grubbing with her hands in the earth in the hope of finding some clue about who the bones had belonged to. Something gleamed in the torchlight.

Sunna realized that she was looking at a large, handsome filigree cross on a chain.

1986

9 October

Sunna didn't say a word on the short boat ride back to harbour. Taking her cue from her, Margrét was equally silent.

There was no reason to betray their discovery to the fisherman. They had left the dirt-covered spades behind to avoid giving rise to awkward questions, and although the man kept darting curious looks at their muddy clothes, he didn't ask what they'd been up to, perhaps put off by their stony expressions. They hadn't brought the necklace with them either, for fear of disturbing the crime scene any more than they already had, but had left it where it lay. Hopefully they'd be able to convince the police to head straight out to Videy tonight, to conduct a proper examination of the site.

Her breathing fast and shallow, Sunna avoided looking at the fisherman or Margrét, staring instead across Faxa-flói bay towards the open sea, out there somewhere in the darkness, in an attempt to calm her agitation. She was so worked up that she could barely think straight, let alone put her thoughts into words.

When they reached the shore, they set off for the car at a run.

Margrét got behind the wheel.

'Bloody hell,' she said, starting the engine.

'Where are we going?'

'To my place,' Margrét said decisively. 'We can grab a hot drink, change our clothes – I can lend you something dry – and warm up a bit before phoning the police. I'm worried they'll think we're nuts if we go charging into the police station in this state and try to get them to believe us. You've got the direct line of the guy who's in charge of the case, haven't you?'

'Yes, both his work and home numbers. They're in my bag.'

Sunna's own instinct was to go straight to the police, but she didn't like to contradict Margrét. Taking a bit of a detour wouldn't make much difference in the long run and, besides, the thought of changing into clean, dry clothes in Margrét's warm, civilized home in Gardabær was tempting in the circumstances. As it was, Sunna couldn't stop shivering from cold, the shock of their discovery and apprehension about what was going to happen next.

They had found Lára, there was no doubt about that.

Margrét switched on the car radio. It was a few minutes to nine and they were broadcasting live coverage of Ronald Reagan's arrival in Iceland. The newsreader's voice competed with the drumming of the rain and the swishing of the windscreen wipers. Sunna closed her eyes, drew a deep breath and tried to focus on what was being said. It all seemed so unreal: the most powerful men in the world meeting here in little Reykjavík, one of them already landed, the very same evening that she and Margrét had found the body of a girl whose disappearance had kept the nation guessing for three decades.

They were almost at Margrét's house when the chimes went for nine p.m., Margrét's digital watch bleeped and the live broadcast came to an end. Margrét switched over to Radio 2 and the car was filled with the sound of Eiríkur Hauksson singing 'Halfway between Moscow and Washington'. The song, an entry in the contest back in the spring to select Iceland's Eurovision contender, had suddenly gained a whole new relevance.

'My parents are home,' Margrét remarked as she pulled up in front of the house. 'They were planning to watch the launch of TV 2 this evening.'

The first day of the new, private TV station! This landmark event had completely slipped Sunna's mind in all the excitement.

'Let's go into the sitting room,' Margrét said. Sunna followed close behind her.

Margrét's parents, who were glued to the television, both turned their heads. 'Hello, you're back? And Sunna too?' Nanna said. 'The launch of the new channel has been a bit of a fiasco. We've been switching between that and the live coverage of Reagan's arrival, as TV 2 had technical trouble. Still, it's quite exciting having a new channel. Jökull and I won't be bored in the evenings any more, will we, dear?'

The former Minister of Justice muttered something in reply.

'Goodness, you're both soaked to the skin!' Nanna exclaimed, apparently only now registering the state of them. 'We've just watched Reagan getting rained on at the airport. Have you been out in that?'

Sunna hung back, letting Margrét speak for both of them.

'We've been out to Videy.'

'Videy?' Jökull finally gave them his full attention. 'What on earth for?' His brows drew together in a frown.

'We were looking for ...' Margrét broke off mid-sentence, either searching for the right words or trying to summon up her courage. 'We were looking for Lára,' she finished, sounding breathless and a little ashamed.

Nanna gasped in astonishment and Jökull shot to his feet. Sunna reflected that even Reagan and Gorbachev had been overshadowed by this latest development.

'You've been looking for Lára?' Jökull repeated. 'Now you've lost me. Is this related to the questions you were asking Óttar and Ólöf?' This last was addressed to Sunna.

'Not directly, no,' she said in a small voice. It was dawning on her what a bad mistake it had been to come back here with Margrét. Her parents were bound to object and make things difficult for them.

She felt a futile desire to run out of this house, to go back in time and take refuge in her brother's arms. Valur would have helped her; they could have gone to the police together; together they could have achieved anything.

'It has nothing to do with them,' Margrét said firmly. 'Sunna's been investigating what happened, following up old clues and new ones, and she worked out somehow that Lára was buried on Videy.'

'What absolute nonsense!' Jökull exclaimed. 'That Lára's buried . . . No one knows what happened to her. She could be alive for all we know – in Iceland, abroad, working, who can say? I can't understand what you were thinking of, Margrét, to let yourself be dragged into this sort of madness.'

'It's not madness, Daddy. We've found her.'

'Found what?'

'We've found Lára.'

'Oh my God, darling, are you telling the truth?' Nanna asked in tones of disbelief. 'Have you really found the girl?'

'She was in the churchyard all along. In somebody else's grave, of course.'

'No, I don't believe it,' Jökull said, sinking down on the sofa. His face was so ashen that Sunna was concerned. Supposing he'd joined the dots like her and worked out that this must implicate Óttar and Ólöf. That the ultra-respectable couple, Jökull and Nanna's friends, had conceivably caused the death of a teenage girl, or at the very least conspired to cover up an appalling crime.

Margrét carried on, undaunted: 'We found her necklace, and after that we stopped digging.'

'Her necklace?' Nanna echoed.

'Apparently Lára always wore the same necklace. It wasn't in any of the pictures of her, but Sunna learned about its existence. There's no question it was her necklace.'

'Did you bring it with you?' Jökull asked.

Margrét hesitated: 'No, we didn't want to destroy any evidence. We wanted the police to see the scene as it is, which is why we—'

'Damn it, you've already disturbed the grave of whoever's buried there, which in itself is a breach of the law. I just don't know what to say . . .' Jökull released a long breath. 'But, if you've really found Lára after all these years . . . It was absolute insanity to go charging off to Videy like that, disturbing graves, but . . .'

'You'll look after us, won't you, Daddy, if the police make trouble?'

Her father nodded distractedly.

'We need to phone them now,' Margrét went on. 'Sunna's got the number of the officer in charge of the case.'

'Yes, could I use your phone?' Sunna asked.

'Of course, it goes without saying. Margrét, show her,' Nanna said. 'You'd better ring straight away. For goodness' sake, this needs investigating.'

Sunna had already dug out the note with the telephone number.

She picked up the receiver with a trembling hand and waited to hear a tone before carefully dialling the five digits, anxious not to make a mistake.

It began to ring.

As she waited, she ran through the possibilities in her head: the policeman might not be home or he might have gone to bed. Though surely no one would have had an early night today of all days, with the American president arriving in the country and the new TV channel going on air?

In that instant, the phone was answered.

Sunna recognized Snorri's voice straight away and introduced herself. 'I'm so sorry to disturb you but it's urgent.'

'Oh?'

'We've found Lára Marteinsdóttir.'

It was past one in the morning.

The police had taken precise directions over the phone but hadn't required Sunna and Margrét to accompany them to the island. Much as Sunna would have liked to watch the excavation of Lára's remains, she hadn't raised any objections. She was exhausted, but her whole body was thrumming with so much nervous excitement that she couldn't go to bed. Instead, once she and Margrét had had hot showers and changed into dry clothes, they joined Jökull and Nanna in the sitting room, where they listened to a radio concert by the symphony orchestra until midnight, then put on a video.

At long last, the doorbell rang.

Jökull went to answer, and Sunna got up and followed him.

Inspector Snorri was standing on the steps, accompanied by a man Sunna recognized from photographs in the papers.

'Good evening.' Snorri had promised to drop by as soon as matters were clearer. 'This is Kristján Kristjánsson, who was in charge of the original investigation.'

'You must be Sunna,' Kristján said.

'Yes, I am.'

'Won't you come in?' Jökull interjected.

'Yes, thanks,' Kristján said. 'I met your brother,' he continued, his eyes on Sunna. 'I was shocked to hear what happened to him. Please accept my condolences.'

'Thank you.'

The doubts had been piling up in her mind as the hours passed. Had she and Margrét made a mistake? Should they have brought the necklace back with them? Supposing it hadn't in fact been Lára's necklace? Could the bones have belonged to someone else entirely? She'd also been tormented by fear that someone might reach the island before the police and dispose of the evidence.

'Well, anyway.' Snorri cleared his throat. 'To cut a long story short, I believe Lára has indeed been found. It's astonishing, quite frankly.'

Sunna caught her breath.

'So it's definitely Lára, then?'

'All the evidence suggests that it is. Sadly, the physical remains and the necklace are consistent with it being the girl. Naturally, we'll need to carry out a more thorough examination, but we're now working on the assumption that Lára is dead; that she lost her life on Viðey and was buried there.'

'She's been hidden there all these years,' Kristján said, more to himself than to the others. 'I've spent more than three decades of my life searching for her.' He sighed.

'It's safe to say that the investigation has been re-opened, and we're glad to have you on board, Kristján,' Snorri said. 'We'll be putting all our energy into finding out what happened.'

'What about Valur?'

'I'm afraid it looks as if your brother's death could well be part of the same case. I think we'll be examining them both in parallel from now on. His death is still unexplained, but we'll now be giving more weight to the account of the witness who claimed he was pushed in front of the bus. It's not inconceivable that he was murdered to stop him investigating any further. Because he'd obviously got pretty close to the truth, like you.'

'Do you think Sunna could be in any danger?' Margrét asked suddenly.

Snorri didn't seem to have considered this. 'Hmm, I doubt it. Though we can never be too careful. Then again, we've got the body now, so disposing of you wouldn't serve much purpose, Sunna. The truth has quite literally been brought to the surface.'

'For the most part, yes,' she replied, trying to sound calm, though Margrét's words had sent a frisson of fear through her. 'But, on the other hand, we still don't know who's behind it . . .'

'Have you made any progress with that?' Snorri asked gravely.

Up to now, Sunna had kept most of her speculation to herself, never quite convinced that she was on the right track. Besides, she had learned from Valur that good journalists keep their cards close to their chest. She was determined to write that article; nothing had changed there. But she could hardly withhold information from the police for much longer.

'I've been looking into it, yes,' she said quietly. 'I understand there was a gang of friends who had regular gatherings on the island. Friends of Óttar's.'

It dawned on her that Jökull and Nanna were listening. She would have to tread carefully, but it was too late for her to withdraw her comment now.

'When was this?' Snorri asked.

'Definitely over the summer of 1955, and it seems likely that they continued the following year, when Lára disappeared. They used to have monthly get-togethers on Friday evenings, but Valur received a tip-off that Lára had died on a Saturday evening. My guess is that they met on the Saturday on that occasion and that some-thing happened. One of the men, I don't know which, had pestered the girl who worked there as a maid the previous summer . . .'

Snorri's face was the picture of surprise. 'Who were these men?' he asked sharply.

Sunna shot a glance at Kristján, who was sitting with shoulders bowed. Was it possible that he had pursued this same lead thirty years ago, only to lose his way in a maze of dead ends?

'Well, Óttar, obviously . . . And several others, I believe. But I warn you that this is partly guesswork, based on my brother's notes and—'

'Go on. We need the names and, naturally, we'll be needing your brother's papers too.'

Sunna felt a moment's reluctance to give up the men's identities: she'd been hoping to make a splash with them in her article. It was Thursday evening now – or rather the early hours of Friday morning – and that gave her less than a week to write the piece if she wanted to publish it in the next issue of *Vikubladid*. It was the only place she'd even consider. In Valur's honour.

'Well,' she said after a pause, 'I believe there were four of them: Óttar, then a developer called Högni Eyfjörd—'

'Högni Eyfjörd? Are you sure?' Snorri asked, raising his eyebrows.

'Apparently, though I couldn't get any clear answers out of him.'

'You mean you've actually spoken to him?'

'Yes, but only briefly.'

'Well I never. All right, we'll look into it. Who else?'

'A businessman called Finnur Stephensen, as in the wholesale company. He died recently, but I spoke to his widow.' Sunna knew with sudden certainty that her next move would be to visit Thórdís. She had a powerful intuition that Thórdís was the only person in possession of the truth who would be prepared to speak up. But she wasn't going to share that suspicion with the police just yet. It was as well to keep at least one ace up her sleeve.

'Yes, naturally, I've heard of him,' Snorri said. 'What's your take on this, Kristján?'

'It's certainly interesting,' the veteran detective said quietly. 'I'd need to refresh my memory about whether those names cropped up during the original investigation.'

'Anyone else? One more, was there?'

'Yes, I believe it was Páll Jóhannesson from the city council.'

'Damn it, that's quite a collection of names you've given me,' Snorri said, blowing out a long breath. 'You'll have to excuse me if I have a hard time believing this.'

But Kristján contradicted him, raising his voice for the first time in the conversation: 'We should listen to her. I have a feeling she's on to something.'

'I've spoken to all of them, apart from Finnur, of course,' Sunna said, 'but I expect you'll have more success than me . . . Those old secrets need shaking up.'

'You can say that again. The nation will be on the edge of their seats when we break the news about the body. And they'll want justice. We'll be uncompromising in our search for the truth, Sunna, I can promise you that.'

'When are you going to make it public?'

Snorri didn't answer immediately; he seemed to be mulling it over.

'Tomorrow – or later today, rather – is probably too soon. At the weekend, I imagine. We want to re-examine the scene by daylight to make sure that everything adds up. It'll be futile to try and hush it up for long, though. The public will start asking questions about what the police are up to on Videy, though the summit should give us a brief respite, as all eyes are focused on that at the moment.'

'OK.' Sunna was starting to think with a journalist's calculation. It would have suited her to be allowed to sit on the scoop a little while longer, to be sure that hers would be the first news story about the body. After all, she reasoned, the police could hardly forbid her to write about what she herself had discovered.

Silence fell in the room. Sunna was hit by a wave of fatigue. Perhaps she'd be able to grab a few hours' sleep after all the excitement. Tomorrow she would make a start on the article – and pay a visit to Thórdís.

It was Kristján who unexpectedly broke the silence: 'Thank you.'

Sunna looked up.

'Sunna, I just wanted to thank you. This investigation has been stuck in a rut for thirty years; there's been no movement, no fresh clues, then you – and your brother, and your friend here, of course – actually manage to find the girl. I've always allowed myself to hope that she was alive, though I don't suppose I really believed it in my heart of hearts. It's such a relief that she's turned up, though; I can't tell you what a relief.'

Sunna, lost for a reply, merely smiled at him. She had a vague inkling of what this moment must mean to him.

'Sunna, you'll stay here tonight, with Margrét, won't you?'

It was Jökull who asked. He made it sound more like a command than an invitation.

'Well, I suppose . . .'

Perhaps it was her tiredness stifling all other thoughts, but Sunna felt the appeal of being able to go straight to bed rather than having to head back outside into the cold and dark. She didn't even have a car. And she could feel her prejudices against Margrét's family melting away in the warmth and comfort of their house. It was so homely and welcoming. And, in spite of her antipathy for him, even Jökull improved on acquaintance. The alternative was to return to her lonely little flat in Hlídar. There was another consideration too, though Sunna kept it to herself: she was frightened, scared of being alone tonight. Someone had murdered Lára, and that same person had almost certainly pushed Valur to his death. It seemed they would stop at nothing to prevent the truth from coming to light: supposing they thought Sunna knew too much?

'We'll continue this conversation in the morning, Sunna, if that's all right?' Snorri said, though she knew it wasn't so much a question as an order. She would have to make a formal statement, hand over all the evidence, take them through every stage of the search for Lára, tell them about Júlía . . . She hadn't mentioned her yet, and no one had asked.

'Yes, that sounds fine. Late afternoon would be better, if that's all right with you.'

'Of course. You get some rest. From now on, we'll be bearing the brunt of the investigation and you can afford to relax.'

The two policemen said their goodbyes.

'I think I'd like to accept the invitation,' Sunna said in an undertone to Margrét. 'To stay the night, if that's OK?'

'I wouldn't hear of anything else.'

'I can easily sleep on the sofa if—'

'You can have the room next to mine,' Margrét interrupted. 'It's the biggest guestroom.'

The biggest guestroom . . . Yet another reminder that for this family money had never been an issue.

Sunna's thoughts strayed to her own parents. She ought to have phoned them and filled them in on the events of the evening, but that could wait. She needed some sleep, and she'd have to summon up her courage for that conversation. Besides, she didn't have any answers for them yet about what had happened to Valur. The phone call would have to wait until tomorrow. Everything could wait until tomorrow.

'Sleep in as late as you like, Sunna,' Margrét said. 'Then you can finish the article.'

'The article?' Jökull asked, pouncing on this.

'Sunna's writing about Lára. She's finishing the work that Valur started.'

'Is she, now?' Jökull said. 'For Dagbjartur's paper?' He frowned, betraying how little regard he had for *Vikubladid*.

'Yes,' Sunna said. She pictured herself going to see the editor on Monday or Tuesday to present him with the finished piece – a front-page scoop, by Sunna Róbertsdóttir and Valur Róbertsson. And while she was about it, she would ask if he had a job for her, until the end of this year, at least. Because her mind was made up. There could be no turning back now. Elías Mar would be shelved while she gave journalism a go.

The world of newspapers appeared to her now in a rosy glow.

As a way out of the dark.

1986

10 October

Sunna could barely crawl out of bed on Friday, she was so mentally and physically drained after the exertions of the previous night. It was getting on for twelve when she stirred and past one in the afternoon before she finally dragged herself up. She had been determined that her first act would be to ring Thórdís or go round to her house, but there was no answer when she tried her number, and then the police called and asked her to come in and make a formal statement.

She and Margrét went to the police station together. The process of taking their statements took longer than Sunna would have dreamed possible and somehow it was evening before they were done.

'Shall we drop in on Thórdís?' she asked Margrét as they drove away from the police station.

'It's far too late. It can't do any harm to wait until tomorrow, can it?'

Sunna shrugged. She was still shattered.

After a pause, Margrét went on: 'Look, shouldn't we leave it alone for a bit, Sunna? We've found Lára. Isn't it up to the police to do the rest?'

It was then that Sunna realized she would have to talk to Thórdís on her own. She needed to get to the bottom of this mystery once and for all, without interference from anyone else.

Instead of responding to Margrét's question, she asked: 'Listen, could you possibly give me a lift home once I've picked up my stuff from your house? I left my coat there, and . . .'

'Why don't you stay with us over the weekend, Sunna? You could do with a rest. You got a good night's sleep in that big bed, didn't you?'

'Yes, sure. But I don't want to—'

'Don't be silly. We could go to the cinema this evening if you like, to the eleven p.m. showing . . .'

'Tomorrow would be better. As it is, I'd only conk out during the film.'

Sunna's thoughts darted briefly to Gunnar. She would have to fill him in on everything that had been happening, but not quite yet. That could wait.

She was so tired.

Tomorrow, she thought. For tonight, she would accept Margrét's invitation.

The evening in Gardabær was very pleasant, in the embrace of that warm family atmosphere that Sunna had been missing since she left home. The TV and radio burbling away in the background – with wall-to-wall coverage of the Reagan–Gorbachev summit – and a late supper for her and Margrét when they eventually got in, and later the aroma of coffee spreading through the house, served with doughnut twists and crisps . . . Everything the way it should be. No heaps of dirty laundry on the floor or half-empty fridge.

Yet, every now and then, she was assailed by a fit of dread that was hard to shake off.

Somewhere out there Valur's murderer was still on the loose.

1986

11 October

Sunna lay awake for a long time. She kept thinking she could hear the rumbling echo of Jökull's voice, but when she sat up and strained her ears, there was silence. When she did finally drift off, it was into a deep and dreamless sleep.

Next morning she surfaced at nine, feeling groggy and only half-awake. The family were up already. Margrét and her mother, Nanna, were sitting at the kitchen table and there was a smell of toast and bacon in the air.

'Good morning,' Margrét said cheerfully. 'Did you sleep well?'

'Very well, thanks.'

'Daddy's gone into town, it's the big day.'

'Sorry?'

'Reagan and Gorbachev, of course. With any luck he'll get to see them today. It's the first meeting of the summit.'

'Oh, yes, of course.' Sunna had managed to forget all about the historic event. Since opening her eyes, she'd had no thoughts of anything but Lára.

'Would you like something to eat?'

'Please. Toast and some cheese would be great, if that's OK.'

'Make yourself at home.' Margrét smiled.

'There's someone I need to meet later,' Sunna said. 'Is there any chance you're going into town or . . . ?'

Nanna replied: 'We can lend you a car, Sunna. We've got three just sitting in the drive. You can take my old one – we haven't got round to selling it yet.'

Sunna accepted the offer. She simply had to finish the job by getting hold of Thórdís. She was convinced that the actress must be Júlía and that she had a story to tell. That her husband's death had changed something, making her want to atone for the sins of others. She couldn't have foreseen the results: Lára had indeed been found, but at the cost of Valur's life.

After breakfast Sunna had tried ringing again, but Thórdís hadn't answered the phone.

Now she was standing in front of the woman's house on Laugarásvegur. It was raining and miserably cold. Parked in the drive was a new-looking Mercedes. The car, the detached house were clear symbols of the couple's success. They had gone far in life, Finnur in the wholesale business and Thórdís in the theatre, everything as it should have been. Or was it? They had been silent for thirty years, leaving Lára's parents to suffer every day, though it had been in their power to put an end to their agonizing uncertainty, however wretched the truth was. Perhaps that had been the very reason for Thórdís's phone call to Valur – because it must have been Thórdís who called. She had a warm heart, Sunna could sense that, yet she had kept her mouth shut all these years until her husband died. Sunna wondered if she had been protecting him, or a secret that belonged to Finnur and his friends? Could Finnur have asked her on his deathbed to reveal the truth? Or had she begged his permission to do so? And who had killed Lára? That was the big question. If Sunna could find out the truth about that, she would also have the answer to a far more important question: who had pushed Valur to his death? Her brother, that good, kind, beautiful boy . . .

The obvious answer to the first question was surely Finnur himself. He had killed Lára. Thórdís knew but hadn't been able to speak out until after he'd died, when she had tried to salvage what could be salvaged.

That theory would work, except that it was impossible.

Because it wasn't Finnur who'd killed Valur. That was self-evident.

Sunna wasn't going anywhere until she got some answers.

She rang the doorbell and waited.

There was a large garden in front of the house and no doubt a similarly generous amount of space behind it. Although it was autumn, there were signs everywhere that the trees and flowers were lovingly tended. There was still the odd splash of colour in the flower beds, the late blooms refusing to admit defeat to winter, and the red leaves on the shrubs lent a touch of warmth in the icy wind. The house, which was painted pale grey, looked well kept too.

Sunna raised the door knocker in case the bell hadn't worked. She couldn't stand here in the rain all day. In the worst case, she would wait in the car. She took a couple of steps backwards and saw that the lights were on upstairs. Thórdís was definitely home. She couldn't hide for ever.

When, shivering now, Sunna started back towards the warmth and shelter of the car, she heard the door opening. Thórdís was revealed in the gap, posing like an actress on the stage, either making her grand entrance or accepting applause at the end of a successful performance. She was wearing a red silk dressing gown, her hair falling in waves over her shoulders like that of a much younger woman, glamorous but dignified, unquestionably the star of the show.

'Sunna,' she said, managing to convey so much with the one word: that Sunna was welcome, that she'd been expecting her, and, simultaneously, that she was very the last person she wanted to see.

'Can I come in?' Sunna asked. She was soaking now.

'I don't think we have any choice but to save you from the rain,' Thórdís said wryly. 'Come in and take off your wet things.'

'We can talk out here, if you like.'

'Don't be ridiculous. Come in. Finnur and I always invite guests into the drawing room.'

Sunna took off her shoes and dripping coat, then followed Thórdís into her formal drawing room.

For an instant, she felt as if she was in the middle of a play, but there was no audience and she had no idea who was directing the drama. But one thing was clear: Thórdís was the leading lady.

'*Rómeó and Júlía*,' Sunna said, once they were seated. It had belatedly occurred to her: Júlía was the Icelandic name for Shakespeare's heroine.

'*Rómeó and Júlía*,' Thórdís repeated.

'You played Júlía.'

'Yes, and I played her well, though I say so myself. That was a long time ago, though. I've lost my youthful bloom, Sunna. I'll never play Júlía again.'

There was such inexpressible sadness in her voice that Sunna was caught unawares. She found herself touched by pity for the woman, when in fact she should be thinking about Lára and Valur. She mustn't let Thórdís play on her feelings. Wasn't it possible that Valur might still be alive if Thórdís had come forward earlier and told the truth?

Or, alternatively, if Thórdís had let sleeping dogs lie and Valur had never received that phone call from her? Then there wouldn't have been any media frenzy about him being on the verge of solving the mystery.

Sunna felt suddenly uncertain about how to approach Thórdís. She couldn't tell whether the woman was an ally or an enemy, but then perhaps the theatre was all about that kind of deception.

'When you rang my brother, you called yourself Júlía, didn't you?'

Thórdís rose to her feet and started pacing to and fro,

not saying a word, a magnificent figure in her silk dressing gown. Then she sat down again, leaned forwards and gazed deep into Sunna's eyes: one actor, one audience member.

'Sunna, I know you've found Lára. The police came round to see me yesterday. Isn't that enough? Can't we just leave it at that?'

'I don't think you quite realize the seriousness of the situation,' Sunna countered, her voice trembling with emotion. 'My brother is dead. That happened after you spoke to him. You sent him a letter. That's why he's dead. Someone pushed him in front of a bus. I could repeat that again and again to the end of time, but it wouldn't change anything. Valur is dead. You've lost Finnur, and that must hurt. I've lost my brother and it hurts so much I can't begin to put it into words, Thórdís. I don't think I'll ever be able to put it into words.'

Sunna's sigh was almost a groan. She was utterly exhausted, hollowed out, empty. She'd slept so badly since Valur died, her mind working in overdrive all day and half the night. All she lived for now was to discover the truth, but suddenly she didn't know if she could keep going any longer. Her last reserves of energy had been used up.

When Thórdís didn't respond, Sunna seized the chance to add: 'And Lára's parents, they lost their daughter. Have you met them?'

Thórdís shook her head. 'No, I've never met them.'

'Then maybe you should go round for coffee one day. They're just ordinary people who've had to struggle in life. I don't suppose they live in an expensive house like this. And they've been grieving for their daughter for thirty years. That's a long time, Thórdís. What have you been doing in that time?'

'I haven't been happy. As you can probably guess.'

'Yes, that's clear,' Sunna said. 'And I know that you yourself didn't do anything to harm Lára. That was somebody else. But staying silent can have consequences. Lára was murdered, you told my brother that. Who murdered her?'

Thórdís buried her face in her hands. 'The poor child.'

'Who murdered her?' Sunna repeated.

Thórdís didn't answer.

'Was it Finnur? Was it your husband?'

'Finnur? No, no, no. He . . .' Her voice broke. Sunna wasn't sure if the play was over or this was merely a different scene. Not that it mattered, since Thórdís's life seemed to be one big performance. But now, apparently, she had made up her mind to talk.

'Sunna, you're not recording this, are you? Everything we say here has to remain between the two of us.'

Thórdís fixed Sunna with a stern look and Sunna shook her head. 'I'm not recording this.'

'Finnur was a good man, I can assure you of that. He didn't necessarily keep good company, but sometimes the bonds of friendship are too strong to be broken. Shared interests, shared secrets. Finnur was a good husband. We didn't have children, but we had each other. And he never hurt a soul. Would never have hurt a fly. He was a tough businessman, which is why we were well off, but . . . we were never OK, though, not really. We were never short of money, the wholesale business is thriving and will out-live us both, but there was always this shadow hanging over everything, Sunna – Lára's shadow. We never dis-cussed it, though we could talk about everything else and always enjoyed each other's company. Finnur was simply in the wrong place at the wrong time. That's how it is sometimes – everything hinges on the cruel irony of fate. That's how it was, Sunna . . .'

'Who murdered Lára?' Sunna asked in harsh voice. She was determined to play this game to the end. She wasn't going to let Thórdís have the last word. She wasn't going to feel sorry for her, not now, not yet.

'I don't know . . . I can't . . . What difference does it make now?'

'It makes *all* the difference!' Sunna had raised her voice. 'The case won't be closed until justice is done. Until someone admits responsibility. They owe it to Lára's par-ents. To me and my parents, my mum and dad. You have to do the right thing.'

'Do the right thing? Well . . .'

'It's what Finnur would have wanted, isn't it?'

'Yes.'

'What did Finnur say?'

'He told me about it immediately after it happened. I wasn't there, you see. And we never spoke of it again. There was nothing we could say. They had promised one another to keep quiet because the girl was dead anyway. That couldn't be undone. And Finnur got trapped in the silence, as we all did. Not a day has passed, Sunna, when I haven't wanted to call Lára's parents and tell them what happened. But I couldn't betray Finnur.' Thórdís fell silent, then cleared her throat. 'You know, it was actually the last thing my darling Finnur said to me before he died. He mentioned Videy, and then I knew I would have to do something. I'm so sorry to have mixed your brother up in it, so dreadfully sorry, but somehow it seemed the most obvious thing to do . . . Yes, it was the most obvious . . .'

'And now he's dead.'

'It's a tragedy, all of it, a tragedy.'

'One thing I don't understand,' Sunna said. 'How come the police never found out that Finnur and his friends were on the island that weekend, visiting Óttar? How come they were never interviewed? Surely whoever ferried them over would have told the police?'

'Óttar had his own boat,' Thórdís replied. 'He used to pick them up himself and take them back to the mainland after their parties, so it didn't matter that he delivered them home in the early hours of Sunday morning. Us wives were the only ones who ever knew they'd been there.'

'Why didn't you both come clean, Thórdís?'

'Life is so complicated, so complicated – all those vested interests. The slightest mistake can have such far-reaching consequences . . . Finnur was tangled up in a web that he couldn't break free of – that we couldn't break free of. The strands stretch out in every direction. One for all and all for one. It was a blood brotherhood, like in the sagas. The only thing they didn't do was actually mix their blood. They helped each other and they all did well out of it. We built up a thriving business. Politics, construction . . .' She broke off abruptly as though she was afraid of saying too much. 'Not one of them dared to stick his neck out and break with the group.'

'Who killed her, Thórdís? If you tell me that, everything will be better.'

Not that Sunna believed this for a minute.

'He attacked her and was going to . . . I can't even talk about it . . . He wanted to take advantage of her, but she fought back. The first the others – his friends – knew about it was that she was dead. He'd gripped her too tight round the neck, he said, pressed too tight . . . They were all drunk, that's just the way it was. And one of them – not Finnur – had the idea of burying her in the churchyard – so it wouldn't ruin all their lives.' She laughed, an icy, uncanny sound. 'But it ruined all our lives, anyway, like drinking poison every bloody day.'

So Finnur was innocent. That's how Thórdís told the story, that's what she wanted to believe. Sunna doubted it had been as simple as that but decided this wasn't the moment to argue with Thórdís's interpretation. She needed Thórdís. And what she needed from her was a name. A single name . . .

Sunna had to finish this herself. She wasn't going to involve the police at this stage, though they would have to be brought in eventually.

She was so tantalizingly close to the truth.

'Óttar, it has to have been Óttar,' she burst out. 'It was his house, he was the person with the most authority on the island. His wife was safely out of the way upstairs, and I suppose he lost control. Assaulted the girl and . . .'

Thórdís didn't say a word for a moment. Then: 'I can't . . . We'll have to solve this some other way, Sunna.'

'Was it Óttar?'

But Thórdís wouldn't answer the question. Instead, she returned to the theme of her guilt: 'I was so desperate to ring them – Lára's parents, I mean. I should have done it years ago. But sometimes you just don't have the courage. They had a right to know where she was. Sometimes I look in the mirror and don't recognize the person I see there. I was better than this. I don't know why it's taken me so long.'

'It's time to end this, once and for all.'

'Sunna, you have to put yourself in my position. Finnur didn't do anything wrong, apart from keeping quiet. He didn't kill anyone. He was just afraid. The boys had always stood together, ever since their schooldays, and it was never a realistic choice for Finnur to betray . . . to betray . . .'

Sunna wanted to scream at Thórdís. Couldn't she understand what a twisted view she had of the facts? She seemed to have convinced herself that she and Finnur had never had a choice, and not only that but that they hadn't done anything wrong, though Lára had been murdered, almost under Finnur's nose. She'd been buried in another woman's grave – and her murderer had walked free. Yet Finnur had held his tongue and so had Thórdís, right up until the moment she decided to make that phone call to Valur.

And the murderer was still walking free.

Wasn't it possible that Finnur had in fact been the murderer, in spite of Thórdís's vehement denials?

That could be why she hadn't said anything until after he was dead, that could be why she didn't want to point the finger at anyone else, because there was no one else . . .

'When did Finnur tell you what happened?'

'Almost as soon as he got home. He was a changed man afterwards, you know. Carrying the weight of a secret like that destroys a person. You probably don't understand that yet, and I can see that you don't have any sympathy for me. That's fine. We're very different, and you're so young. You'll learn, in time.' There was a patronizing note in her voice. 'But I'm not after anyone's sympathy. I'm of no importance in this matter.'

'Thórdís, did Finnur kill her? He's dead – you don't need to lie for him any more.'

At this, Thórdís lost her temper. 'I've answered that question already, perfectly clearly,' she snapped. 'My husband didn't kill anyone. I swear it.'

'Yet you won't help me. All I need is a name, then I can go to the police. Then there's a chance of justice being done.'

'I need time to think. Stop trying to rush me.'

'Óttar?'

Thórdís shook her head. 'I asked for time to think.'

'Högni? It would be no surprise to anyone if he had something to hide . . .'

'I'm not saying a word, Sunna. Not now. You can say all the names in the world if you like, but it won't do any good. It's not important who was on Videy.'

'It's *vitally* important, Thórdís. *Vitally* important.'

Thórdís got to her feet.

'I need more time, Sunna. Thank you for your visit. It was helpful to talk things through.'

'Páll . . . ?' Sunna continued stubbornly, scrutinizing Thórdís's face for a reaction every time she produced a name, but the woman was icily impassive, decades of acting experience coming to the fore.

Then, as if there had been a sudden gear change, Thórdís seemed to relent.

'I agree with you, Sunna, if that makes you feel any better.'

'What?' Sunna said, confused.

'You said I should do the right thing,' Thórdís went on. 'That was a good point. This matter has to be finished – and I'm going to finish it. I'm—'

Sunna interrupted her: 'Does that mean you're going to tell me the truth?'

'I'm going to sort out this mess in my own way. I'm going to confront . . .' She broke off. Had she almost let the name slip? 'I'm going to confront him and persuade him to give himself up.'

'And you think that will work?'

'I'm sure it will.'

'But what if . . . he . . . What if he killed my brother too? Do you really think it'll be that simple?'

'Trust me, Sunna. And now I'm afraid I'll have to say goodbye.'

Sunna rose slowly to her feet. 'Why not just tell me, and I'll go straight to the police? Then they can take care of everything.'

'No, that's not how it works. I want to keep Finnur out of this. He doesn't deserve to have his name in the papers. And what we've discussed here today is confidential, of course, as I said at the beginning. No one must know what we've talked about. I'll deny this conversation ever took place if you try to report it.'

Sunna had to admit defeat. There was no way of budging the woman from her course. 'Thanks for agreeing to talk to me,' she said dully.

'I didn't exactly have a choice.' Thórdís smiled.

'Just be careful.'

'Careful?'

'You said you were going to confront a murderer.'

'I'm not afraid of anything, Sunna.'

1986

11 October

Sunna sat in the car for a while, feeling completely at a loss. The conversation had developed in a totally unexpected direction. Thórdís had said far more than Sunna had dared hope, yet she had refused to reveal the one thing that mattered.

So they *had* been there, the group of friends, on Videy, thirty years ago, drinking heavily, and one of them had turned out to be a dangerous predator. Dangerous enough to murder a young girl. Yet they had all kept quiet. That's how it worked, one for all and all for one. What was it Thórdís had said? Like blood brothers in a Viking saga.

They had got on with their lives as if nothing had happened; they were in their sixties now – those who were still alive – all of them comfortably established. They had helped each other to accumulate wealth and build up their networks of useful connections. And all that time Lára

341

had been lying alone in her cold grave. The murder had been horrific enough in itself, but the complicity of the men – and Thórdís, and perhaps the other wives, Ólöf and Gunnlaug, too – was no less appalling. Their secret had been safely buried and forgotten, while Lára's parents were left empty-handed, never knowing what had happened to their daughter.

Sunna wondered what on earth she ought to do now.

She studied the house, that beautiful home; Thórdís and Finnur had presented such a smooth, flawless appearance to the world. But no chain is stronger than its weakest link and now that link had buckled and possibly even broken. It was obvious that Thórdís was tortured by guilt, and no wonder, but did she really deserve any praise for coming forward now, so long after the event? Sunna had mixed feelings; on the one hand, she was grateful to Thórdís for exposing what had happened on Videy, even though she had chosen to do so in this eccentric manner, but, on the other, Thórdís had triggered a series of events that had probably cost Valur his life.

Sunna tried to marshal her thoughts. Should she go back to Margrét's house, or home to her flat? Or straight to the police and tell them the whole sorry tale? The puzzle had almost been completed; all that remained was for someone to supply the last piece. The police would almost certainly be interviewing the three surviving men that day anyway, if they hadn't already done so. One of them must surely confess.

Högni, Óttar or Páll?

She didn't like any of them.

Carrying around a secret like that for three decades must have taken its toll, but she doubted they had ever been truly nice men or noble characters in the first place.

Which of them had lost control? Assaulted a fifteen-year-old girl, throttled her and watched her die?

And who had pushed Valur to his death? Who had *murdered* her brother, and how would she react when she found out?

The only course open to her now was to go to the police, to speak to Snorri – and perhaps Kristján too – and report her conversation with Thórdís, point by point. Sunna had done everything she realistically could to solve the case.

She turned the key in the ignition and the radio quickened to life. The announcer on the ten o'clock news was saying that the most prestigious news agencies in the world had now congregated on Borgartún, waiting for the two world leaders to appear on the steps outside Höfdi House. Never had Reykjavík played a more prominent role in the international press.

Just then, she noticed that Thórdís had emerged from the house and was walking towards her car, apparently totally unaware that Sunna was still sitting there, watching her. The actress had changed into a black dress and white coat, cutting as impressive a figure as the queen on a chess board, ready for her next move.

Sunna thought quickly. The one obvious course of action was to follow Thórdís, who wouldn't recognize the car and would presumably be unsuspecting.

If, as she'd said, Thórdís was going to face up to the murderer, Sunna should be able to find out his identity by following her.

Thórdís drove off down Laugarásvegur, then turned left into Sundlaugavegur.

The news had finished and a cheery DJ was introducing a brand-new song, 'Moscow, Moscow', written by the Icelandic group Strax in honour of the occasion.

Moscow, Moscow, hurry up, it's almost news at nine . . .

As she listened to the catchy tune, it dawned on Sunna that Thórdís was heading in the direction of Borgartún and Höfdi House. Could she in fact be on her way to catch a glimpse of the two leaders?

Moscow, Moscow, can't you hear me, waiting on the line . . .

At the junction with Borgartún, however, it became clear that the road was closed to traffic. Thórdís made a U-turn, then parked illegally on the pavement. Sunna pulled into a spot not far away, all the time keeping a close eye on the actress.

Thórdís was definitely making for Höfdi House. This was very odd. Given the urgency of confronting Lára's killer, it seemed unthinkable that she could be taking time out to go and watch the events at Höfdi. But Sunna wasn't going to risk letting the woman out of her sight, despite the rain that was now being lashed against the car windows by the wind. She snatched a glance at her watch: a quarter past ten. The view that met her outside made her feel as if she was in some big foreign metropolis. There were police officers on every corner, no doubt accompanied by members of the American and

Soviet secret services. Countless cars, limousines and four-by-fours lined the road. Getting out into the blustery wind and rain, Sunna made her way towards Höfdi, catching sight of the horde of reporters as she drew closer. The eyes of the world were trained on Reykjavík all right.

Although Thórdís never once looked over her shoulder, Sunna kept at a discreet distance behind. She saw the woman approach a policeman and speak to him. Could Thórdís be intending to go to the police herself? No, clearly she was trying to gain access to the closed-off area. And, to Sunna's astonishment, she managed it, because now she was through the barrier.

Sunna was quite close to the house herself by now but couldn't see the two leaders anywhere, only bodyguards, police and a crowd of Icelandic politicians and officials, some of whom, though not all, she recognized. Everyone was waiting for Reagan and Gorbachev. The world was holding its breath . . . Could this meeting succeed in bringing the Cold War to an end?

Had Thórdís really come all this way just to see them with her own eyes, or did she have another motive?

If she had come here to confront somebody, it could only be the city councillor, Páll.

Sunna recalled her uncomfortable meeting with him in his office. Her gaze swept the crowd, but she couldn't see him anywhere, not at first glance, though the members of the city council must be here, like the rest of the establishment.

Could it really have been the respectable city councillor

who had watched Lára give up the ghost, then talked his cronies into burying her secretly in the churchyard? The thought made Sunna shudder.

She had now reached the security cordon that had briefly delayed Thórdís before, and was faced with the same police officer.

'This is a closed area,' he said, his expression grumpy in the rain.

'I'm here for *Vikubladid*,' she said firmly.

'*Vikubladid?* Oh, OK, hang on ... Have you got a press pass?'

And then it came back to her that she had slipped Valur's press ID into her bag when she cleared his desk at the office. She rooted around and finally found it, taking care to keep her fingers over the name.

The policeman nodded. 'OK, but stay well back. No one's allowed too close.'

'Will do.'

Then she saw from the sudden surge in the crowd that something big was happening.

A black car drove up to Höfdi and out stepped none other than Ronald Reagan.

Sunna halted, her breath catching in her throat.

She had never expected to see the president of the United States with her own eyes, to be a first-hand witness to such historic events.

The president greeted the press with a smile, then continued up to the house without answering any questions.

Looking round, afraid that she might have lost Thórdís,

Sunna saw her still worming her way through the throng. She started trying to work her way after her. But a moment later a hush fell on the crowd again as another car drew up to the house, carrying Mikhail Gorbachev, of course. Reagan reappeared on the steps and greeted the Soviet General Secretary. Sunna stood there as if turned to stone, watching. It felt so unreal.

When she snapped back to the present and flung a frantic look around, Thórdís had vanished.

Hell!

Had she lost her?

How could she have been so careless?

She scanned her surroundings but could see nothing but a wall of police officers in the direction where Thórdís had been heading. The press had begun to move and disperse as well, since they couldn't expect any more photos of the leaders for a while.

Where on earth could the woman have gone?

And then Sunna caught sight of Thórdís's white coat, vanishing inside a modern office building on the other side of Borgartún from Höfdi. The crowd was tightly packed there and it was hard to move anywhere fast, but Sunna did her best, squeezing between people and cars. Her heart was pounding, partly for fear of losing Thórdís, partly for fear of what would happen next. She might be about to come face to face with Valur's killer.

It took her two or three precious minutes to reach the building. She swept through the door, without pausing to ask for permission, and discovered a hubbub of conversation inside, with English, Russian and Icelandic voices vying to be heard, belonging to reporters from all over the world, she guessed. This must be the press centre for the summit meeting. Which begged the question, what could Thórdís possibly want here? Were there offices based in the building? Or could the city councillor Páll be here for an interview, perhaps?

She looked around. Unable to spot Thórdís anywhere, she set off at random, peering into room after room. Everywhere there was noise and bustle; she overheard snatches of conversations, all relating to the summit, news or pictures. And she sensed yet again the buzz, the appeal of this life. It would be amazing to be here in a professional capacity, though of course not every day in the life of an Icelandic journalist could be this thrilling.

Thórdís seemed to have vanished into thin air.

There was only one office left in this part of the building, in the far corner. The door was unmarked. Sunna felt a sudden rush of foreboding. The sensation was similar to the one she had experienced on Videy, an intuition that the truth was just around the corner. For a second she raised her fist to knock, then came to her senses and ripped the door open without any warning.

And there was Thórdís, her face a mask of terror, cornered by a man who appeared to be pinning her against the wall. He was in mid-flow – Sunna didn't hear exactly what he was saying, but his voice was raised – doubtless he was confident that the clamour outside would drown out any sound – and, with all eyes on Höfdi, there would be no witnesses if a dark deed was committed in a windowless office on Borgartún.

The man's head jerked round as Sunna burst into the room, leaving the door wide open behind her.

As his eyes, widening in alarm, met hers, she saw that now it was his turn to be afraid.

1986

11 October

Sunna froze.

For an instant, her brain couldn't process what she was seeing.

In front of her stood Dagbjartur.

'Sunna . . . Sunna . . .' he stammered.

She had seen, for a split second, the savage fury in his eyes, but now his expression was that of a man who had no moves left, who knew the game was up.

Four or five.

Hell!

That's what Gréta had said.

Óttar and some of his friends. *Four or five, no more than that.*

Foolishly, it hadn't occurred to Sunna that there could have been a name missing from the list.

Óttar, Högni, Páll, Finnur – and Dagbjartur.

She stumbled a few steps backwards, out of the room, without taking her eyes off the editor for a second.

She stopped the first person who was passing, a woman in a hurry.

'Sorry, but could you phone the police for me or find a police officer outside and ask him to come here at once?'

'What?'

'Please, it's extremely urgent. I need a policeman here now.' Sunna's voice and manner were more calmly assertive than she would have believed possible in the circumstances, but she mustn't falter now. Not when she was confronting Valur's killer; when she had looked him straight in the eye and felt the grief and rage fighting to break through to the surface.

Turning back into the room, taking care to block the doorway, she said with cool authority: 'Leave Thórdís alone.' She sensed that she had the upper hand now. She wasn't afraid of Dagbjartur – it was too late for him to try anything.

He let out a groan, his eyes darting around frantically in search of an escape route, and ran a hand over his bald scalp. It was then that Sunna remembered something else Gréta had said: the man who harassed her had had red hair. The description didn't fit any of the other four men – unless Högni was a redhead under the hair dye – but perhaps Dagbjartur's hair could have been red before he lost it?

'I wasn't going to hurt her,' he said lamely.

'You attacked me, you bastard!' Thórdís shouted, her fear dropping away to be replaced by outrage.

It was then that Sunna knew the game was well and

truly up. Thórdís wasn't going to protect Dagbjartur any more, and he must have realized the fact.

'First Lára, then Valur, now . . . you nearly did for Thórdís too.'

'It wasn't like that, I wasn't going to . . .'

'You attacked Lára on Videy, we know all about that. We've found her body.'

Dagbjartur stared at her, his eyes bulging, then abruptly hid his face in his hands.

The minutes were ticking by, but still no policeman appeared. Sunna stood braced in the doorway, waiting.

'Did you and your friends bury her together?'

He nodded.

'In Arnfrídur's grave.'

'Some woman, yes. Arnfrídur Leifsdóttir. We just picked her at random.'

'And Valur was on the trail.'

'Thanks to Thórdís,' Dagbjartur said, his voice thickening with anger again.

'All of you?'

'What?'

'Did you all take part in burying the body? In covering up the crime?'

'Yes, it was the only thing we could do. Finnur always found it the hardest to get over. He was a good man. Kind-hearted, but weak.' Dagbjartur turned to meet Thórdís's eye. 'But even he didn't say no to the opportunities, to the money. We stuck together.' His eyes moved back to Sunna. 'They're all as guilty as I am, those friends of mine. I gave them good press; they financed my papers.

Páll pulled all the political strings he could for us, Finnur and Högni raked in the profits, everyone played their part.'

'But Lára died.'

'It happened in the heat of the moment. Tragic, I know. She was so young, so beautiful.'

'And then Valur.'

This time there was a delay before Dagbjartur answered.

'You've got to believe me, Sunna – I didn't mean to hurt your brother, you've got to . . .' Dagbjartur broke off momentarily, too choked up to speak. 'I just wanted to keep an eye on him. I was worried, afraid he'd get too close to the truth. I couldn't let that happen. It even crossed my mind to go out to Videy and dig up the body, but . . . It just wasn't realistic – it would have been too big a risk. Valur seemed so sure of himself, so convinced he would solve the mystery in time for the next issue, and he'd started mentioning my friends by name. Then . . .' He trailed off again, heaved a deep breath, and continued: 'Then I saw him, standing at a crowded bus stop, and a bus coming full tilt, and I . . . I tripped, and crashed into him – honestly, it was an accident, I never meant to . . .'

'No way was it an accident,' Sunna retorted, her voice icy with disgust and rage. 'You'd prepared it very carefully, hadn't you? You leaked the story to the TV newsdesk that Valur was on the trail so that everyone would know and there would be no reason for suspicion to fall on you. That's true, isn't it? That's what really happened, isn't it, Dagbjartur?'

He didn't answer, but she could tell from the flicker in his eyes that she'd got it right.

It took all her self-discipline to stop herself from attacking the man then and there.

She drew a deep breath, fighting back the tears. This wasn't the time or place to weep for Valur. There was a faint consolation in knowing that Dagbjartur faced a long sentence in jail.

'You were friends,' was all she said, her voice tight.

'He worked for me. You don't go into the newspaper business to make friends. And of course I didn't mean to kill him. I actually gave him the green light to sniff around the bloody case and go delving into the past. But the whole thing spiralled out of control. At first he was just rehashing news from the archives – that happened every few years and didn't bother me: the secret was safely buried and would never come out. There were too many interests at stake – all the other people who knew about it had too much to lose.' He threw a quick glance over his shoulder. 'I didn't know Finnur had blabbed to his wife,' he said contemptuously. 'I should have guessed. The rest of us knew how to keep our mouths shut, though of course Ólöf knew something. That was unavoidable.'

'Did you never, for one minute, think about Lára's parents?'

'What was I supposed to say to them?' Dagbjartur asked in an aggrieved tone. 'That she was dead? They must have realized that. Was I supposed to direct them to Videy, to the grave? People would only have linked it to Óttar, and in the end someone could have made the connection to me, though you and Valur didn't manage that. The good old gang from school . . .'

'What about Valur? Is it no big deal to you that my brother's dead? How does it make you feel?'

Dagbjartur didn't answer.

Thórdís had been standing like a statue while they were speaking, silently watching Dagbjartur and Sunna, her eyes eloquent with emotion. The thought struck Sunna that this was just like another play to the actress. But just then her thoughts were interrupted by a commotion in the corridor behind her and Sunna looked over her shoulder to discover that two police officers had turned up.

'Has something happened?' one of them asked.

'This man . . .' Sunna pointed at Dagbjartur, her finger trembling. 'Dagbjartur Steinsson – he attacked this woman, Thórdís, and . . .'

Then she remembered what Thórdís had said when they met at her house on Laugarásvegur. *Talking to Valur seemed the most obvious thing to do.* She had put it something like that – of course, it had been *because* Valur worked for Dagbjartur.

'Is that true?' the policeman asked. 'Did he attack you?'

Thórdís nodded. 'He certainly did. He tried to kill me.'

'I got here just in time,' Sunna said, the wind suddenly going out of her. She felt utterly depleted. 'And that's not the only thing: Dagbjartur has confessed to two murders as well.'

'I'm sorry?' The policeman looked stunned. 'Murders?'

'Yes,' Sunna replied with icy coolness. 'He killed my

brother, the journalist Valur Róbertsson. And he killed a young girl on Videy in 1956. Her name was Lára Marteinsdóttir.'

'Lára? The girl who disappeared?'

'You'd better speak to two of your colleagues, Snorri Egilsson and Kristján Kristjánsson – they're in charge of the investigation. They need to . . .'

Sunna broke off, her head spinning. Somehow she staggered past Thórdís, past Dagbjartur, and sat down on the floor in the corner. She watched, hazily, as the police officers escorted Dagbjartur out of the room.

Her mind was flooded with memories of Valur, ordinary moments that hadn't been important at the time but meant everything now. His smile, his zeal for his job. Dagbjartur had made a mistake in underestimating Valur. Of course Valur would never have taken on such a big story without doing things properly, and now it was up to her to finish what he had started.

'We're taking Dagbjartur to the police station on Hverfisgata,' one of the policemen said, as they were leaving the room. 'Can you two meet us there?'

'We'll be there,' Thórdís assured him. She turned to Sunna. 'I'm so grateful you came, that you . . . well, you followed me. Didn't you?'

Sunna nodded.

'I rang the paper to speak to Dagbjartur as soon as you'd left,' Thórdís explained. 'They told me I could find him here . . . and . . .'

Sunna closed her eyes again, feeling too weak with reaction to answer.

'Everything's going to be all right, dear,' Thórdís said gently. 'We'll give a statement, then you can go home and rest. Is there someone I can call for you?'

Sunna didn't answer for a moment, then she said: 'Gunnar, yes, you can call Gunnar.' She'd meant to say Margrét but changed her mind at the last minute. 'Gunnar Gunnarsson, who came round to see you with me the first time.'

'Do you know where I can get hold of him? Do you have his number?'

Sunna tried in vain to remember it, but her mind was in too much turmoil. 'He's in the phone book . . . Gunnar Gunnarsson, theology student.'

'We'll sort it out,' Thórdís said.

More than anything, Sunna wanted to go home, to sleep, then, as soon as she'd recovered her strength, to start writing.

But the article would never appear in *Vikubladid*, that much was certain.

1986

1 November

Almost without warning Christmas was around the corner.

Sunna had gone for a walk through the centre of town, lingering for a while in front of the window display of a tourist shop on Hafnarstræti, with its festive decorations, including the thirteen Yule Lads of Icelandic tradition.

She was on her way to her favourite haunt, Café Mokka, but this time, instead of Valur, it would be Gunnar she shared her coffee and waffles with. He had come to be an increasingly important fixture in her life during the last few weeks. She even found it charming when he went on about theology, but then she supposed she'd always had a bit of a crush on him. He'd been by her side the week the world was turned upside down, when Dagbjartur was arrested and the Icelandic people had got to hear the truth.

The evening of the day the article was published, Gunnar had invited Sunna to the theatre. And although she wasn't much of a theatre-goer, she had accepted with alacrity and succeeded for that one evening in forgetting about everything else. For two or three short hours, miraculously, her thoughts hadn't once strayed to Valur or Dagbjartur or Videy.

This evening he had invited her to the last night of *Il Trovatore*, performed by the Icelandic National Opera. Again, this wasn't something Sunna would usually be interested in, but she had let him persuade her. Their relationship was getting off to a slow, unhurried start. She wasn't in any rush, and her article – her and Valur's article – had stirred up such a media storm that she could do without any more excitement for the time being. However, she had managed to convince Gunnar to go out dancing at Hotel Borg after the opera, as it was Saturday night, after all.

In the end she had chosen to publish the article in *Morgunbladid*. Margrét's father, Jökull, had strongly recommended it, and as a result Sunna had agreed to meet the two editors over coffee. They had convinced her that a piece like this – a major story in every sense of the word – belonged in the country's biggest newspaper, and, as a bonus, they had offered her a trial job at the paper, starting in the New Year.

She had sat there listening to their terms with cool composure, aware that she was sitting on the scoop of the year, then asked: 'It'll definitely go on the front page, won't it?' Though she knew perfectly well that the front page of *Morgunbladid* was traditionally reserved for international news.

This had given the editors pause, but eventually one of them replied: 'Yes, of course.' And with that the deal was done.

The story appeared on 18 October, exactly two months after Valur's death. Sunna was allowed to choose the date. In the event, she had to share the Saturday paper and front page with the President of Iceland, who had gone to meet the Pope at the Vatican, but at least she was in good company. The headline was accompanied by three pictures, of Lára, Valur and Sunna, and both brother and sister were credited as the authors.

She had worked day and night to polish the text.

Dagbjartur had confessed, but she hadn't wanted his photo on the cover – in her opinion, the inside pages were good enough for that bastard and his cronies, the accessories to his crime. Ólöf and Thórdís didn't get off lightly either. They all bore a share of the blame for covering up a murder, there was no question of that. Iceland was rocked by the scandal and there was a feeding frenzy in the press after the article appeared. The story was still headline news. Sunna had been interviewed on both TV stations – *the messenger of truth*, one producer had called her – and the case triggered a major debate on the importance of combating corruption in Icelandic society. Politicians from all parties jumped on the bandwagon; Páll had been forced to resign as city councillor, and Högni Eyfjörd had lost contract after contract. From what Sunna had been told, he was facing bankruptcy. They also had the threat hanging over them of being arrested as accessories to a crime. But, incredibly, Thórdís had managed to dodge most of the criticism, presumably because the actress was a national treasure, and Sunna had credited Thórdís with putting her and Valur on the trail, however late in the day.

Now, as Sunna walked through the city centre, she was aware of passers-by recognizing her, surreptitiously watching her and whispering to each other. So this was what it was like to be famous – or as good as. She didn't mind; she reckoned she could get used to it.

Dagbjartur was in custody and *Vikubladid* had not come out since the Reagan–Gorbachev summit. All the staff on the paper had quit, one after the other, as none of them wanted to work for Dagbjartur, and other newspapers had launched investigations into *Vikubladid*'s finances and the alleged funding received from Óttar, Högni and the late Finnur: the five schoolfriends' back-scratching pact had certainly been comprehensive. Dagbjartur had mostly stayed in the shadows, avoiding public links to the others, but it seemed he had used the papers he'd edited to protect all their interests over the years. His one mistake had been to allow Valur to spend so much time on Lára. Disastrous over-confidence, Sunna thought to herself. She had the impression Dagbjartur had believed himself untouchable, confident that the secret that had been successfully hushed up for so long would never come to light. It was possible that he'd also thought it safer to be in control of anything that was written about Lára.

When the extraordinary revelations about Lára's murder appeared, the Icelanders were quick to forget Reagan and Gorbachev, the new TV station, the city anniversary and everything else that had recently dominated the news. But one day, sooner or later, interest in the story would fade. Sunna was ready for that. She planned to take it easy until Christmas, maybe finally pop round for that coffee with Elías Mar, and tinker a bit with her dissertation.

She would give Gunnar a chance too and see where things led.

For the first time since Valur had died, she sensed in herself a stirring of happy anticipation. She was looking forward to Christmas, in spite of everything, and planned to spend the holiday up north in Húsavík with her parents. And in the New Year, she was going to throw herself full tilt into the world of journalism, full of self-confidence and zeal to make a difference.

As for the dissertation, well, she'd finish that one day.

There was no hurry.

Afterword

It was in January 2020, over a lunch to chat about our mutual interest in crime fiction, that Ragnar first pitched the idea of a story about an old disappearance on the island of Videy, set largely in the 1980s. As it happens, we're exact contemporaries and both remember the decade as a carefree, happy time. We were ten years old when all the stops were pulled out to celebrate the City of Reykjavík's two-hundredth anniversary and we were right there in the thick of it when everyone was trying to get a piece of the 200-metre-long cake. We also remember the '80s as a time of rapid change in Iceland. And as we're very different people, with differing views, there was a certain freedom in writing about a bygone era with its own set of social issues unrelated to those of today.

Shortly after that lunch, the pandemic struck, transforming all our lives. During this period, it was therapeutic to be able to turn our minds whenever possible to Lára and the mystery of her disappearance. Our writing of the book was a leisurely process, free from external pressure, performed in stolen moments between other tasks, and undertaken largely as a way of amusing ourselves with a shared interest.

Finally, in the spring of 2022, the end of our project was in sight. Although we continued to argue about some points right up to the last minute, we can honestly say that the book has given us immense enjoyment, which we hope will come across to the reader.

While researching the background we pored over old newspapers, reading about the people and issues of the day. But while some named individuals who were prominent at the time have walk-on roles in the story, all the main characters are our own invention. Needless to say, we also had tremendous fun reminiscing about all aspects of life and culture in the mid-1980s, from the music to the food.

Inevitably, writing about the past is a complicated business and despite our best efforts our book may well contain some factual errors about Icelandic society at the time. We have also taken the liberty of rejigging certain minor details in the service of the plot.

Readers may be amused to know that Sunna's conversation with Elías Mar about his translation of an Agatha Christie novel – and the disapproving reaction of an eminent composer to Elías Mar's previous Christie translation – is based on a real exchange that Ragnar had with the writer.

Many people are involved in turning a book like this into a reality, including our brilliant publishing team at Penguin Michael Joseph in the UK and Bjartur & Veröld in Iceland, our wonderful translator Victoria Cribb, and our families, who provided helpful advice and read through the text for us. We also owe huge thanks to all the friends who read the book in manuscript: Björn Gíslason, Halldóra Björt Ewen, Hulda María Stefánsdóttir and Víkingur Heiðar Ólafsson. Any errors are entirely the responsibility of the authors, but we ask readers to bear in mind that the story is fiction from beginning to end. Last but not least, we sincerely hope that our readers have enjoyed the tale and the experience of being taken back to the Reykjavík of 1986.

REYKJAVÍK, SUMMER 2022

KATRÍN JAKOBSDÓTTIR
RAGNAR JÓNASSON

Pronunciation Guide

In Icelandic the stress always falls on the first syllable.

Character's names

Arnfrídur Leifsdóttir – ARDN-free-thoor LAYVS-doh-teer

Baldur Matthíasson – BAL-door MAT-tee-ass-son

Dagbjartur Steinsson – DAAK-byar-toor STAYNS-son

Eiríkur – AY-ree-koor

Elías Mar – ELL-ee-as MAAR

Elísabet Eyjólfsdóttir – ELL-ees-a-bet AY-yohlvs-DOH-teer

Finnur Stephensen – FINN-noor STEFF-en-sen

Gudrún Reykdal – GVOOTH-roon RAYK-dal

Gunnar Gunnarsson – GOON-nar GOON-nars-son

Gunnlaug Haraldsdóttir – GOON-lohg HAA-ralds-DOH-teer

Halldór – HAL-dohr

Högni Eyfjörd – HURK-nee AY-fyurth

Jökull Thorarensen – YUR-kootl TOR-rar-en-sen

Júlía – YOO-lee-a

Kamilla Einarsdóttir – KAA-mil-la AY-nars-DOH-teer

Katrín Gudjónsdóttir – KAA-treen GVOOTH-yohns-DOH-teer

Kiddi – KID-dee

Kristján Kristjánsson – KRIS-tyown KRIS-tyowns-son

Lára Marteinsdóttir – LOW-ra MAR-tayns-DOH-teer

Laufey Karlsdóttir – LOY-vay KARLS-doh-teer

Margrét Thorarensen – MAR-gryet TOR-rar-en-sen

Marteinn – MAAR-taydn

Nanna Thorarensen – NAN-na TOR-rar-en-sen

Ólöf Blöndal – OH-lurf – BLURN-dal

Óttar Óskarsson – OHT-tar OHS-kars-son

Páll Jóhannesson – POWTL JOH-han-nes-son

Snorri Egilsson – SNORR-ree AY-yils-son

Steingrímur – STAYN-gree-moor

Sunna Róbertsdóttir – SOON-na ROH-berts-DOH-teer

Sverrir – SVERR-reer

Thórdís Alexandersdóttir – THOHR-dees AL-exanders-DOH-teer

Valur Róbertsson – VAA-loor ROH-berts-son

Placenames and other words

Árbær – OWR-byre

Arnarhóll – AARD-nar-HOHTL

Austurbær – OHST-oor-BYRE

Austurstræti – OHST-oor-STRYE-tee

Borgartún – BOR-kar-TOON

Braudterta – BROHTH-tair-ta

Bylgjan – BIL-kyan

Esja – ESS-ya

Faxaflói – FAX-a-FLOH-ee

Gardabær – GARTH-a-BYRE

Grafarvogur – GRAAV-ar-VOR-goor

Hallgrímskirkja – HATL-greems-KEERK-ya

Hlemmur – HLEM-moor

Hlídar – HLEETH-ar

Höfdi – HERV-thee

Húsavík – HOOSS-a-veek

Hverfisgata – KVAIR-vis-GAAT-a

Kárastígur – COW-ra-STEE-goor

Kópavogur – KOH-pa-VOR-goor

Lækjargata – LYE-kyar-GAA-ta

Laugarásvegur – LOH-gar-owss-VAY-goor

Morgunbladid – MORG-un-BLAA-thith

Reykjavík – RAY-kya-VEEK

Skólavördustígur – SKOH-la-VURTH-oo-STEE-goor

Skúlagata – SKOO-la-GAA-ta

Tjarnargata – TYARD-nar-GAA-ta

Videy – VEETH-ay

Vikubladid – VEEK-oo-BLAA-thith

Vísir – VEE-sseer